- - APR

Limitless

Out of the Box, Book 1

Robert J. Crane

Limitless
Out of the Box, Book 1

Dedication

Dedicated to my wife, who somehow always believed my potential was limitless.

Chapter 1

Two Years Later

The alley smelled of blood and fear, the stench and signs of death spread all over the red brick. It was a backstreet in Chelsea, a barely passable gap that wouldn't have qualified as an alley in America. A car might have been able to squeeze through, but only one of the smaller models that were popular in London.

London. Again. I'd wanted to come back, but not like this.

I took another sniff of the smells drifting through the alley. Blood was the easiest to identify. I had a lot of experience with blood. I had a lot of experience with fear, too, but the smell of fear I scented here was different. The sort of thing you'd catch in a toilet, if you get my meaning. Each step I took, my heavy boots thumped on the cobblestones.

I passed under the yellow crime scene tape as though it was something I did every day. It wasn't, but I had done it enough to not even feel the thrill of unease or anticipation anymore. From just the smell of this place, I could tell it was going to be messier than the stuff I was usually called in to consult on.

I rounded the corner into a narrower space, a dark offshoot of the alley that was even smaller and more foreboding than the one I'd followed thus far. There was a man waiting for me just around the corner, wearing a tan trench coat to protect him against the April chill. He had a mess of light brown hair that was styled in such a way that I knew he had either spent an abundance of time on it or almost none at all.

"Ms. Nealon, I presume?" He spoke with a British accent, of course. He looked to be in his late twenties or early thirties, and was tall enough. He was a wearing a white dress shirt with the tie just a little loose around his neck. He wore his trousers pretty well, I had to say, even from the front. He rested his hands on his hips expectantly, standing sentinel in the middle of the narrow passage.

"I'm Sienna Nealon, yes," I said, giving him a short nod. I wasn't really in the mood for pleasantries, but for him I made an almost unconscious exception.

He gave me a beautiful smile, and I felt my patience growing by the moment. "I'm Detective Inspector Matthew Webster." He offered me a hand, which I stared at only for a moment before I shook it quickly and without ceremony. "If you'll follow me?"

"Sure," I said, following him. I'm not much for gawking, but I was cursing his trench coat every step of the way.

"Delivery man found the remains early this morning," Webster said. "He actually walked around the scene for quite a while before realizing there even was a body. Trudged through carrying fresh produce into the restaurant's rear entrance here." He gestured to a solid steel door built into the wall.

"Okay." I listened to his commentary as I trailed behind him. I rubbed a hand over my face and stifled a yawn.

He glanced back and caught me before I could finish covering my mouth. He gave me a brief look of contrition. "I suppose they woke you in the middle of the night to get you over here so quickly."

"Caught me about an hour after I'd turned in, yeah," I said, trying to shake the sleep out of my head. I gave him a tight smile. "It's not unusual, though. Go on."

"Right." He turned and kept walking, just a few more feet to what I assumed was the scene. I didn't see much, but the blood smell was more pronounced here. "We found the largest part of him here."

"Part?" I asked. I hadn't exactly gotten a ton of information before I'd flown over. "So, the victim was in pieces?"

Webster looked at me, lips pursed as he concentrated. "What exactly did they tell you?"

"Almost nothing," I said, stifling another yawn. "State Department called my agency, requested me for some sort of murder investigation that you boys in the Met had cooking. They call, I go." That's the way it was. The way it had been for two years now, moving at the beck and call of the U.S. government.

"They really didn't tell you anything?" Webster looked a little pained. He kind of had angel eyes. His empathy was touching.

"I get called all over the place, and I'm rarely told anything until I'm there," I said with a shrug. "Hazard of the job." Or at least it was nowadays.

"I suppose there aren't many people with your particular set of skills at this point."

I looked him right in the eye. "There aren't any."

"Right. I suppose," Webster said, averting his eyes. "So, yes, we have a body. The commissioner called your State Department for a different reason than you think, though—"

"So this isn't a metahuman crime?" That was my job, policing the people who had powers beyond those of normal humans. Usually my jurisdiction was limited to the United

States, though. I'd only consulted with foreign governments a few times.

"Well, we think it might be," Webster said, bobbing his head slightly left and right as he answered.

The alley was empty save for the sick smell and us. "You already moved the body?"

"Couldn't leave it out," Webster said. "We assumed that you'd be the better part of a day arriving, so the scenes of crime officer already cleaned up and did their work." He flashed that smile again; I still liked it. "Imagine my surprise when you show up four hours after the commissioner made her call."

"It would have been less, but your government made me land in an empty field north of London and ride in via car," I said, staring at the crusted brick on the wall next to us. I glanced at the heavy steel door at the back of the restaurant, noticing hints of blood here and there throughout the scene. "So, the body... how many pieces?"

Webster blanched. "A lot. More than I've ever seen."

"That's messy," I said and knelt next to one of the spots of blood that had already dried. "Victim's name?"

"Maxwell Llewelyn," Webster said, and he squatted next to me. I felt a cold, clammy chill run up my spine that had little to do with the London weather. "Sound familiar?"

Shit. "Yeah, I knew him." I couldn't place the face, but I remembered the name. "He was a meta, all right." One of us, we few who remain.

"We gathered as much," Webster said, looking quite comfortable squatting down next to me. His coat dragged on the alley floor. "Checking up on him, we found his travel arrangements to America a couple years ago. Seeking sanctuary from what happened when you lot had that crisis—"

"Yeah, he was one of a group I tried to protect during the war," I said. Webster blinked when I said it. Most people didn't think of what had happened as a war. Then again, most normal humans didn't even know it was happening until it was already over. I let my finger drift over the blood that caked the ground, watched it flake at the tip of my finger.

"I'm a little surprised he ended up dead in an alley," Webster said. "Aren't your people supposed to be stronger, faster, all that?"

"We are," I said. "Some of us are stronger and faster than others. Max was low on the power scale. Not much of a fighter, either. We had him doing secretarial work until he and the others decided they'd rather hunker down and hide from the rest of the war on their own." I stood, leaving the blood behind. "I don't know what I'm looking at here, other than a murder scene. Maybe it involved a meta as the killer, maybe not. A normal human could have overpowered Max, potentially, in a few ways—"

"Well, that's actually not why we called you, either," Webster said, breaking my concentration. I stared at him, at that chiseled jaw. "There's a little more going on here than that—"

"Listen," I said and ran a hand along the back of my neck. "I like to help as much as the next person, but my agency is a bit maxed out at the moment. Besides, I'm not the person you should be talking to on this." I glanced toward the mouth of the alley and saw a hint of the grey day that waited out of the darkness. "There are a few metas over here who were closer to Max than I was. I'll put you in touch with them. Maybe they can tell you what he was up to."

"Why are you whispering?" he asked, leaning toward me a little conspiratorially.

I shrugged. "Because of the EU ban on metahumans in your countries."

His eyes ticked slightly left, then to the right. "I don't know if you've heard, but the UK isn't doing very much to enforce that ban."

I chuckled, humorless. "Then you're the only ones who aren't."

He matched my chuckle with a low guffaw. "It's a bit of that old American invention, 'don't ask, don't tell,' around here. Brussels went a trifle mad with sanctimony after that Italian incident. It was your brother who did it, wasn't it?" He said it like *whaddinit?*

"My brother, yeah," I said, peering back at him. It wasn't exactly a secret, since that little incident had been reported on every major news station in the world, and my name got dragged into it even though I'd been safely at home, in Minneapolis, at the time.

"Anyway, we've had more than a few barneys with Brussels from things like bends in bananas to whether inmates have the right to vote, though, and I reckon one's coming up about their stance on metas." Webster shifted, pushing his hands down in his pants pockets, elbows out. He was a wonderful specimen, standing like that, a crusader for justice and whatever.

"That's a nice blow for equality," I said, almost yawning. "Still, I don't think I can help you with Max. I'm not much of a detective, and I only knew the victim in passing. Like I said, I can put you in contact with a couple of people over here who worked with him in the past."

Webster made a *tutting* noise. "By any chance, are you talking about your friends Janus and Karthik?"

I blinked and felt a slight chill. There was a chance he could have picked those names up off the same list that he'd found Max on. "Yes. Why?" A chance.

"Ah, well," he said, shifting his attention back to the puddle of dried blood at our feet, "that's why the commissioner called your State Department asking for you. See, their names did come up when we started looking into poor, bloody Maxwell here, but they'd already been brought to the attention of the Metropolitan Police weeks ago."

"For what?" I asked, frowning. Janus and Karthik were many things, but criminals?

Well... not exactly.

"Missing persons," Webster said, and he dropped his hands into the pockets of his trench coat, snugging it tight. "They were reported missing six weeks ago by another person on your sanctuary list—Rory Kilmeade—and we haven't been able to ferret out a peep from either of them since."

Chapter 2

I let Webster give me a ride back to his headquarters in his car. It was one of those smallish British ones, might have been parked in the alley for all I knew. I stared out the rain-dotted window as he drove, mulling over what he'd told me.

Janus and Karthik were missing. One or the other would be suspicious enough, but both? And in the short span of time before an acquaintance of theirs turns up as a dismembered corpse? Beyond suspicious. There was a connection here, and the only thing troubling me was whether it had something to do with them being metas.

"Did you know them well?" Webster spoke into the silence. The only sound other than the engine and his smooth, British voice was the clicking of his turn signal as we prepared to make a right.

"Janus, yes," I said. "Karthik, a little less so. I worked with them both for a while during the war, but Karthik left before the end." The heat blew faintly out of the car's vents. Janus…

… he'd stayed with us to the very end.

"Can you think of any enemies they might have had?" Webster said, wheeling the car to the right.

"I'm sure they had them," I said. "But I don't know who they might be, specifically." With Janus, especially, the list could go on for pages.

"Anyone from *your* rogues' gallery, perhaps?" Webster said this with a smile.

If anyone else had been asking, it might have sounded smug and slightly asshole-ish. He managed charming, which was why I answered as sweetly as I could. "I don't have much of a rogues' gallery, I'm afraid." Like that was a bad thing. I felt my face straighten into hard lines, and I looked back out my window. "They pretty much all ended up dead."

We lapsed into another silence. While that admission might have shut other, lesser men up for a good long while, Detective Inspector Webster was back at it relatively quickly. "So... you've been to London before?" It didn't come off as much of a question.

I didn't bust him on it, though. "Just the once," I said. "It's a beautiful city."

"After we managed to dredge up the file involving the passports," Webster said, shooting me a sly look, "I looked at some of the criminal reports filed around the same time as your friends' departure from England." He paused. "Saw something about a teenage girl in a traffic collision with a car up near Russell Square. She mangled it so badly that the engine dropped out."

I kept a straight face. "I hope she's all right."

"Something in the same area," he went on, "some sort of foot chase in a hotel nearby. A fracas in the National Museum a few days later—"

"Oh for crying out loud—" I muttered.

"There were an awful lot of murders that cropped up around that time." He was probing. I didn't even glance at him. "Lots of shootings."

"Century—the people behind the war," I said, "they hired armed mercenaries to wipe us out. It got messy." That was an understatement.

"Maybe you can tell me all about it sometime," he said, and he sounded genuinely hopeful.

"Sure," I lied. I might have had diplomatic immunity now—maybe; I was a little fuzzy on how these things worked—but there was no way in hell I was going to revisit the good old days with a detective inspector. There was dumb, there was stupid, and then there was confessing all your sins to the local police. I was dumb and occasionally stupid, but I didn't plan on sinking to the third level.

"Here we are," he said, and we passed a sign that proudly proclaimed NEW SCOTLAND YARD. Just like on the TV. Or telly, I guess they called it. I shook my head as we entered a parking garage.

I followed Webster into the building, on my guard but trying not to look it. He kept glancing back at me like I was going to bolt at any second. He gave me a reassuring smile each time, and I was practiced enough at social niceties that I responded in kind. In reality, though, I was feeling a little more like the cat in the dog pound after his discussion of unsolved mysteries.

"Right this way," he said, holding a door for me as we entered a bullpen filled with activity. There were a lot of plainclothes police officers inside on phones, their accents so thick they melded together into a fascinating audio stew that even my practiced ear couldn't sift through.

The smell of coffee lingered in the air, the cheap kind, brewed in a pot that had probably been around since the Brits had ruled half the world from their island. People were hunched over their desks, looking at paperwork, staring at computer screens. It was like any other office I'd been in, except for the atmosphere of tension that underscored it all. That wasn't something you'd see in a copy machine repair shop. Unless massive layoffs were coming, maybe.

"Have a seat over here," Webster said, guiding me over to his desk. It was clean and neat, not a file left out. There was a desk calendar and a computer monitor, both perfectly positioned. Nothing else inhabited the space, not a picture of family, not a school diploma, nothing. If he'd told me right then that it was a temp desk and he was only using it for now, I wouldn't have questioned him.

I stopped short and took a seat in the chair alongside as Webster stripped his coat off, folded it in half and hung it on the back of his chair. I decided that the careless look of his hair had to require tremendous effort, and his otherwise natty appearance suddenly made more sense. The man kept things neat.

I leaned against the back of my seat as he sat down in his own. I watched him as he rolled it into place and shook the mouse to wake his computer. He slid out a drawer to reveal a keyboard and logged in, glancing at me out of the corner of his eye as he did so.

Did I mention he had angel eyes?

"Ah, here we go," he said, causing me to look away. "Looks like the medical examiner has had his say on this."

"Let me guess," I said, dryly, "the cause of death was being fileted into tiny pieces."

"Actually, it looks like a heart attack," Webster said, focused on the computer screen. "I don't know exactly how he made that determination, but it would appear the dismemberment happened post-mortem."

"Wow," I said, thinking that one over. "Chopping someone up just to dump their body in an alley—"

"Where it would almost certainly be discovered, keep in mind," Webster said. He twisted his lips as he read the screen, and tapped one finger idly on his clean desk. "They didn't even make an effort to dispose of it, and with it—him—in that many pieces, it would have been easy to at least try."

"A public display of some sort," I said, thinking it through. "But who would do something this messy...this brutal...?"

"I'm not exactly a profiler," Webster said, sliding back in his chair, which squeaked as he did so. He regarded me in a posture that looked lazy, but his eyes were intent. "This mess, though, I mean… it could be personal, someone with a grudge, or it could be a serial killer…"

"Or neither," I added. "Or both. Did your examiner find any DNA at the scene?"

"Not a bit other than the victim's." Webster shook his head. "The scene was short on blood compared to what you'd find in a human body, so the victim was definitely killed somewhere else and brought here."

My head spun with the possibilities, but I kept myself upright in the chair. Personal score? Random killing? Disappearances of metas? I stared straight ahead as I considered it, then turned my head to meet Detective Inspector Matthew Webster's brown, soulful eyes with my own. I could see he had some questions. I just had one, really.

What the hell was happening here in London?

Chapter 3

The old man screamed when he got cut, and that didn't bother Philip Delsim at all. He took a leisurely path away from where the bastard hung upside down from his chained ankles and picked up his bone-white china teacup and saucer from the table they rested upon. He saw the red from his thumb smudge a bit on the saucer, and that drew a frown. He should have known better than to take a sip before washing his hands. This was a messy endeavor, after all.

The screams were a delicious sound; they caused him to prickle with anticipation all across his skin. They were a symphony of a sort, high and primal, primitive music that harkened back to the days of instinct. Philip had discovered early on that he liked the sound of this particular kind of music, though he'd rarely had a chance to listen to it in the last few years.

The world had changed, after all. Gone were the days of setting a leisurely pace of life. The digital age, they called it. Life moved frenetically, everyone feverishly scrambling to speed up. Philip took another sip of the tea, which hadn't gone cold, fortunately. Not yet, anyway. He preferred to do things at a slower pace, take his time. Do the thing right.

Make them suffer.

The last one had suffered greatly, and for a long time, too. Why, he had barely remembered his name at the end of it. It was all wet croaks from a voice so strained it might as well have been broken. Philip took a sniff of the Earl Grey in his cup and found it quite the joy in contrast to the scent of blood and fear that suffused the room in which he stood.

"You know," Philip said, placing the cup and saucer back on the table and turning, slowly, to face the old man hanging by his ankles from the ceiling, "I'm rather enjoying seeing you bleed." He adjusted his glasses, wire-framed spectacles that he loved because they looked at least fifty years out of date. "Seeing you suffer. I could enjoy watching this for years to come."

"You… would," the old man croaked. It caused Philip to raise an eyebrow. Not many people could lose as much blood or skin as this fellow had and still remain cheeky.

Philip tried to recapture his sense of joy, though the subtle hint the old man had thrown at him nettled more than a little. "But I'm afraid I just don't see a very long future for you." He made a vague gesture with his hand, and the old man screamed again, this time from the pain. Philip had made him scream from terror at least a few times, and those were choice screams indeed, especially from a tough old bastard like this. "It'll be memorable until the end, though. At least for me."

Philip took a step closer and ran a hand down the old man's chest. Knife work had exposed tissue to the air that was not supposed to be out and breathing. It was messy, really, but there wasn't much to be done for it. He reached further up, came to the hip and thigh, where the damage done by yesterday's handiwork had started to heal. "I can't imagine you'll enjoy it, but I can assure you that I'll find the whole process immensely satisfying." Philip smiled.

And then he jabbed a finger into the newly knitted flesh and started peeling it off in a long strip.

The screams followed, and that was all to the good. Philip found himself humming along with them, trying to match the pitch as best he could while he worked, tirelessly, on the old man, burying himself in his efforts and barely noticing the mess he continued to make.

Chapter 4

"So you have no knowledge of who might be behind this?" Webster asked me. I was getting a little chilly sitting in New Scotland Yard, but the faint hope in his eyes as he asked the question helped keep my disappointment at bay.

"Not a clue," I said, giving him a short shake of the head.

"Is it possible—" he started, and I cut him off.

"*Anything* is possible," I finished for him. "Absolutely anything at this point. Which is the problem, really. You could have a random act of violence. You could have a planned act of violence. A mugging and abduction gone horribly wrong, a revenge killing that—"

"Hang on a minute," Webster held up a hand to stop me. "What if we operated from the assumption that this killing is connected to your friends' disappearances?"

I shrugged my shoulders. "So what if we did? I guess at least then you'd have something to work on."

"That's the spirit," Webster said and flashed me a smile. He turned back to his computer and pecked at the keys with one finger on each hand. I watched him coolly, pursing my lips. He glanced up at me and made a faint noise, an embarrassed guffaw. "Never have learned how to use a keyboard."

"Me either," I said, taking my eyes off of him and letting them roam around the bullpen. I caught a hint of interest as he cocked his head at me, waiting for further explanation. "They didn't offer typing classes where I did my schooling."

He returned his attention to his half-assed typing. With a sigh, I leaned over. "I think I've kind of reached the limit for how much help I'm going to be able to give you on this."

His eyes flicked to me in surprise. "What about your friends?"

I felt my stomach rumble just a little. "I don't know if you could call either of them friends. Acquaintances, co-workers maybe—"

"War buddies?"

"Maybe," I said. "Whatever the case, you've got an investigation started and… frankly, I'm a little out of my depth here. I don't think there's going to be much I can do for you on this, and I've got a world of trouble waiting for me on my desk back in Minneapolis." That was entirely true. I was presently inundated, working about eighty hours a week for less pay than I'd ever worked in my life. I mean, I was head of an underfunded agency that was in charge of policing metahumans across the United States, and while we were a small part of the population—about five hundred or so—we were not a quiet part.

Plus, a lot of the crap that flowed my way had nothing to do with metahumans, but I had to investigate to rule it out anyway. That was fun. I'd been called down to Ohio one time because of reports of some sort of fish-type meta living in a local pond. It was actually some weirdo who liked to take naked swims with a shark fin attached to his back. That image was forever seared into my mind; they didn't make a mental bleach I could wash it out with, unfortunately.

Like I said: crap flowed my way. And that was one of the milder examples.

"I've got a list," he said, and I heard a printer nearby spin to life, working on something. "Last known addresses for these people you dealt with—"

"Refugees," I corrected. "We granted them sanctuary, after all, so really they were refugees."

"Right, these people," Webster said, and he scooted back in his chair just around the corner of the cubicle and returned a second later with a piece of paper clenched between his thumb and forefinger, "they're out there." He glanced at the paper. "They could be in danger."

"I'm sure you'll warn them," I said warily. Wearily, too. Those two always came together for me somehow.

"I've got to talk to them all," Webster said, making the paper dance as he held it out in front of me. I couldn't decide whether he thought the way he was doing it was enticing or if he was just trying to hypnotize me.

"Yeah, we call that 'canvassing,'" I said. "I've done it. It's not the fun part of police work."

"I could use some help," Webster said.

I sighed. "Not to be an ass, but so could I. I'm one of two—count them, two—responders to metahuman threats for the entire United States." I had really felt the "entire" part of it over the last two years. "I have a stack of investigations on my own desk about six inches thick that I'm supposed to be working on, and just about the time I get it down to halfway, the U.S. State Department sees fit to loan me out to some other nation whose metas were nearly exterminated so I can deal with whatever threat they're facing. Which is fine, except that when I get back, my little pile of folders will have increased back to a full six inches or more." I joked with my brother—the only other responder to meta threats at our agency—that our caseload was more prolific at breeding than rabbits.

And on the rare occasions when our folders turned out to be filled with something serious, it was usually hairier than rabbits, too.

Webster studied me with a practiced eye. His finger traced that rugged jawline as he seemed to consider what I said. "So working this one case with me would be like a holiday of sorts." He smiled. His smile was boyish and damnable and *arrghhhhhh*—

I rubbed the bridge of my nose and shut my eyes. I had a perpetual headache these days. My brother kept insisting that I go to the doctor for it, but I hated my doctor and knew what she'd say anyway—it was stress. Or the product of my abilities. Or an impending brain hemorrhage.

Part of me was rooting for the last one.

I pulled my hand back slightly and looked out at Detective Inspector Matthew Webster with one eye only. He gave me that smile and cocked his head invitingly. "Arghhhh," I said, aloud this time. "Fine. I'll canvas with you." I saw his smile widen in victory. "But if we find nothing, I'm out of here so fast it'll shatter your windows from the sonic boom. Deal?"

"Absolutely," Webster said and stood, tugging his long tan coat free of the chair and then sliding it back under his desk. "Shall we, then?"

"We shall," I said and followed him out. And I wondered why the hell I was doing this.

Then I saw him walk in front of me with the coat folded over his arm instead of blocking the view of his backside, and I knew exactly why I was doing it.

Chapter 5

Webster broke the silence as we rolled along the London streets. "You know, I saw you on the news." I glanced to the side and he blushed, briefly, before expounding. "When it happened, you know."

"You and everybody else in the world," I said. This was all old hat to me by now.

"The whole world, eh?" Webster smiled. It was disarming.

I looked away in order to keep composed. "I went to China for a diplomatic mission last year, trying to foster cooperation because they lost pretty much all their metas at the opening of the war. This guy on the street recognized me and asked me if I could turn into a flaming dragon for him." Technically, I could do that. I'd done it on footage that had millions of hits on YouTube. Of course, I hadn't known I was being filmed at the time, and I hadn't done it since.

Webster paused before answering. "I suppose it's a rather impressive party trick."

I just blinked, looking straight ahead out the rain-dappled windshield. "I think that's the sort of trick that would send most people with any sense running from the party."

"I suppose I've never been all that sensible," Webster said, turning his attention back to the road. I glanced at him out of the corner of my eye. He was smiling faintly.

"Know your limits," I said, keeping an eye on him.

"A wise practice in general," he replied. "Do you follow your own advice?"

"I have no limits," I said quietly, looking back at the road as he accelerated through a green light.

"You say it like it's a bad thing."

I paused before answering, giving it some thought. "It's not an easy thing, that's for sure. Finding out you've got power—real power, the kind that has a real purpose behind it—and knowing you have to use it responsibly? It's not quite as glamorous or glorious as you might imagine."

"If you'll forgive me saying so," Webster said, nudging the car gently into a turn, "you sound like you're a bit... worn out."

"Probably."

"Maybe you should seriously take that holiday. An actual one."

"Can't," I said. "Every time I leave for a few days my life gets measurably worse. There's only so much of me to go around, you know."

"So you do have a limit," he said, and I caught him smirking faintly.

"My patience is certainly limited." I kept it relatively gentle, and by his expression I could tell he took it as banter. Which was good. Seriousness was my biggest drawback, and frankly, he was right. I did have limits. Except in the area of metahuman power. No one could match me there, at least no one I'd met in the last few years.

In that one area, I *was* limitless.

"So you're... super strong, right?" Webster was eyeing me again. I was familiar with this sort of curiosity. I'd been on the receiving end of it more times than I could count when I went out in the field and had to cooperate with local law enforcement, other federal agencies, or even just people on the street.

"Yes."

"And then there's the whole dragon bit," he said. "The flames are a nice touch, by the way."

"Thanks," I said. "But the fire is an independent thing. I just combined them when I had to kill Sovereign, that's all."

"You shot some sort of light at him, as well," Webster said. "Some kind of web or something."

"It's a net," I said. "Made of light. It's pretty strong, tough to break out of." I'd used it a lot lately. For the last couple years, actually. It was my non-lethal option for confining and restraining.

"And you can fly?"

"It's how I got here so fast," I said.

"You flew over without a plane?" Webster looked slightly astonished. "I mean, I knew they picked you up outside the city. When you said you'd flown into an empty field, I assumed—"

"It's a nine-hour flight from Minneapolis," I said. "Only leaves during normal airport operating hours. I wouldn't have been here until tomorrow if I'd gone commercial." I ran a hand back through my long, dark hair, which still felt a little frizzed even though I'd tried to contain it in a ponytail while I rode into London in the Foreign Office car.

"That means you must be able to fly at ridiculous speeds," he said, not taking his eyes off of me. I gestured toward the road. He looked back with a hint of contrition but kept stealing glances at me.

"Supersonic, yeah," I said. "At least until I hit the coast of Ireland, then I had to turn it down a little bit."

"My God," Webster said, shaking his head. "Why not just fly right into the middle of the city?"

"Your government," I said with a slight tug of a smile at the corner of my mouth. "They didn't want me flying where I can be seen. Apparently they want to sleep with me, they just don't want to be seen with me the next morning."

"Ah, yes, well," he said, clearing his throat—out of embarrassment, I suspected. I thought his next question was going to be some variation of "What else can you do?" but he kept it in check. After a moment's silence, he followed up with a question I did not expect. "So, with all that power at your fingertips, why did you decide to run yourself ragged working for your government?"

I opened my mouth and it hung like that for a moment. *That* was not a question I was used to getting. I had an answer anyway. "Because if I didn't," I said, "who would?"

He looked over, met my eyes, and nodded once. I would have sworn I saw a hint of sadness or something within them, but I wrote it off as me not knowing him very well. We lapsed into a comfortable silence, lulled by the quiet tapping of the rain at the windshield and the gentle thrum of the car's engine as we drove onward.

Chapter 6

Philip had to take a good long scrub after finishing with the old man. He wasn't dead, the crotchety old bastard, but Philip suspected he wanted to be. No one could lose that much skin and be sanguine about it. Except in the other sense of the word sanguine, of course—the bloody one.

"This is it?" he asked, taking a good long look out the window of the car. It was raining of course, as the London sky was prone to do, grey clouds hanging in a low ceiling over the scene. But he could still see the small house across the street. He had to look across the driver to see it, a worn-down brick house far on the outskirts. They'd been driving for a while to get here.

"This is it," Liliana Negrescu said to him, her low, harsh voice tinged with a Romanian accent. She'd been living in London for years, he knew, but showed little sign of ever fully adapting. She was a sharp-faced girl—and she still looked like a girl, except in the darkness, where she looked like a scary, hard-edged witch he wouldn't care to trifle with. Her dark hair was pulled back tight, and her black eyes flitted to look at the house.

"All right," Philip said, buttoning his tweed jacket before he opened the side door to get out. "Quick and quiet is the name of the game, then. You take back door, I'll take front."

She acknowledged him with a slight hiss that was almost a signature for her. Liliana didn't speak all that much, and when she did, it was straight to it. He liked that about her, but it was hardly her biggest selling point.

The knives: those were her biggest selling point.

They were both out of the car in a moment, moving quickly but casually. They kept to human speed, but when they reached the door just off the short drive, Philip knocked while Liliana disappeared along the side of the house without a sound. She wore street clothes. In them, she looked surprisingly normal, as long as one did not stop to ponder the vast darkness of her eyes.

Philip took a sniff of the wet air, a few drops of rain coming down on him as he stood outside the screen door, waiting for someone to answer it. He forced a smile onto his face. He was small of frame, and his glasses made him look even less intimidating, he thought.

If only they knew, no one would ever open the door for him.

The white door clicked open just a crack, inward. Philip kept the smile perched on his lips and angled his head to look in. There was a face there, that of a young man. Angus Waterman was his name. He was slightly paunchy and had a mane of red-brown hair. His eyes were small. He reminded Philip of a rat hiding in a hole and staring out at a threat.

"Yes?" Angus Waterman asked. Philip had the feeling he was looking at him as one would stare at a door-to-door salesman. He was going to be ever so disappointed.

"Mr. Waterman?" Philip asked and waited patiently for the answer. He already knew, of course, but this was the game to be played.

"Yes," Waterman replied, still looking cagey. "Can I help you?"

"I doubt it," Philip said smoothly, his smile broadening. "You can't even help yourself, after all."

Waterman took a moment to register the surprise before he attempted to slam the door. Philip managed to brace a hand in and stop him. Waterman was a weak meta, his physical strength so low on the scale that a strong human might have been able to overmatch him with a little effort.

And Philip was no human.

The door flew back open, Philip's hand pressing an imprint into the wood as if it were wet clay. Waterman ran. Philip already knew exactly how that was going to play out. He stepped inside and closed the door gently behind him. No need to make a scene, after all. He wiped his feet on the mat, listening without much interest. It was all so terribly predictable, unfortunately. Took some of the fun out of it.

The scream was exactly as he'd known it would be when it came, the sound of Angus Waterman catching a punch to the throat. It cut off when Liliana landed a blow to the side of his head that knocked Waterman's infantile brain into unconsciousness.

Philip, meanwhile, stepped into the kitchen. The kettle was boiling, just as he'd known it would be. He took a moment and poured a cup, taking his time as he heard Liliana in the back of the house. Philip knew what Waterman's future entailed, and it involved a stint wrapped up in a rug. "Hit him again," Philip called as he stirred a lump into his tea. "Otherwise he'll wake up in the trunk and make a frightful ruckus."

There was a short, sharp grunt of acknowledgment from the other room, followed by a dull thump. Philip felt a tingling sense of satisfaction and took his first sip of the tea. He made a face. It was quite cheap.

There was the sound of a car outside, and Philip froze. He reached out to his surroundings and felt a sense of urgency as the realization hit him, something he hadn't predicted yet.

The police would be here in seconds.

And they had help.

Her help.

"Liliana," Philip called, icing the sense of discomfort he felt, "the police are arriving and shall be knocking momentarily. Be a dear and ready poor Angus for his journey." He reached into his breast pocket and pulled out the item Antonio had given him for just such an occasion. He could sense that it was going to make one hell of a bloody mess, but then, by day's end, Angus Waterman wouldn't be much in need of a house anymore. "I'll need a moment to prepare for them before we set off…"

Chapter 7

I still wasn't used to riding on the wrong side of the car or the wrong side of the road. We were in a town called Hounslow, on a street of brick homes that were called townhomes in America, sharing common walls with the residences immediately next to each house. There were breaks in between every other dwelling that allowed for tight alleyways. The space next to the house we were going to— domicile of one Angus Waterman, whom I didn't remember at all—had been planted with a bank of trees. They didn't have much space to work with, but it was a nice break between houses.

"You remember Angus?" Webster asked as we crossed the street. There were cars parked evenly down both sides, only a few scattered spaces available.

"Not really," I said. "I'm not that good with... uh... people," I added, just being honest.

Webster must have thought it amusing, because he let out a low chuckle. "Think he'll remember you?"

"Probably," I said. "I do tend to make an impression." I froze before the white door and noticed it was just a hint ajar, with a palm print pushed into the wood. I stared at it for only a second before I pulled my gun.

"What the hell!" Webster started and took a step back. He looked murderously angry, and suddenly I was glad the pistol was in my hands, not his. "What is that?"

"A Sig Sauer P227," I said, keeping my weapon at low rest as I sidled up to the door.

"You can't have that here!" He muted his outrage to a respectable level in terms of loudness. The fury oozed with every word, though, unmistakable. "Handguns are illegal."

"Yeah, well, his door is open, and my mental alarm is going off because someone has clearly forced entry," I nodded to the indentation in the door. "That's something it would take meta-strength to do. Now, are you coming in, or am I entering on my own?"

"You can't go into someone's house with a weapon drawn!" He was nearing apoplectic, but at least he was being quieter about it. "It's burglary at least—"

"Come in and catch me, then," I said, and shouldered my way into the entry without looking back.

"Dammit—" Webster said, but he was right behind me. And not preparing the handcuffs, thankfully.

I slid into the entryway and found myself in a small room, only a few feet long. I could hear the scrape of shoes across the tile ahead and the faint hiss of water just done boiling. I doubted Webster heard any of it, and I was going to look like a real ass if it turned out that Angus had just left his door open and had made that palm print in wood himself.

He hadn't.

I stared at the guy standing across the kitchen from me. He wore a black ski mask, in contrast to his neatly pinstriped suit and tie and the cup of tea he held oh-so-properly in his hand. Except for the mask, he might have been any distinguished British gentleman. A pair of older spectacles perched on his nose reminded me of Janus, but even through the mask, I could tell he was younger.

"Hello, Sienna," he said in a classic example of a sophisticated British accent. Every syllable was perfectly pronounced, none of the rough edges or balled-up phrases that fell out of Webster's mouth. "I must say, I'm surprised to see you here. Surprised and pleased."

"Can't say the same," I said, surveying the kitchen as I came in. My pistol was still at low rest, but I could snap off a shot at him in milliseconds if I had to. "You're not Angus."

"Indeed I am not," he said as I made room for Webster, who followed behind me wordlessly. He had a baton in his hand now, and it took me a second to register that that must be what they gave British cops instead of guns. I gently thumbed back the hammer on my pistol and felt a lot better about my chances to stop this guy than Webster's.

"Where's Mr. Waterman?" Webster butted in. He still looked angry, but it had transferred to the man in the mask instead of me, which was a lot cuter. He had kind of a flush in his cheeks—

Ahem. Never mind.

"You just missed him," the masked man said and took a sip through the slit that exposed two thin lips. "I'm afraid he has a rather urgent engagement that will be keeping him occupied from now until the end of his life, which shall be arriving very soon."

"You're the murderer," Webster said, voice gone cold. "You're under arrest—"

"You must keep him around for his looks," the man in the ski mask said, looking me straight in the eyes. They say the eyes are windows to the soul, and if that was the case, this guy had a serious case of empty rooms lurking behind his. I couldn't see anything in them, not a flicker, not a hint, save for maybe just a little scorn or anger; I couldn't tell which. "Because he certainly doesn't have a bloody idea what he's up against, does he?"

"Do you?" I asked, not looking away from those cold, pitiless eyes.

"I've long been an admirer of yours, Miss Nealon," he said in that cultured tone. "You were the first of us to really open the worlds' eyes to what we're capable of." He chuckled lightly, an utterly humorless sound. "Of course, it was such a dramatic display that I don't think they really know what *all* of us can do, even going on two and half a years later. In any case, it seems rather fitting as I go public with this endeavor of mine to let you know that I'll be killing you—"

I raised the gun and squeezed the trigger without waiting for another word. The pistol roared twice with the fury of the .45 ACP rounds nestled in the magazine. I saw Webster blanch next to me, ducking away from the gun as it belched fire out the barrel.

But the masked guy? He dodged both shots, disappearing into the darkness of the hallway behind before I'd even finished my double tap.

"After him!" Webster said, rushing forward. He recovered quickly. I strong-armed him back, catching his chest as I slipped into line with the hallway where the masked man had disappeared. It looked empty, but appearances could be deceiving. I heard movement in the back of the house and took four hurried steps across the kitchen after him—

And failed to notice the tripwire hidden in the darkness until my ankle caught it.

The world exploded around me as a bomb went off with the fury of thunder and lightning striking all around me. I barely had time to register what it was before the flash of flame lit the room, then the world dissolved into smoky darkness as I fell to the ground, pain dragging me into unconsciousness.

Chapter 8

Philip had already made it out the door when the bomb exploded, catching that little twat in the blast. Antonio had called it his version of a claymore mine, whatever that was. All Philip cared about was that she was down, the little bitch, and she wouldn't be following him.

"Come on, come on," he urged Liliana. She followed in his wake, Angus Waterman rolled into a long, unsightly rug on her shoulder. Philip licked his teeth nervously, striding down the side of the house, feeling tree branches claw at his arm as he passed. It was a curious sensation, like someone was dragging wet fingers across the outside of his coat. He noticed it, detached from the sensation, as he followed the path.

He pulled the ski mask off and pocketed it just before he came into the open in the front of the house. He paused, running fingers through his lightly mussed hair, smoothing it back into place. The street was quiet, not a hint of movement anywhere. The grey sky hung above, foreboding, as though it could hint at the destruction he'd just unleashed in the house behind them.

"Is she dead?" Liliana asked in that flat voice of hers. Did she have a hint of nervousness in it?

Well, who wouldn't? "No," Philip said, not stopping as he stepped off the curb. "She heals quickly as well, so we need to remove ourselves from the situation before she gets a chance."

"When will she be up again?"

Philip felt a brisk charge of annoyance prickle across his skin. "I don't know." That wasn't exactly true, but he didn't have time to delve into it at the moment. "Soon enough. We need to be fully prepared before we face her." Liliana did not argue with him. She knew better.

There was no sign of traffic, no sign of anybody. The bomb going off in Waterman's house had left his ears ringing slightly, but his hearing was better than most, and he had been closer to the blast than anyone in the neighborhood. "Let's go."

They crossed the street and Philip opened the boot. Liliana dumped her burden inside without much in the way of ceremony or mercy, unfurling the carpet to spill Waterman out. He hit his head on the metal edge of the boot as he fell, probably compounding his unconsciousness. Philip reached out, waiting to see if that would cause a problem. Once he was sure it wouldn't, he glanced up and down the street again, then made for the passenger door while Liliana slammed the boot closed. The sound echoed up and down the quiet Hounslow street.

"Did you kill the copper with her?" Liliana asked as she slid into the driver's seat and started the car. Philip could smell the faint hint of something burning and wondered if he'd started a fire with the bomb. That would be delicious, but alas, not fatal for the girl in question.

"No," he said, shaking his head. He knew the answer by instinct, of course. "He's merely rattled, like a soldier in a war zone. He'll be out the door in about thirty seconds. I suggest we be around the corner by then."

Liliana nodded once, already turning the ignition key. That was something Philip had long admired about her. She was ruthlessly efficient. Probably the product of her Cold

War-era training. She had the car moving seconds later, and they turned the corner just in time by Philip's reckoning.

"What now?" Liliana asked.

Philip felt a gentle sense of euphoria fall over him. He'd just poked the Met squarely in the eye with a sharp stick, and it gave him more than a little thrill. They had no idea what they were dealing with, not even a hint. "They'll move quickly, so we'll need to be quicker still. They've guessed what we're up to, but the structure of the situation will work against them."

Liliana's dark eyes found him as they drove on. "You mean the fact that they're hiding?"

"That's the structure of the situation, yes," Philip said. He could feel his lips curl. "Now they think all we care about is killing these swine." But there was more. So much more. "That could work to our advantage."

Liliana gave him a perfunctory nod to say she understood. She didn't truly, though. He'd seen that much from looking into her eyes. "What about Waterman? Do you want me to start on him?"

"Start, but not finish," Philip agreed. He took a sniff of the car interior, and he wondered, not for the first time, if someone had been smoking in here. Probably Antonio. The bomb maker seemed like the sort to indulge every now and again. "Make sure the old man watches it all."

She made that hiss again, the one of acknowledgment, and settled into silence. That worked well for Philip, though, because he had plans to make. Plans that now included that girl, Sienna Nealon. He hadn't seen her coming, and that was a rare thing.

But then again, a surprise like this…knowing who she was and what she'd done…it was quite enticing. The very idea of besting her, killing her… it would make the ending of this whole thing all the sweeter.

Chapter 9

I awoke in pain. Lots and lots of pain. Screaming, flames-licking-my-body pain.

For the record, there were no actual flames. It took me a while to realize that, though, with the haze of smoke and debris scattered all over the place.

Angus Waterman's kitchen looked like someone had come through with a sledgehammer and liberally smashed to pieces all the parts of the décor they disliked. There were holes in the walls, the doorframe had been widened by several inches, and the old white refrigerator bore battle scars.

And did I mention the pain? Oh, the pain.

I wanted to scream, but I didn't. Pretty sure I was making a wailing noise of some sort, though. I sat up and looked down my body to see that I was missing a leg.

Yep. Missing a leg. It was just gone. Below the knee, it had disappeared.

I noticed stains on the wall as the world came into focus and the smoke began to clear. It took my addled, agony-burned brain a moment to realize that the stains were my blood.

"Wolfe," I gasped, interrupting a sound that was akin to a cat yowling. "Need… your help."

Normally I could have gone without vocalizing the thought, but missing a leg was throwing me off my game.

35

"Dear God," Webster said, his voice artificially exaggerated by what I assumed was the ringing in his ears. "Hold still!"

"Not really in a state to go anywhere just this second," I said through gritted teeth. I pulled the power of Wolfe, a serial killer whose soul I had absorbed years ago, to the front of my mind. I could use his power when he was with me like this. I could hear his thoughts, too.

He was exceedingly violent, so one of these things was more useful than the other.

This time he stayed blissfully quiet, probably figuring I wasn't in much of a mood to deal with him. He was right: I wasn't. Not with the agony that came from the bones growing back where my leg had been.

"You're bleeding very badly," Webster said, still talking louder than I thought was necessary. In spite of all the damage, there wasn't much noise at this point. I heard an engine starting somewhere in the background. It was either that or my back teeth grinding against each other.

"Tell me something I don't know," I muttered. I could see the bone of my shin growing back, extending down into the empty space my right leg had once occupied. The explosion had mangled my left as well, chunks of meat missing where I'd had a calf once upon a time. The holes were knitting themselves even as Webster fretted over me, doing little to nothing by my reckoning.

"You have to hold still!" he cried again, turning his panicked face to look at me. His eyes were warm even though they were wide, and I had my mouth clamped shut by now, unable to say a word. My lip was bleeding from where I'd caught my teeth on it biting down.

"Just give me a minute," I said, forcing my mouth open. My voice did not sound nice, just agonized.

"A minute?" Webster looked at me, agape. "You need medical attention. I need to call for an ambulance."

"Just give me… a minute," I said, shaking my head. The bad guy, whoever he was, had been brighter than I would have given him credit for. He'd dodged two bullets and run, catching me in a trap that actually worked. That never happened anymore.

I watched the bones of my foot extend as they grew, muscle and fibrous tissue chasing behind them. A layer of pale skin crept down my calf, pink and fresh as it settled, turning back to the snowy white color of the rest of me as it finished wrapping around my foot. Toenails sprang from each toe, and I wiggled them one by one.

Somewhere in the middle of all that, Webster caught on and stared, dumbfounded, at my newly grown foot. My pants had been shredded to mid-thigh by the explosion, exposing way, way more skin than was really appropriate. Partially protected by the explosion hitting my right side, hints of my left pant leg fluttered down to my knee like a tattered flag. The denim was soaked with blood, probably from where my femoral artery had been severed by the blast.

"My God," he whispered. I was surprised he got that much out.

"I said give me a minute." I flexed my new foot and worked my way to standing. My left boot was still mostly intact, whatever debris the explosive had used missing it from about mid-calf down. The top looked a little dog-eared, though. I hobbled into the next room, feeling the press of splinters and drywall fragments on the plantar surface of my foot.

I found my other boot in the hallway beyond. I picked it up like it was nothing, and turned to see Webster still staring at me, openmouthed.

"What?" I asked, dumping the severed foot out of my boot. It landed on the floor with a loud *thunk* that I suspected even he could hear.

His jaw moved up and down several times before he got a word out. It was kinda cute. "You… you can do that? Regrow a leg?"

"I can do a lot of things," I said, slipping the boot back on. "Right now I'd like to catch the bastard who just made it necessary."

Webster shook his head. "He's gone."

I stared at him. "How do you know?"

"I went running outside to check once I saw you'd lost a leg. Saw a grey car going 'round the bend too fast for me to read the plate or get a make."

"Hmm," I said. Blood squished between my toes in the boot I'd just recovered. I turned over my severed foot, looking for my ankle holster and backup gun.

"What are you doing?" Webster asked. He was almost back to normal volume now.

"Trying to find something." The Walter PPK I habitually carried strapped to my ankle lay underneath it, the band a little dog-eared but still mostly intact. "Here we go." I pulled the pistol out of the holster, examined it to make sure there was nothing blatantly wrong with it, and made a mental note not to fire it until I was sure the barrel was clear of debris and the weapon was undamaged.

"You brought *two* guns to London?" Webster looked sick—and not just from the display of gore, I'd wager.

"I would have brought more, but I can only carry so much across the Atlantic, y'know?"

He was not amused. "You're in violation of our laws."

I shrugged. "I can leave, if you'd like."

"You can lea—" He looked near-ready to explode, but he suppressed whatever he'd planned to say a lot better than I would have in his situation. "You can't do that."

"Leave?" I asked, looking down again at my tattered clothes. He didn't know it, but I wouldn't have left now if I'd had to surrender both guns and one of my hands to stay. Mr.

Ski Mask had taken a leg from me. I had a score to settle. "Or carry a gun?"

"Both," he sputtered. "I need your help. But you can't carry a handgun around London."

"If you need my help, then you'll deal with the fact that I go everywhere armed," I said. "Me and my guns, we're part and parcel, one and the same."

He made a noise of frustration. "You bloody Americans." He placed both hands on his hips, squaring out his elbows and causing the trench coat to billow. "This isn't my decision. It's up to our commissioner and the Foreign Office."

"Great, why don't you bump that up the chain of command?" I pushed past him, heading toward the door.

"Where are you going?" he asked.

"I figured you wouldn't want me contaminating your crime scene any further," I said, stopping at the entry to the kitchen and keeping my hands to myself to avoid doing just that. "I'm going to wait in the car until your crime scene unit gets here and you've had a chance to sift through the place for clues." I shot him a smile and hoped it was dazzling.

I got a look back that told me it was anything but, and I ducked around the corner to head out of the house, grimacing in discomfort that was not just physical.

Chapter 10

Philip slammed the door to the warehouse shut after the car had pulled in. The door slid on a rail and clattered like a train on tracks as he closed it. The grey daylight of the London afternoon vanished as he did so, and it took a moment for his eyes to adjust to the darkness. He could feel the smile on his lips, though, as he turned to look at the car's boot.

"Mr. Waterman," he said, taking slow, joyful steps toward the back of the car. It was practically a dance. "Your moment is coming swiftly, and I think you should prepare for it."

Liliana opened and closed her door, watching him as he made his way over to the boot and opened it. Angus Waterman was still inside, still unconscious, black bruises layering the side of his face. Even a weak meta such as he would heal from them in little time, but unfortunately for Angus Waterman, it was not time he had. "Can you see his future?" Liliana asked, those dark eyes looking even blacker in the low light of the warehouse.

"Indeed I can," Philip said, staring at Waterman. His pudgy body was angled in such a way that Philip felt certain he would awaken with a severe pain in his neck. "It will be gruesome and it will be short. Though not nearly short enough for Mr. Waterman's taste."

Liliana hissed, this time in apparent pleasure. He'd seen the knives at work and knew what she could do with them. He gestured, and she reached into the trunk, dragging

Waterman's unmoving form from it and placing him into a fireman's carry. She walked as if he were no more of a burden across her shoulders than a mink coat. The fat oaf likely wasn't.

"String him up next to the old man," Philip said, passing one of the supporting struts that held the corrugated metal roof on the warehouse. "Let him wake up to a glimpse of his future."

Liliana did not nod, just headed toward the far corner of the room, to the door of the soundproofed chamber where the old man currently resided. It made Philip smile, just thinking of what was to come. "Oh, and Liliana?" She turned to look back at him. "Give him a poke or two to... get the juices flowing, will you?"

That drew a smile out of her.

Philip sashayed his way up the nearby metal stairs, his leather shoes making a sound with every step. He opened the old wooden door to the offices in the middle of the warehouse, listening to the window rattle in the frame as he did so. He stepped into a room lit by a single dull bulb shining overhead, which cast illumination down upon a man hunched over a desk, hard at work on something.

He had tanned skin and dark stubble that extended up his cheeks and across his bald head. Though his back was turned, Philip could picture the nightmare-black goatee that rested on his unsmiling face. Philip approached carefully, not making any loud noises or sudden moves as he walked, thumping his feet gently against the concrete floor to announce his presence to Antonio Ruelle.

"You don't have to do that," Antonio said, not looking up from his work. "I could hear you come in."

"I don't like to chance surprising you when it's possible you could be working with something delicate." Philip mimed an explosion with his hands. "Not that I don't enjoy seeing your fine pyrotechnic work; I just don't want to see it quite that close."

Antonio grunted, though Philip was hard-pressed to tell whether it was in amusement or simple acknowledgment. Philip could see the man's hands now, and the burn scars that gave the skin a rippled look caught his attention once more. To see a metahuman with scars was an odd thing. Antonio wasn't a particularly strong one; still, whatever had done that to him must have been truly magnificent to leave such marks.

"I found good use for your makeshift claymore," Philip said, and he could hear a touch of singsong happiness in his voice as he said it.

"Did you?" Antonio did not look up from his tinkering.

"I did," Philip said. "We just happened upon Sienna Nealon and an officer of the Metropolitan Police."

That got Antonio to look up. His eyes flashed and the hands ceased work immediately. "Are you sure it was her?"

Philip held up a hand to his chest, faux-wounded. "How could you doubt me?"

"Of course," Antonio said, clearly chastened. "Did you kill her?"

"I think I'll need something a bit… stronger for that, don't you?" Philip asked. He bared a smile. "Besides, I don't think it's her time. At least… not yet."

Chapter 11

I probably looked like hell, but I didn't care. I sat with my legs exposed, hanging out the side of Webster's car. My boots reached up to mid-calf, partially shredded at the top, long-sleeved jacket covering my upper body, arms folded across my midsection. If I took my jacket off, I'd probably look a little like the palest cowgirl at the rodeo because my jeans were now cut-offs. And I really didn't have the thighs for that.

I watched the police swarming all over the place with their distinctive yellow vests and funny hats. I looked at their belts as they passed back and forth and saw nothing but those batons and some pepper spray. I studied them through slitted eyes, like a huntress watching prey. I had the "Don't talk to me" vibe in full effect, though at least part of that was motivated by a deep desire for a nap.

They are all of them prey, Wolfe's voice said in my head.

I didn't bother agreeing with him. When you feed a stray animal, you just encourage it to come back for more.

Besides, sadly, in this instance, I couldn't find fault with his opinion.

Webster was milling around, bouncing back and forth between conversations with a few other plainclothes officers on the scene. One of them came up to him and greeted him with a smile. This guy was a little over the weight limit, if you know what I mean. His stomach over hung his belt by a couple inches. He looked young, like late twenties, similar in age to Webster, and when I saw the grin from the DI that indicated familiarity, I could tell even from fifty feet away that theirs was more than a casual acquaintance.

So I listened in. Because I can do that. Powers, you know.

"Can't believe the carnage in there," the big guy said to Webster. "An actual bomb?"

"It was," Webster said with a sharp nod. "Took her bloody leg right off."

The big guy glanced over at me and I looked away. "She looks all right now. Fit, even. Very fit, actually. Bit chunky 'round the thighs and trunk, but not bad." Just the way he said it, with drool running over the words, left me with little doubt about what *fit* meant to him. "Is she the one—"

"Yes," Webster cut him off. "She's the one from the news."

"I saw her on that interview from the American network, talking about powers and people and all that. It's all a bit mad, innit?"

Webster's reaction was not so subtle. "I've just seen her get a foot blown off and watched it grow back in seconds. Mad is not quite the right word, Dylan."

"Bloody hell," Dylan said, and I watched the blood drain from his face. "Like, grown from a stump?"

"Like magic," Webster said. "Bone stretching out, muscle and skin coming back, like watching a time-lapse video."

"I should get her to talk to my brother," Dylan said, pensive. "He's a git. Lives in council housing on account of losing his leg to a train—"

"I don't think she can teach your brother to grow a new leg," Webster said with a hint of impatience.

"I look at her like that, I can just about feel one growing on me—"

What. A. Pig.

"Oh, God," Webster said, turning his back so I couldn't see his expression. "Will you just leave it out?" It was at this point I got up and started toward them.

"Oh, honestly, mate, don't get so worked up. She's just a piece of arse—"

I arrived a second later, to the surprise of Dylan, whose mouth gaped open at my sudden blur of speed. "The only piece of ass I see around here is a hole, and it's you," I said.

"Bollocks, you heard that?" Webster asked, turning to me incredulously.

"Uh, yeah. It'd be hard to miss Sir Bacon Fatback here calling me 'very fit' and talking about how his little twig is stirring into motion for the first time in years."

"Oh, shit," Dylan said, hands falling to cover his groin. "You got the bloody x-ray vision, too?"

I glanced at him with a look of pity. "No. I just assumed you had a tiny, tiny penis because of the way you talk about a woman whose clothes have been shredded by a bomb blast." I gestured at the crusted blood that had dried on my knee. "Clearly the thought of red wings doesn't even turn you off, you're so hard up for—"

"Okay, well, let's just veer off that topic," Webster said, adopting the pose of a conciliator. I scowled, and he blinked away. "We're... uh... almost done here. Dylan was just coming over to tell me what SOCO found."

"SOCO?" I said it back to him, because it made not a damned bit of sense to me.

"Scene of Crimes Officers," Dylan said helpfully. And snottily.

"Well, Dylan," I said, turning my attention back to This Little Piggy Who Trod on My Nerves, "tell us what your British equivalent of CSI found that could aid in our murder investigation, and do so without looking at my chest." That snapped his eyes north again.

"Right," Dylan said, sounding slightly professional. Slightly. "Ah, not much. No mobile phone, no calendar or computers in the house—"

"You think the kidnappers took them?" Webster asked.

"Or Angus never had any," I said.

"There is a phone in the house, a landline," Dylan said, taking a notepad out of his trench coat pocket. As the sky started dribbling on me, I started to realize why they were both wearing coats. My leather one looked especially beat up next to my cut-offs. I wasn't much for shopping, but I'd need to do some, and soon. "I'm getting the calls to it traced."

"That's making yourself useful," I said. "What else can we find out about this guy?"

"We can ask the commissioner to make some introductions at the Foreign Office," Webster said. "Perhaps get some answers from them on any other travel records, but I'm not hopeful."

"Forensics are going over the remnants of the bomb," Dylan said, shrugging as he closed his notepad. "I don't know what they'll be able to give you, but it's at least a few hours off." He glanced nervously at me. "Um… about that foot… do you want it back?"

"Why?" I asked. "Are you going to do something perverted to it if I leave it here?"

"What?" He looked offended at that, eyebrows arching up even as his pupils dilated. "No, I'm asking because I know you Americans get bloody paranoid about people watching you, and I didn't know if you didn't care about leaving it behind or you just can't be arsed to get it."

"Can't be *what*?" I asked with a laugh. "Arsed? What does that even mean?"

"Bothered," Webster said, looking a little chagrined.

"No, I don't care," I said, looking evenly at Dylan. "I left enough of my blood in there that if your government wanted to clone me or whatever, they won't have any problem getting a sample."

"This is without a doubt the oddest conversation I've ever been involved in," Webster said, shaking his head.

"It is a bit surreal," Dylan said.

"That's a big word to come from such a small mind," I said.

"Oh, piss off," Dylan said, and before I could take his advice, he turned and did it for me, dodging into the crowd of officers milling about.

"He's a charmer," I said.

"That's just Dylan," Webster said, still shaking his head. "He doesn't mean anything by it." He had a hand planted on the back of his neck, like he had an itch where his hair started. "He just doesn't know what to make of you, that's all."

Dressed like this, I couldn't totally blame him. Still, he got no points for anything he'd said. "I need clothes."

Webster's eyes dragged south before coming up to meet mine, and I caught more than a hint of discomfort. "We can stop at a—"

"Great," I said, heading toward the car. Didn't even bother for him to finish. I didn't need eyes in the back of my head to see him looking as I walked away. But only because I could see his reflection in the bumper of a nearby car.

Chapter 12

"Still think you need my help?" I asked as we cruised through the streets of London on our way back to New Scotland Yard. The rain had let up, thank the heavens. I didn't remember it being quite this bad when last I'd been here.

"Now more than ever," Webster said tensely from the driver's seat. His fingers were white-knuckling the steering wheel. "Without you, I'd probably have been butchered by our suspect."

"Yeah, I'm not sure why he ran," I said, mulling it over. We'd stopped off at a department store that I didn't catch the name of, and in spite of some frowns from the proprietress due to my attire and a certain amount of bendiness due to a crack in my only credit card, I'd managed to get pants and a new shirt. I'd wanted a trench coat to go along with everything, but I couldn't find one that fit. The lady behind the counter had apologized profusely once I'd cleaned up and paid, but they just didn't have anything in my shorty short size. Ah, the challenges of being a woman of average height. So I stuck with the beat-up leather coat. It wasn't like I could ruin it much more wearing it in the rain, I supposed. "He had us. All he had to do was come right back through the door while I was out, and he could have finished me."

"There's an element of play to this whole thing," Webster said, tapping his finger on the wheel. "I mean, what he did to your friend Max—"

"Max wasn't my friend," I said absently. I didn't say it like I was indignant or upset, just stating a fact. Max wasn't my friend.

I didn't really have any friends. Not anymore.

"Well, what he did to Max was just brutal. And dumping the body like that? He had to know it'd be found. He even made sure it was identified."

"Serial killers like attention," I said. "Or so I'm told." *Right, Wolfe?* I got a growl in my head in reply.

"Maybe he's playing with you, too," Webster said, finishing his thought. "Maybe you're part of his game now."

"Maybe," I said, not convinced. "Or maybe we've watched a few too many serial killer movies. Don't these guys—I mean, don't they typically want to keep getting away with it?"

"One would presume," Webster said, and the car slalomed slightly. He looked over at me, a little red. "Sorry. I just don't understand it. It feels like there's more here, obviously, lots of pieces we're not seeing. But what he did to Maxwell Llewelyn makes it feel like there's some rage in there."

"I don't really understand sickos," I said, shaking my head.

"I, uh…" Webster started, and I could see the hesitation. "You've uh… had to kill a few people, right?" He froze, then adjusted. "In the line of duty, I mean?"

I sat very still for a moment and felt my mouth go a little dry. "Yes. In the line of duty." Not the whole truth, but never mind. "But I've never mangled a corpse." Mangled a few before they became a corpse, but never afterward. "I agree, what he's doing to them is vicious. Do you have a serial killer division or something?"

"Or something," Webster said. "Not sure they'll be interested in this one. It's being kept rather quiet, naturally, since metas are involved."

"Right," I said, feeling my sarcasm had not been put to enough use today, "because you wouldn't want to devote time and resources to stopping people from dying unless they're full-on human."

"That's not quite fair," Webster said.

"I totally agree; it's very unfair to the people who are being killed."

That shut us both up until we were back in the parking garage at New Scotland Yard. We entered the building in silence, and I followed his billowing trench coat down the halls and into the wide-open bullpen where his desk was located. He hesitated as we walked in, and I caught him looking across the bullpen to one of the offices that ringed the room.

There was a woman standing in the doorway making a come-hither gesture with her finger and showing absolutely no emotion otherwise. Except sternness, if one could class that as an emotion. That was present.

"I think this is where I leave you for a bit," Webster said, his expression a little contorted. He took one step and then halted as the woman with the stern face shook her head and altered her finger's direction slightly to indicate me instead.

"Or maybe this is where I leave you," I said, brushing past him. He stood between two desks in an aisle partially obstructed by a chair. Seemed like a fire hazard to me, but I did my best to get past him without knocking him over. I held him at a distance as I passed, my hand brushing around his back through the trench coat. I didn't feel anything. Promise.

I made my way over to the waiting woman. She wore a fancy uniform, one with bars on the collar and everything. "You must be the commissioner," I said as I approached.

"Mary Marshwin," she said, not offering a hand. Whether it was because she knew what my touch could do or because she was simply uninterested in shaking my hand, I didn't know. Her face made me lean toward the latter. "Come in."

There was a hint of a Scottish accent in her voice and no warmth whatsoever.

I breezed into her office behind her and halted just inside the door. We were not alone.

A well-dressed gentleman in a double-breasted suit stood as I walked in. A rich aroma of tobacco smoke wafted off of him, but not the kind that offended my sensitive nostrils. He had a perfectly groomed mustache, and his hand reached out to me in a gesture of friendliness, his smile already wide, though a little limited by a hesitancy I caught behind his eyes. "Alistair Wexford, Ms. Nealon. I am the Foreign Secretary. Welcome back to the United Kingdom."

"Glad to be here," I said as I took his hand. His handshake was warm and firm, and it broke after an appropriate interval. "Though not because of the circumstances, obviously." I hesitated, wondering how that sounded. "I just mean it's nice to be back to merry old England, which I enjoy—"

"Quite," Wexford said with that tight smile. I was actually a little grateful to him for cutting me off before I started babbling. That was always a possibility in strange company. I'd done it once in front of Congress, which had been deeply embarrassing. "Perhaps you're familiar with your ambassador from the United States?"

"Ryan Halstead," the other man said. He was still seated in front of the desk. Mary Marshwin moved toward the chair across from him. Halstead exhibited about as much interest in greeting me as he might in greeting a mosquito. His tone was bored and perfunctory, and he turned his head to look away from me after announcing himself, as though I were worthy of no more notice than a bug.

"Please, have a seat," Wexford said, offering me his chair. I smiled at him and shook my head.

By this time, Commissioner Marshwin was back in her seat. It looked like it could lean, but she was in it straight, her back as stiff as the drink I wished I had in my hand right at that moment. "Now that the introductions are made," Marshwin said, "perhaps we can get down to brass tacks."

Personally, I thought she looked like she was sitting on the brass tacks, but I kept that to myself. "Sure. I have to admit, I'm a little surprised to see everyone here—"

"It's best to have these sorts of discussions prior to there being any misunderstandings," Wexford said, apologetically. I liked his brand of diplomacy; for a guy so high up the ladder, he seemed genuinely decent, which, in my experience, was not usually the case.

"Or to put it another way," Halstead said, his tone and bearing giving away the fact he was a classless asshole, "it's better we get you straight on what the hell's happening here before you stick all of our tits in a ringer again."

I let my eyebrow creep skyward on that one. Marshwin coughed gently, as though she'd never heard that sort of language before. Wexford's smile dimmed just a hint.

"My tits aren't in any ringers just yet," I said, keeping a measured tone. "Trust me, I keep track of these sort of things."

Halstead turned his head around just enough to acknowledge me. He had the smirk of an asshole. "You may not realize it yet, but the next time you go before Congress, you will." He turned back to Marshwin as if I were no longer there. "She's a little slow."

I resisted the urge to jam a hand down his collar and lift him up by the back of his neck. "I'm sorry," I said, and I think my tone conveyed the fact that I wasn't remotely sorry about anything, ever. "Did I miss something? Because so far the only thing that's happened is that I've come face to face with a meta who's killing UK citizens, and I lost my leg trying to apprehend him." Wexford made a sympathetic noise and looked down at my legs. "I got better," I assured him, wondering if anyone else got the Monty Python reference.

"Let me tell you what you've done," Halstead said, his sneer settling as he shot Marshwin a *she's-so-stupid-let-me-*

educate-her look that was not reciprocated. Fortunately. "You've brought a handgun into the United Kingdom—"

"Two, actually," I said.

"—you've prompted an exchange of gunfire—" Halstead went on.

"I'm the only one who shot," I corrected.

"A UK citizen has been kidnapped—"

"And I tried to retrieve him, at great cost to life and limb," I said. "Or at least at the cost of one limb."

"WILL YOU SHUT UP, YOU SILLY LITTLE BITCH?" Halstead lost his shit. He came to his feet, face inflamed, and poked a finger that hit me just below the collarbone. I let him. Once. "I am the ambassador for the United States of America, and I will not have you make a mockery of us by shitting all over the laws of the United Kingdom, you prissy, high-minded little—" He jabbed at me again.

Less than a second later, he was screaming and grunting on the floor, his wrist twisted in a lock on the outside of my leg. I had my foot, the newly grown one, resting lightly on the side of his head, and his face was buried in Mary Marshwin's carpeting. She was on her feet, hands on the edge of the desk in mild alarm, but she hadn't made a move to grab her phone, which I considered to be to her credit. Wexford was standing a bit stiffly, but he did not look particularly upset. Maybe he hadn't had time to get there just yet. Maybe he was secretly glad to see Halstead with his face buried in the floor.

"Excuse me for just a moment," I said to both of them, apologetically, "this is an internecine dispute."

Wexford cleared his throat and regained his powers of speech first. "Quite. Well."

"Listen, dipshit," I dropped the formality as I turned my head to speak down at Halstead, "I don't know whose lower backside cheeks you kissed to get this post, but let me make something plain to you. You may be the Ambassador of the

United States to the United Kingdom, but I am the am-*badass*-ador. I'm here to help them, and you're being a dick. So, we're going to listen to what our hosts have to say for a few minutes, and you're going to learn to love the flavor of Ms. Marshwin's carpet while we do. Understand?" I inwardly cringed at the inadvertent double entendre, but I had a feeling no one else caught that one, so I ignored it. My brother would have been laughing had he been here, though.

"*Mmmrgh—!*" he started to say, his face half-buried in the pile. I pushed him down harder.

"I'll take your silence as an answer, all right?" I kept one hand on his sleeve, keeping him in place, and used the other to brush my long hair off my face. "Sorry about that," I looked up at Marshwin and Wexford. "You have concerns?"

Mary Marshwin looked to Wexford, then back to me. She didn't just look taken aback, she looked taken to the next damned county. "I don't wish to incur your wrath—"

"If you want me to surrender my guns, I will," I said. "Under protest, since we're dealing with at least one meta who has proven himself dangerous, but I'll do it. If you want me to leave, I'll do that. In spite of what this dickhead thinks, I'm here to help you, and I'll comply with what you want as best I can." I felt my face go stiff. "But this guy—the one I just ran across, the villain, not the moron drooling in your carpet—he's dangerous. Truly vicious and well equipped. He's a genuine threat. Probably the first one I've run into in two years."

"I don't have a problem with you keeping your weapons," Mary Marshwin said—of course—sternly.

"We would ask that you be careful in discharging them, though," Wexford added, sounding slightly apologetic.

"Much appreciated," I said.

"It's no less than we've done for others of your law enforcement branches over the years," Wexford said with a dismissive wave of his hand. "We do have another concern, though, and it's about your…" He coughed, delicately, and looked to Marshwin.

"We don't want you flying over the city of London," Marshwin said. "At all."

"London is a no-fly zone," I repeated back to her. "Got it."

"And do try to keep the bloodshed to a minimum," Marshwin said, emotionless. "We've had some problems in the last few years with spots on our reputation due to police actions that have resulted in deaths. We'd like to try and get these bastards alive if possible." I got the sense from the way she said it that "bastards" might have been Mary Marshwin's strongest epithet.

"Yes, alive would be best if possible," Alistair Wexford said with an apologetic tinge to his smile. "I'm sorry if that puts you out, but—"

"I'll do what I can," I said. I looked down at Halstead. I could see half his face, and his lips were partially visible. "Hear that? That's how you make a polite request of someone." I shook my head at Marshwin and Wexford. "I love your British manners. No one can deliver bad news quite like you folks can."

"Would you mind letting him loose?" Wexford asked. "I hate to impose, but… we are responsible for his safety while he's here…"

"Sure," I said, and let him go with a final, not-so-gentle crank of the arm that elicited a grunt of pain. "Since you asked nicely."

"What will you do now?" Marshwin asked, her spine just a little straighter now that Halstead was out of my grip. It was the only hint of how stressed she must have been while watching me manhandle him.

"Follow your boy Webster's lead," I said, cracking my knuckles now that my hand was free of Halstead. I popped each of them in turn, eliciting a wince from Wexford and an even stare from Marshwin. "Track this guy down. Stop him."

"Very good," Wexford said, still with that tight smile. He looked a little like a butler who'd been told he was done for the night. "We entrust this investigation to your capable hands, Ms. Nealon."

"At least somebody does," I said, nudging Halstead with my toe as I turned to leave. He grunted, clutching his arm and wrist to his side. Wuss. I hadn't broken them or anything, though soft tissue damage was a possibility.

"And Ms. Nealon," Wexford said as I hit the door, opening it.

"Yes?" I asked, turning about.

"Do be careful," Wexford said with a faint smile tinged with worry. "I should not care to see you come to additional harm while assisting us."

"There's nothing these pricks can do to hurt me." I smiled and shut the door.

Chapter 13

I snuck up on Webster without him even realizing it. He was studying something on his computer, staring at it like it contained the very secrets of life. He had on earphones and was bent over as if he were listening to the very secrets of the universe.

Or he could have been watching porn on the internet. He was certainly hunched over enough for it.

The bullpen had cleared out; the few windows provided a sweeping view of the darkness falling outside. The smell of coffee that had been so strong earlier in the day had faded along with the volume of noise in the room. I saw other people coming in now, maybe the night shift, and heads were down as people worked on computers or paperwork. I approached Webster.

When I got close enough to see his computer, I knew why he had the headphones in. He was on YouTube, watching an interview from NNC, the National News Channel. It was a couple years old, but I recognized it immediately.

Since I was the one being interviewed.

I could remember almost every word like it had happened yesterday. I watched the interviewer, Gail Roth, asking a question, and even without reading her lips, I knew what she was saying. That moment was etched in my mind, along with the slightly burnt smell of the hot lights in the studio, the scent of the makeup they'd spackled on my face that made me feel like a geisha, and the sense that the air conditioning in the room was in a perpetual and losing battle with the heat coming off the lighting rigs.

"Why you?" Gail Roth asked me. I watched her lips flap in time with the question, and I could hear her words in my head. She had blondish-brown hair and enough of the look of youth still about her that she wasn't going to be kicked off the national newscasts for the crime of aging just yet.

"Why not me?" I asked as the camera shifted angles to catch my reaction. I had gently taken Gail's question and lobbed it back at her. Reed had taught me how to do it, said it was a sales technique called a porcupine. I hadn't asked him how he'd known that.

"You're... nineteen years old?" Gail asked, and waited for my nod. "You've just saved millions of people from a tyrant who supposedly had enough power to take over the world—"

"Yes, he did," I said, interrupting her to confirm that little fact for her. Sovereign definitely had the power to take over the world. I'd seen what would have happened if he'd gotten his way. Enough power was not his problem.

Gail paused, eyes searching me as she made a face to play for the camera. "You have to understand, for the viewers at home... we're taking a lot of this on faith. Everyone's seen the footage from the battle over Minneapolis, which was— incredible. Scarcely believable. The sort of thing you'd see in a Hollywood summer tentpole, not the evening news. You turned into an enormous, flaming dragon—"

"I'd just like to point out," I said, interrupting her again, "that the camera adds ten pounds, and there were an awful lot of cameras pointing at me that day. Like... all of them, I think."

"You turned into a giant dragon," Gail Roth said, not breaking away. Her gaze was annoyingly penetrating. And not in any kind of good way. "You burst into flames. And you killed a man—"

"A very bad one, but yes," I said, nodding. "Again, just for the record, I did try very hard to get him to surrender first."

She settled into her chair, shifting to the right. "What were you talking about with him up there? While you were fighting?"

"Geopolitics," I said with a straight face. "State-of-the-world-type stuff."

She blinked once, and that was all the reaction she gave that the answer might not be what she expected. "How so?"

"Well, Sovereign was of the opinion that people are in need of… stewardship," I said. "That they should be made to fear in order to keep them between the lines. That he could build a better world just by imposing his will on all of us. I politely disagreed, telling him that you can't stomp on a person's free will and freedom like that. Then I disagreed less politely. With punches to the face."

"You have a real wit," Gail said, and it didn't sound entirely like a selling point the way she said it.

"As you pointed out, I'm nineteen," I replied. "You're just lucky I'm not answering, 'Totally!' and 'OMG!' to everything."

Roth turned her head down to look at her notes at that point, leaving about a half second of dead air. I remembered taking that moment to catch my breath. I could feel the sweat rolling down my back from the nervousness. "How long had you known this 'Sovereign'?" She frowned. "Did he have a real name?"

"Marius," I said, nodding. "His name was Marius. I'd known him for about a year, on and off? He came to me under false pretenses." Very, very false pretenses. "He'd introduced himself as an ally, as a friend. It was only later I found out he was behind everything—"

"You realize that the concept of a giant conspiracy to keep this secret of metahumans under wraps is… well, it defies most peoples' ability to believe?" Gail asked me. She did it a little haltingly.

I was ready for this one. "I know how they feel," I said. "I felt the same way myself when I learned about the secret. I was raised as normal as anyone." *You know, except for being locked in my house until age seventeen.* "When I found out the truth about what I was, it was an eye opener. But I quickly found out that not only were there people out there with powers beyond those of normal humans, but there was this whole other world under the surface, and there were bad things brewing in it that wouldn't just go away if I ignored them."

"Back in January of 2012 there was an incident in the city of Minneapolis," she said, looking back to her notes. "A man—"

"A beast," I said, ignoring the growls of protest in my head.

"—killed two hundred plus people while putting the city under a kind of siege," she finished. "Was that a metahuman incident?"

"Yes," I said. It had been. I took a breath, hoping her follow-up didn't go in the direction I didn't want it to.

"A week later, the city of Glencoe, Minnesota, was destroyed in a blast not dissimilar from what you unleashed in northern Minnesota at the close of your war." Now she was turning toward accusing. "Was that you?"

"No," I said, shaking my head. "That was Aleksandr Gavrikov, a meta with a very similar power." Exactly the same power, in fact. Because he was in my head, too, now.

"Another incident in western Kansas a few months later," Gail said, flipping through her notes. "Hundreds of square miles on fire. An incident in the British museum, where the security camera footage shows you fighting with undisclosed adversaries—"

"I can explain that one," I said, feeling like I was rapidly losing control of the situation, "those were Sovereign's allies. Well, some of them were, at least, and—"

Gail's voice overpowered mine. "You seem to have been involved in a lot of... incidents. Orlando Airport. A plane crash outside Bloomington, Minnesota. Some sort of battle on the freeway. The destruction of a warehouse—"

I felt my fingernails dig into my palms, drawing me from that moment, the moment when I could feel all control slipping away, back to the present, and a bullpen in New Scotland Yard where I was watching it all unfold on a screen. There was a tightness in my chest as I remembered the moment, and I looked away, trying to clear it out of my mind. I didn't to be reminded of that interview, of what had happened during it. Because of it. Not now.

"Hey," I said, ripping Detective Inspector Matthew Webster out of his interview-induced coma with a tap on the shoulder. He fumbled, the headphones popping out of his ears before he could watch things on the screen go from bad to worse for me.

"Oh, oh," Webster said, flushing as he fought to spin back around and stop the video. "Oh. All right, there you are."

"Here I am," I said. "And there I am." I gestured toward the monitor, and he clicked the mouse rapidly toward the "shut down" command without even bothering to close the browser window. "And where are we?"

He blinked in confusion as I saw his mind try and catch up. "Oh, right. Ah, we are nowhere. No other hints of any of your friends around the city. We sent out units to all the last known addresses and came up a bit dry. It looks like the rest of them are in hiding, but perhaps your friend Angus didn't get the message."

"I told you, they're not my friends." I let out a slow exhalation. "So, what do we do now?"

"Well, I don't know about you," he said, standing, pulling his trench coat off the back of his chair, "but I'm at a dead end for the night and bloody tired."

"Right," I agreed. "We should get some rest and come back to this tomorrow. Call me if something comes up in the meantime?"

"Certainly," he said. "I've got your mobile number." He frowned. "Is your mobile still working after that explosion?"

I reached into my pocket and pulled it out. The screen was a little cracked, but it lit up when I pushed the button. "Looks salvageable."

"Are you going to check into a hotel?" he asked.

"Yeah, I'll just—" I reached for my credit card in my back pocket and pulled it out with a snap. It emerged as half the card it used to be.

"Well, damn," I said, staring at my half credit card. "I hope they'll still accept it."

"Is the RFID still intact?" Webster asked, leaning down to peer at it.

"The RF-what?" I held up the half card and tugged the other half free from my pants pocket. They were too damned tight. Always. Pants were not made for my hips.

"There's no RFID on this card," Webster said with a shake of his head. "It uses the magnetic strip, and that's snapped clean in half. You're not going to get them to accept this because no one can read it."

"Son of a bitch," I muttered.

"You can just stay at the U.S. embassy," he said, putting his coat on. "Doubtless they have some extra space."

I glanced back at Mary Marshwin's office, where I'd left the U.S. ambassador in a pile on the floor. "Yeah... that's... probably not going to happen..."

"Perhaps you could ask the commissioner for a housing allowance," he said.

I looked at the door of her office. The lights were still burning, and I hadn't heard anyone leave. "Maybe."

"No cash?" Webster asked, pulling my attention back to him.

"I didn't exactly have time to hit the bank before I came over," I said. I could feel the fatigue settling on my bones. I'd been awake for over twenty-four hours, and I'd flown here, which took a toll. Especially at supersonic speed.

Webster had his coat on now, and it had bunched up on his shoulders, crooked lines that told me he was tense. "I'd suggest you could stay with me, but I've only got a one-bedroom flat." My heart raced a little at the mere suggestion and fell at the next words he said. "It's truly a disgrace, though, an utter mess. I think I might die of embarrassment if you saw it, actually."

"It's fine, I'll figure something out," I said. "I'll just... grovel to your Foreign Secretary. Maybe he'll come up with something. Or try and get someone from my office to send me a wire transfer—"

"I rather doubt you'll find a Western Union open at this hour," Webster said apologetically. His face was crumpled, and I watched it loosen. "There is one other option," he said. I could tell he was still running it through his mind.

"Oh?" I was open to just about anything, even a youth hostel at this point. (Not the torture porn kind.) The thought of having to ask Marshwin or even Wexford to set me up with pocket money for a hotel was about as appealing to me as the thought of drinking straight out of the Thames. "What did you have in mind?"

Webster looked embarrassed for just a flash. "Well, my mum has a place on the outskirts. It's got an extra room, it's not too far, and she's a bit lonely..."

"Your mom?" I asked, in just a little disbelief. I thought about it for a quarter of a second, and the image of me pushing Halstead's face into Mary Marshwin's carpeting came back to me. "Sounds good," I said.

"A word of caution about my mum, though," he said, and I could tell that some regret was already settling in. "She's a bit… um…"

"It's fine," I said and tried to give him a reassuring smile. "Whoever she is, trust me when I tell you that she's probably an absolute angel compared to what I've dealt with in the past myself."

Chapter 14

Philip could smell the fear in the room. He liked that smell. The scent of piss and blood, the anticipation of what was about to happen. It made him quiver under his suit. He wasn't going to get his hands dirty, not on this one, but he was more than happy to stand back and let Liliana do her level best to make Angus Waterman scream until his head burst.

"I got nuffing to tell you," Angus said, his Adam's apple bobbing from where he sat tied to a steel chair. It had a nice aesthetic, Philip had thought when he'd bought it. It wouldn't look out of place in a modern flat.

Or here, bolted to a concrete floor, with a shuddering, naked, fat-arsed man attached to it via steel handcuffs.

"I don't need you to tell me anything, Angus," Philip said, giving him a thin smile.

"Oh?" Angus looked from him to Antonio, who stood in the corner in the shadows, arms folded as he leaned against the wall. The bomb maker looked thoroughly bored, as if he might keel over from the tedium right there. "Then why are you bothering with me?"

Philip took a breath as a way to measure his response. Then he took another. Fear was created in those moments between words, in that heady silence that came before Angus saw something that would take his own breath away.

Like now.

Liliana pulled the old man along on the chains suspended from the ceiling. He was hooked upside down, still, long strips of skin still missing and the muscle beneath exposed under a thin layer of blood. He hung, well, just a lump like the sides of beef and pork that had probably been suspended in this very warehouse when it was open for operation. It was handy, having the ceiling tracks so they could pull someone along like that.

The rattle of the chains drew Angus's head around just in time to see Liliana dragging the old man into his view. Angus's face drained of the slight color it had possessed before, and he was left smacking his lips together. "What is this?"

"This is your future," Philip said, not letting even a hint of a smile creep out. "Though I daresay yours is perhaps not as long, torturous or even robust as his."

Angus's lips pursed together hard and Philip enjoyed the sight of it. The bigger man was clearly fighting for courage. But there wasn't much courage to be had here. After all, courage sprouted from hope—hope that one could accomplish something, hope that maybe he would be able to hold out for rescue.

There wasn't any of that here.

And Philip was going to enjoy every minute of watching Angus come to that very realization himself.

"Is that…?" Angus's voice sounded small at first, then gained in strength. "Is that you, Janus?"

The old man made a feeble croak. "Yessss…"

"Good God, what have you done to him?" Angus's look went to a more deeply horrified place.

"Flayed him," Liliana said in that dead tone. It caused Angus to look over at her, as though he were taking notice for the very first time that she was even here.

"You bastards," Angus said, which was unexpected. Philip almost snorted a laugh, to see this little pig try and stand up on its hind legs in defiance. "You're all a bunch of right bastards." He spat at Philip. "You're an arse." He looked to Liliana. "You're a twat." He turned his gaze to Antonio in the corner. "And you're a prick."

Antonio came off the wall slightly, a perplexed look crossing his dark features as he turned to Liliana. "What's the difference between a twat and a prick?"

"It is no great surprise to me…" Janus said from where he hung upside down, bleeding to the floor, "… that you would not know the answer to that."

Antonio started toward the old man, but Philip stopped him with a simple motion of the hand. "His future is not that bright," Philip said. "Let him bask in the pain." He snapped a finger at Liliana and she produced a knife, which she stabbed into the old man's thigh. A high-pitched scream cut the air. She ran the blade down through the meat, and the agonizing noise continued.

But now Angus added to it with a sound of his own— feverish, heavy, high-pitched breaths drawn all too quickly.

Ah. There was the fear.

Philip watched as Liliana pulled her blade from Janus, and with a nod he beckoned her on to Angus. The little piggy did better than he would have expected, lasting almost a full thirty seconds before he let loose his first scream.

After that, he did not stop until it was over.

Chapter 15

It was a simple brick house with a lovely yard—I think they call them gardens over here—and a white picket fence ringing the whole thing. If the sun had been shining instead of grey clouding out the twilight, it would have been idyllic. We parked on the street and got out, still wordless, Webster having fallen into a deep hole of reticence after we got in the car at New Scotland Yard.

I suspected he was afraid of the same thing all big, strong, proud men were afraid of.

That his mommy was going to tell me embarrassing stories about him. Or show me pictures of his naked butt from childhood. Which I didn't care about. Because I was more interested in his naked butt as an adult.

That didn't need to be said, though.

He went through a sequence of emotions as we walked up to the front door. They played out on his face one by one, and the common theme undergirding them all was fear. I knew because when it came to mothers, I was deeply familiar with fear. I knew all about it.

"Listen," he said, pausing on the step just outside. The hesitation was a force of its own, his lower lip jutting slightly. It was kinda cute. "My mum…"

"Is she some kind of heinous villain who's going to cut me off at the knees?" I asked.

"No, nothing like that," he said with a shake of the head. "Besides, you've already had that happen once today."

"Is she cruel? Will she lock me in the basement and never let me out?"

"What? No," he said, mildly horrified.

"Then we're fine," I said and knocked on the door for him. He looked a little jarred as I did it but swallowed his pride and knocked himself, a little louder, as though I hadn't just done it.

"Just a minute!" came a high voice from inside, muffled by the doors and walls between us. I could hear someone bustling across wood floors in a hurry. When the door swung open, we were faced with a delightful, matronly lady who stood partially obscured behind the door. Her hair was tinged with red, making it a light auburn. She already wore a smile before she even saw Webster, but it brightened immediately once she laid eyes on him.

"Matthew!" she cried out in joy and had him in a great hug a second later. She crossed over the threshold without even taking notice of me, and she buried her head on his chest. She was shorter than him by a head or more and looked to be an inch or two taller than me, if that. She carried with her a faint scent of sweet perfume that reminded me of grandmothers I had passed in various stores.

After a solid minute of hugging him, she came off and saw me. "Oh, and who is this?" She asked with a twinkle in her eyes. "Matthew, have you brought a—"

"She's working with me, Mum," Webster said before she could finish her thought. "Sienna Nealon, this is my mum, Marjorie. Mum, this is Sienna Nealon."

"It's lovely to meet you, dear," she said and hugged me, too. I felt her arms envelop me and was utterly powerless to stop her. She was warm and sweet, and I couldn't remember the last time I'd been hugged.

Then I remembered and felt a lump in my throat.

"Oh, let me look at you," she said, breaking off. "Any friend of Matthew's is welcome in this house, of course." She hurried back inside. "I wish you'd called, though!" She disappeared through the door. "I haven't had a chance to straighten anything at all, the place is a dreadful mess."

Webster gestured for me to enter, and I did. I found myself in a hallway that led past a narrow staircase. To the right was a sitting room that opened into a small kitchen. Overstuffed couches filled the sitting room, and bookshelves filled with books lined the walls. Each shelf was neatly arranged from tallest to shortest book. There were two perfectly folded blankets on the back of each couch.

My eyes fell to a table just to my right in the entry; it had freshly cut flowers from the garden, bright yellow and red ones, and when I let my finger run idly across the surface of the table, it came back completely free of dust.

Clearly, Ma Webster and I had differing ideas about what constituted a "dreadful mess."

"I've got Lancashire hotpot on," she called from in the kitchen. "The kettle's almost boiling as well, if you'd care for some tea." Her head popped around the entry to the sitting room. "Sienna, was it?"

"Yes, ma'am," I answered.

"Mum," Webster called as he shut the door and locked it, "Sienna's come over from the States. She's uh… in need of a place to stay for the night."

I heard something clatter in the kitchen. "An American, dear?" Her head poked out again and she still wore a genuine smile. "Any friend of Matthew's is welcome here, of course." She straightened. "Oh, but the spare bedroom is in a terrible state, I'll need to clean it immediately—" She froze. "Oh, the hotpot!" She disappeared back into the kitchen.

I glanced at Webster. "Yeah, your mom is a real terror. I see why you warned me about her."

He cringed. "She's a lovely person, really. She just… maybe tries a bit too hard."

"To what?" I asked, bereft of a clue. "To please others? God, what a failing that is."

"It can be a bit awkward," he said, clearly a little embarrassed.

"Oh, how you have suffered," I said, "having a mother who endears herself to other people."

"It's harder than you think," he said. "Every one of my friends liked her more than me. She always had biscuits for them, always had extra dinner—and apparently she continues the tradition, even years after I got my own flat—I can't even count the number of my former girlfriends she keeps in touch with in spite of me being done with them for years and years."

I raised an eyebrow at him. "Oh, yeah? Are there are lot of those?"

He grunted and looked a little flushed. "The point is, it's not easy to live in her shadow."

"I've got some biscuits before dinner," Marjorie said, appearing from the kitchen with a tray of cookies. A pot of tea sat in the middle of it, and three cups with saucers were arranged around the tray. She made her way to the overstuffed couches and bid us enter with a wave as she set it upon the table in the middle of the room. "Well, come on, then. The tea will get cold."

"Truly, I know no one with a burden as great as yours," I muttered to Webster as I came into the sitting room.

"One lump or two, dear?" Marjorie asked.

"Two, I guess." I didn't really do tea, so I didn't know what was better. I liked my coffee sweet, though.

"And one for Matthew—" Marjorie started.

"None for Matthew," he corrected.

"Oh, that's right," she said and rapped her knuckles against the wooden table's edge. "I forget that you're watching your weight. Good heavens, though, Matthew, I do worry that you're not eating enough. You're a growing lad—"

"All my upward growing is done, Mum," he said as he seated himself on the sofa next to her. "Now it's all horizontal growth."

"Of course," she said, almost resigned. "But I've always maintained that a girl likes to be with a man who has a healthy appetite and a reasonable waistline." She looked at me. "What do you think, Sienna dear?"

I had a hot cup of tea about two inches from my mouth when she asked. "Uh… sure."

She beamed at me and picked up the plate that had the cookies on it. "Biscuit, dear?"

Chapter 16

Angus was dead. Philip had watched it happen, oh so slowly. It was really a joy to watch, especially knowing what Angus had represented. What he'd been a part of.

"Messy," Antonio opined. He didn't usually stay to watch, preferring to spend his time in the office mucking about with his toys. He'd stayed for this one, though. It was as though being called a prick had awakened a primal desire within the man to see some suffering.

Well, there had been plenty of that.

"Where's the next target?" Liliana asked. Her arms were bathed in red from elbow to fingertips. Philip wondered if part of that was her ability, causing the blood to cling to her. He glanced at the corpse of Angus Waterman, then looked back to Liliana. No, it was probably just the nature of what had happened that caused her to be so soaked.

"We have a wide open field," Philip said, his arms crossed in front of him. He'd kept his distance so as to keep his suit free from the bodily fluids that had spattered throughout the chamber. "I have a clear line to each of them."

"Are you concerned that the police will find them?" Antonio asked.

"No," Philip said. "It's a very slight possibility, not likely at all." He dealt in possibilities, in the chances that the things he saw coming would reach fruition. It was a very segmented way of looking at life, he knew, but it was his advantage. It was what made him unique.

It was what made him invincible.

"No," Philip said again. "They'll keep. What we need to do now is take this trail that we've been so neatly laying for the Metropolitan Police—and now Ms. Nealon—to follow and introduce a red herring for them to chase before we carry out tomorrow's business." He tapped his chin, giving a slight nod of acknowledgment to Antonio. Liliana had an idea about how to do that. "Something that will... shall we say... up the chaos quotient? Make our ultimate goal a bit easier to achieve by taking their attention away..." He glanced at Liliana. "I believe you might know someone who fits that description."

She was not smiling, but it was apparent in her bearing that she had something in mind. "Chaos?" she asked in that dark, satisfied voice. "I think I know someone whose bloody death will cause more than a little chaos..."

Chapter 17

I'd never had Lancashire hotpot before, and I ate like I'd never eaten anything before in my life. Like I hadn't had ten of those biscuits Marjorie had offered me. And two cups of warm, sugary tea.

"Gracious, dear, slow down," Marjorie said to me with a smile. "There's plenty enough for you, and if it's not enough I can make you something else—"

"It's plenty, Mum," Webster said. "There's still half the pot left, and I'm done."

I glanced at Marjorie's plate. She had what I would consider a half portion, and she'd had barely three bites of it. She had a nervous energy about her, like she was ready to get up and start bustling about, cleaning something or making something else. She stayed seated, though, shooting a reassuring smile at Webster before cutting a slice of potato no bigger than my thumb in half and gingerly chewing it.

She made me feel like a horse eating from a trough by comparison.

"Sorry," I said, slowing down. "It's just been a little while since I've eaten. And this is... very good." I dabbed my mouth with my napkin and found a lot more layering my lips than lipstick. Which I never wore.

"I'm glad you like it, dear," she said with a gentle smile. She took another impossibly small bite and took five minutes to chew it. If I ate like she did, I'd never have time to work. "So, what brings you over here from the U.S.?"

"She's investigating a series of murders with me," Webster said. He caught my frown at answering for me and blushed. "Sorry."

"Well, that's a bit frightening," Marjorie said. "I don't care for that work Matthew does, but I suppose someone has to keep us safe." Lines creased her face, making her look older.

I could smell the Lancashire hotpot, the delicious scent of the onions still making my mouth water two servings later. "At least he's good at his job."

"That's very true," Marjorie said and put down her fork to stroke Webster's arm. He grunted in acknowledgment. Personally, I wouldn't have been able to spare the seconds of putting down the fork, but Marjorie was clearly very different than myself. "What exactly is this dreadful murdering that you're looking into, dear?"

I waited to see if Webster would answer for me, but a shared glance told me he'd learned his lesson. "A metahuman was killed," I said, waiting to see what her reaction would be. "And another one kidnapped."

"Oh, heavens, that is dreadful," Marjorie said, shaking her head. She stared a bit closer at me, and I waited for it. Waited. "Oh!" she said at last, and it sounded a little joyful. "It's you, you're her!"

"I'm her," I said. She'd taken longer than most people to recognize me.

She reached over and slapped Webster's arm, causing him to look up in surprise. "We have a veritable celebrity in the house, Matthew! And you didn't even think to make mention that you were coming over! I don't even know why you have one of those mobile phones if you won't even use it to tell your mother you're bringing over such a famous guest…"

Webster, for his part, looked suitably chastened. His eyebrows arched downward, and his fork paused in its ascent to his mouth. He'd eaten maybe—maybe—a quarter of the enormous portion his mother had dished out for him. I'll admit, I was eyeing it like a hungry dog. Or like I imagine a hungry dog would look at it, if that dog had a taste for Lancashire hotpot. Because of the change in time zones, I didn't even know what time it was when I'd last eaten, so it was totally justifiable, right?

Marjorie made an exasperated noise and got up from the table. She went straight to the freezer and began to rummage through it. "Famous company come all the way from America to my house, and I don't even have a decent dessert to put on the table... Matthew, if your guest wasn't here, I'd give you a right piece of my mind..."

He looked a little disquieted at that.

Me? I was thinking about dessert.

Chapter 18

To Philip's eyes, the flat he was looking into was not all that different from his last. A bit more posh, perhaps. A bit more upmarket than Philip's had been, before he left it in favor of the warehouse. But it was clearly a place of refinement, in a higher-class neighborhood. As he entered the building with Liliana at his side, he made note of the lobby, of how it looked. Plush red carpeting that the feet sunk into.

Yes, it was truly a lovely place. A place where he might have wanted to live after this was all over.

But what they were about to do was going to make that well nigh impossible, unfortunately.

Besides, he'd have enough dosh to afford something better once this was finished, anyway.

The man behind the security station just inside looked up from his desk as Philip and Liliana made their way toward him. There were only a very few probabilities floating around for how this would go, and they narrowed all the way up until he rose from his seat to greet them and presumably ask who they were here to see—

Then Liliana produced a knife with a flick of her wrist and ripped the poor bastard's throat out with a hard slash.

Philip knew which direction the blood would spatter and sidestepped it at the last moment. Liliana was always considerate and very seldom messy when she didn't want to be, but the guard's movements didn't exactly help her. The guard clutched at his throat and made a wheezing, gasping, sick sort of noise as he fell back behind the desk. Philip counted the seconds until he was sure the man had expired.

No more future for that one.

He started moving again, and Liliana followed him. Philip paused for a moment and shouldered his way into a nondescript door just beyond the elevator banks. It contained a half dozen surveillance monitors, cameras showing a dozen hallways. It also provided a wonderful view of the guard, still making his final twitching motions in the lobby.

Philip pressed a button with his knuckle and a CD ejected with a whirring noise.

"Is that it?" Liliana asked.

Philip concentrated for just a moment. "That's it. No backup recording, nothing to catch these lovely images." He made a vague wave toward the monitors and paused on the image of the desk guard, now still. "Without this, it's quite dead."

Liliana almost smiled at the subtle joke. "Fifth floor."

They rode the lift in silence. No music played, thankfully; low-key Muzak was not exactly Philip's cup of tea. At the fifth floor, they exited. He stopped her just before the fourth door, gently backing her toward the wall of the hallway. He feigned kissing her, pressing her head back, turning his face so that he could not be seen. He heard the faint sound of a door opening, then closing. Footsteps traced their way toward them, and he heard a cough. The footsteps receded toward the elevator, and when he heard the ding, he gently put an arm on her elbow and tugged her away so that they man who'd passed by them had no chance to look at their faces.

"Sorry," he said.

"Don't apologize," she said in that cold tone, "you know what needs to be done. I am at your disposal."

He felt a slight thrill at her words. Not because they hinted at something suggestive—he knew they didn't—but because the simple command of such a chilling instrument as Liliana Negrescu was a heady thought for him. This was power, real power, and to be able to wield her body, her skill, her very life the way that bitch Sienna Nealon might pull a gun, well... that was more than some American whose instinct was to shoot first would ever understand.

"What's his name?" Philip asked as they reached the door. It was a wood-frame, solid panel, nicely carved. It suited the building, that was for certain.

"Dmitriy Alkaev," she said, and he caught a hint of that joy in her voice. Deep within. "He's Chief of Station—head of the spies for the Russians in London. Works in the embassy."

"Well, then," Philip said with a smile, "this should start a bit of a diplomatic incident."

"It will start more than that," Liliana said with that chilling joy as she kicked in the door.

Philip waited for her to enter, and by the time she had, he already had a sense of Dmitriy Alkaev. It only took seconds for Liliana to cross the main room and reach Alkaev, where he rested in a leather chaise, a bottle of vodka by his side. "A drunken Russian," Philip said as he entered the room. "What a terrible stereotype to perpetuate." He kept his hands clasped behind him.

"What... is this?" Alkaev said in a heavy accent. Liliana had him by the throat, gripped tight, fingers already pressing heavily into his neck. He tried to speak again, but his words were cut off by the pressure.

"This is a slaughter," Philip said, pacing to the edge of the room. The room was plain, far from ornately decorated. In fact, in spite of it being a fine flat in a fine building, one might have assumed that this man was poverty-stricken by the state of his possessions. Philip glanced around. Not a single book. Not a hint of culture. No paintings. His eyes fell on two posters of nude women hung in the far room. They weren't exactly Botticellis; they looked more like a pair of Page 3 girls. He sniffed his nose at the affront to good taste. "Liliana, you will have to let him breathe at some point."

"He can breathe through his nose," she said simply.

"Very well, then," Philip said and picked up a dress shirt that was hung, wrinkled, upon the back of a chair in the dining room. Philip took another brief glance at the nude pictures on the wall and shook his head. He pinched the shirt between his fingers and handed it to Liliana, placing it in her gloved hand.

She crumpled the shirt, smashing it into a ball less that the size of her fist. She did this while Alkaev watched, horrified, unspeaking, a low squealing noise coming out of his mouth.

Philip made his way back to the door, lifting it off the ground and settling it into the frame. It leaned slightly off-kilter but rested in place. "That should keep the prying eyes out," he said, leaning against it. He turned in time to see Liliana stuff the shirt—compressed by her strength into a ball—into Alkaev's open mouth. Philip did not know this Alkaev, had not heard of him before today, but he knew one thing for bloody certain: Dmitriy Alkaev had angered Liliana Negrescu at some point in the past.

And Philip would not have cared to trade places with him for all the vodka in Russia.

The torture began, as it always did, at the point of a knife. Alkaev cried and whimpered and begged, each in turn, each sound suppressed by the makeshift gag. The television blared, deafening Philip as he stood there, back against the door, watching Liliana drag Alkaev around the apartment as she did her work. It was a thing of beauty, really.

"Just like the others, yes?" Liliana asked as she played with her new toy.

"Well… perhaps with one slight difference," Philip said with a smile. "To keep things interesting."

An impressively brutal hour later, she was done.
And so was Dmitriy Alkaev.

Chapter 19

I felt full to bursting, splayed out on the sitting room couch with Marjorie Webster across from me. She was staring at me intently, and I felt a little uncomfortable. Not just from all I had eaten, but also because… well… I was uncomfortable being stared at.

"What was it like, dear?" she asked, finally getting around to asking what I suspected she'd wanted to all along. Webster was upstairs, sorting out the spare bedroom with new sheets at her request. I got the feeling that those bedroom sheets were probably as clean as could be and hadn't been slept in since the last time she'd changed them, but Ms. Webster commanded, and her son grudgingly went up to do as he was told.

"What was what like?" I asked. I suspected I knew what she was getting at, but it never hurt to narrow things down.

"Saving the world," she said quietly.

I forced a smile. "Not everyone believes I did."

"That's rubbish, that is," she said, a rock-hard certainty underlying her words. "I don't care what any flat-earther thinks. The world changed on us. People still argue that no man has walked on the moon. I don't pay much attention to them, either." She leaned forward, hands resting on her knees. "So, what was it like?"

"I don't know," I said, shaking my head. "Scary. Exhilarating. Gut-clenchingly frightening."

She gave me a slow nod. "I can imagine a few of those feelings went right together."

"I was afraid at the time that I was going to be outed and thrown in jail," I said. "Or turned into some kind of scapegoat or freak show."

"But you weren't," she said. "They called you a hero. The President gave you a medal."

"Yeah," I said with a nod. "But… it didn't look like that was what was going to happen at the time. And Sovereign…" I shook my head. I was so over talking about that dipshit. "He was a real piece of work."

She gave me a curt nod and averted her eyes. "And your young man?" She looked up, and I caught a hint of slyness. "That blond fellow who helped walk you out of your house afterwards?"

"How did you know he was my…" I saw a spark of laughter behind those eyes, and I knew I'd been had. "He's not my boyfriend anymore," I said simply.

"Oh, I'm sorry to hear that, dear," Ms. Webster said, and I caught genuine regret in the way she said it. "Sometimes it works out for the best, though. And you're so young! It's better to be unfettered when you're that age. I'm sure he'll treasure the memories of your time together, though."

"I don't think so," I said, feeling a slithering sense of guilt crawl up from my stomach.

"Oh, it ended that badly, did it?" She seemed more regretful for asking about it than anything.

"Well, it didn't end well," I said. "But… I'm sure he doesn't remember me at all anymore. Not that way."

"Nonsense," she said. "A fine-looking lass like you would be impossible to forget."

"No." I felt the color drain from my face. "Not impossible."

Not for someone who could remove memories.

"What was the problem, dear?" she asked, jolting me out of my trance. "I had more than a few dust-ups with

84

Matthew's father, God rest his soul, but we always managed to work it out in the end—"

"It was work," I said, cutting her off. Why was I telling her this? I hadn't told anyone this. My brother was good enough to keep his mouth shut after Scott had left the Agency, at least about my love life. "I work a lot," I said, answering her inquiring gaze.

"Work is important," she said, and I got the feeling she was choosing her words carefully to avoid tripping over them.

"I agree," I said.

"So what was the problem?"

"He… didn't always want to be competing with my job," I said. I smoothed the wrinkled leg of my pants.

Marjorie's gaze pierced deep, and her eyes did not move off me. "But it's more than a job to you, isn't it, dear?"

"Yes," I said, feeling it. "Yes, it is. It's everything I have."

"Surely you must have friends?" This with just a hint of concern.

"I did," I said, smoothing that pant leg again. Was that a crease or a wrinkle? "But they all moved on to other things." I felt a bitter taste in my mouth. "They all have lives."

She inclined her head just slightly. "And what do you have?"

I felt a sharp pang inside. "A purpose. I—" I stopped when I heard motion on the stairs, and Matthew descended with a furious clomping like a goat shambling down. Or a cow. Or a—something heavy. Something that didn't wear a trench coat.

"Got another mess on our hands," he said as he swept into the sitting room. That trench coat really billows. It's cool. And a good look for him.

"Did they find Angus?" I asked, rising to my feet. Marjorie was a little slower to get up.

"No," he said. "Someone different. Flat in Westminster, body torn to pieces and flayed—"

"Matthew!" Marjorie said, flinching away with a look of horror.

"Sorry, Mum," he said, contrite. "Looks like Maxwell Llewelyn all over again, but this one was done in his own home."

"Let's go," I said, already sweeping out of the room. He headed me off, opening the front door before I could get to the knob myself. Or, more accurately, I let him open the door for me. Like a gentleman.

"I'll make sure to leave a light on for you, Sienna dear," Marjorie called after me. "And I'll turn down your bed if Matthew hasn't already—"

He shut the door before I could thank her.

Chapter 20

Philip watched the crime scene via the London surveillance cameras. It had been easy enough to get access; it was something he'd figured out early on by having Liliana go to work on one of the engineers. Making his way into the system had been the easy part.

Sifting the damned data? That had been impossible. Which was a shame, because that had been what Philip had wanted when he'd set out on the project. To have something watching at all times, in the moment? That was just one more step toward invincibility.

Still, it had its uses. He could tap into any camera in the city that was linked to the network, and he could shut them down as needed. He'd done just that on their way to and from every site thus far. With all the cameras in the city of London, it would be impossible to notice the few of them that went offline while he was moving.

But now he was watching. He had eyes on the door to the apartment, could see the Metropolitan Police buzzing about. He'd watched the crime scene unit go up a few minutes earlier. He didn't envy those fellows their jobs today; Liliana had left such a suitably impressive mess that even walking in the door was sure to contaminate the evidence at least a little.

Here he would sit; here he would wait. She'd be along shortly, he was sure of it. That was the whole reason he was watching, after all. To see her.

Because she could be the sweet capstone on this whole endeavor. The little plastic figurine on top of the cake.

Sienna Nealon.

Her death would be the sweetest triumph of them all.

Chapter 21

I got out in front of the building and looked up. It wasn't out of place in the London landscape. Big, impressive facade with Greek columns and lots of marble. It was only about four or five stories high, too, which also seemed the standard for much of the city. It looked classy, though, unlike a few places I'd been.

"This is a twenty-thousand-quid-per-month flat," Matthew said, adjusting his coat. He looked faintly nervous, and I wondered why.

"I assume that's a lot," I said. He gave me the pitying look I reserved for morons. I guess that's a lot.

I followed him into the lobby. We found the first corpse behind the security desk. Guy had had his throat slashed and bled out right there. There were dried, bloody handprints in the carpeting where he'd struggled to hang on to life with whatever little strength he'd had left.

"Looks like he died first," I said, "and because he was in the way."

"Keen detection skills you've got there," Webster grunted as we made our way to the elevators. We waited until one dinged and stepped inside. "What did you talk about with Mum?"

"Oh, she showed me naked baby pictures," I said casually. He froze, eyes wide.

The elevator doors opened onto a swarm of cops in the hallway. Every door was flung wide, neighbors being questioned, the whole damned floor turned out for this event. It was probably the most excitement this building had ever seen.

For their sake, I hoped they never saw anything more exciting than a torture murder.

"Detective Inspector," came the familiar voice of Alistair Wexford, standing behind a knot of officers ahead of us. I started a little, a bit surprised to see him there. It took me a second to realize Mary Marshwin was standing in his shadow, her eyelids looking lined. "Ms. Nealon," said the Foreign Secretary, acknowledging me with a nod of the head.

"Minister," Webster said urgently, his voice respectful. It was an ass-kissing tone of voice. I knew it because I couldn't deny I'd had to use it myself now that I had people to report to. Not like I used it often—I was my agency's director of operations, after all, and my supposed boss was in Washington, D.C., firmly ensconced at the top of the Department of Homeland Security—but I had a job to do, and the less friction I got from the executive and legislative branches of the government, the better off I was. Speaking gently and taking some of the needles out of my words was a small price to pay to be left alone most of the time.

I had enough shit on my plate without knocking it off the table and having to clean it up because I'd been impetuous. That thing I'd done to Ambassador Halstead was like the Sienna of old and was probably a reflection of my irritation with the bureaucracies I had to answer to now.

"What are the foreign secretary and the commissioner of the Metropolitan Police doing here at a simple murder scene?" I asked as we walked down the hallway toward Wexford and Marshwin. They were standing in front of an open door; the Commissioner to one side with an unobstructed view and Wexford a little to the right, where he couldn't easily look into the apartment. I got the sense that this was not a fun time for him.

"The victim was a Russian national," Wexford said, a little stiffly, and—if I wasn't imagining it—a little pale. "He was a diplomat with their embassy."

"Yay for international incidents," I said with a fake enthusiasm. "What did he do at the embassy?"

"I don't know offhand what his official title was," Wexford said, "but unofficially I am informed that he was chief of station for London."

"I don't know what that means," Webster admitted.

"Head spy," I said. "Was he a meta?"

Commissioner Marshwin gave me a tired look. "We wouldn't know."

"Let's assume he was," Webster said. "It's a tenuous tie, I'll grant you, but assuming he was, then we've got our motive. They're killing metas."

"And assuming that he's not, we're now at a place where there's no pattern," I said. "Unless this was a deliberate attempt to skew the pattern. I mean, going from ex-Omegas that were with me in the old fights to a Russian diplomat? *Très* strange, eh?"

"There is something else," Wexford said, and his complexion definitely changed on this one, going sheet-white. "Something that would indicate a tie to you, Ms. Nealon."

I stared at him blankly. "I don't know any Russian diplomats."

Commissioner Marshwin gave me a hard look. "It's entirely possible he didn't know you, either… but…"

I caught a lot of something lurking behind her words. "But what?" I shouldered my way closer to them, passing Wexford to get a look into the apartment.

Marshwin didn't bother to answer me. She didn't have to.

The room was a bloody, bloody mess. Like nothing I'd ever seen before, which was saying something since I had one of the world's most prolific serial killers sitting inside my head. For spite, he used to give me flashes of his greatest hits, the kills he was most proud of.

But this…

This was just…

… it was…

Butchery.

I could tell where the torso was because that was where the balance of the crime scene investigators were. It wouldn't have taken metahuman vision to see the name carved into the exposed muscle. And it certainly wouldn't have taken metahuman vision to see it written on the walls in five—no, six—different places around the apartment, including on a tasteless nude picture hanging on the dining room wall.

Sienna Nealon.

My name.

Carved into the body.

Written in blood.

Everywhere.

Chapter 22

I pride myself on having a strong stomach, but I got right the hell out of there as soon as I could. It was one of the single grossest things I'd ever seen, and I'd seen a lot. I could hear Webster shouting behind me, but I didn't care.

I made it out the front door of the building before my stomach emptied its contents. The nasty, acidic taste mingled with the remains of Lancashire hotpot made me even sicker, overwhelming my sense of smell. Cops were all around me, polite enough not to mock or laugh. Maybe some of them had been sick, if they'd seen it. I'd made it down several flights of stairs and out the door before I'd heaved, so that was something.

"You all right?" Webster asked, delivering the obvious and expected question.

"Do I look all right?" I asked, spitting the last bits out and rising to my feet.

He handed me a cloth handkerchief. "You look all right, yeah. 'Cept for that little spot of sick, there…"

I dabbed at my lips. "Better?"

"Much." His nose wrinkled. "Mind stepping over this way? The smell—"

"Yeah." I passed him without waiting, just breezed by on my way to the curb.

He followed a few seconds later, lingering behind me as I stared out across the street to the square beyond. "So… how are you enjoying your holiday so far?"

I took a breath. It felt like blood was still draining from my face. "Holiday? That's what you Brits call a vacation, isn't it?" I glanced back at him. "Because this isn't a holiday to me. Unless there's a Dismembered and Inscribed Corpses Day on the calendar that I'm not remembering."

"I take it you've never seen anything like that, either?"

"My name carved into a brutalized corpse and painted on the wall in their blood? No. No, I've never seen that before."

"It's going to be all right—" he started.

"Liar," I cut him off.

"Well, I was trying to be reassuring."

"Reassurance is for idiots," I said. "We've got a killer who's murdering people I know. Two people I knew well are missing—probably dead, given what we've seen so far. Now this guy is leaving me love notes at the scene of the crime." I ran a hand over my sweaty, chilled forehead and realized I still had Webster's handkerchief in my hand. I offered it back to him and he shook his head, so I pocketed it. "This is serious business. This guy has a plan for something. He has a motive. He has some connection to me that I don't understand, and I don't like mysteries."

"I do," Webster said. I shot him a look, and he shrugged apologetically. "I wouldn't be in this line of work if I didn't find some appeal in untangling the knots."

"Maybe this has something to do with Omega," I said, "or maybe it doesn't. Maybe this guy has Janus and Karthik, maybe he doesn't." I was trying to reason it out, but it was like a giant, thousand-piece puzzle with nine hundred and ninety-eight of them missing. "We need answers."

"I agree," Webster said. "So far, this bloke's been near to a ghost as I could imagine short of him wearing a sheet and saying, 'Whoooooooh.'"

That shook something loose in my head. "The thing about those ghosts is that they're always hiding for a reason. We've got a few strings to tug on. Maybe we can yank the sheet off his head."

"This isn't Scooby Doo, you know." Webster sounded reassuring. Again. I let him get away with it because he was cute. And well meaning.

"But it's not random acts of violence, either," I said. "He's a meta, that's definite. He's targeted at least two former Omega members; that's not random. There's something going on behind that sheet."

Webster looked like he was going to grudgingly admit something he didn't want to admit. "Maybe. But this is a serial killer sort of pathology of the like I've never seen. These crimes are not only shockingly brutal, but amazing in their sheer viciousness. I've got people pulling local surveillance, maybe we can a spot this bloke on camera."

"That'd help," I said. "While you're doing that, there's another string I can tug on."

"Oh?" he asked. "What's that?"

I sighed. "One I don't particularly want to pull."

Chapter 23

Katrina Forrest had been Janus's longtime companion. They had history. They had background. They had sex, which was still icky to me because he was thousands of years old and she looked barely legal.

But she was also the closest thing to Janus I could find without finding the man himself.

I'd heard rumors through Reed that she'd parted ways with the old man a year or so earlier. I didn't really keep up with her because... well... because Kat and I weren't exactly bosom buddies. But Reed, my darling brother, he kept the feelers out with everybody. He was the spider at the social center of a little web, keeping the little strings to all my old friends, who were now scattered to the winds. It was just as well. Someone in the family had to be warm and caring.

I think it was just surprising to everybody that it was him. Not because they'd have expected it to be me, but because Reed wasn't exactly the warm and inviting type, either.

Still, his mom wasn't my mom, and that probably made a world of difference.

I'd called him asking for the number and he'd given it to me immediately. I had it dialed into my phone and was just staring at the lit faceplate, almost willing the "Vodafone UK" signal bar to die down in the upper left hand corner. I so did not want to make this call. And not just because of the absurd cost-per-minute of doing it.

But I pushed the green button anyway, and a few seconds later it started to ring.

She picked up on the fifth ring or so. I'd lost count after three, really, a feeling of dread filling my guts. It wasn't like Kat and I had left things on bad terms. I just hadn't spoken to her in almost two years and didn't know what I was going to say.

It turned out that I didn't really need to worry about that.

"Hey, girlfriend!" she said, perky as ever she was. Kat was a peppy person by nature. I was not. This was reason eight hundred and fifty million why I had not stayed in touch. "How are you doing?"

"Up to my ears in shit and trying to keep my mouth closed." The response was natural.

She giggled, but it wasn't because she was enjoying my pain. Probably. "Sienna, you're always so funny. How are you always so funny?"

"Because without humor and sarcasm to soften my words, I'd be called a bitter old hag by everyone. Listen," I said, "I'm in London."

"Oh?" She perked up a little bit at that. How was that even possible? I'd assumed she'd reached max perkiness years ago. "You know Janus is in—"

"That's why I'm calling," I said.

"Oh, you want to look him up while you're in town?" she asked casually. "I can give you his number. I'm sure he'd love to get together with you—"

"Kat," I said, and I could hear the warning I put into my tone. "Kat, there's a problem here that you should know about."

"What?" That took some of the perk out of her.

"Janus is missing," I said. "And people from that group of Omega refugees we brought over to the States are turning up dead."

There was a predictable silence on the other end of the phone. "What do you mean he's missing?"

"Missing," I said. "Gone. Untraceable. Karthik, too. Do you know what he was up to over here?"

"Sienna, he can't just have gone missing—"

"Kat, focus," I said. She was a scatterbrain, and if I let her run the conversation she'd drag me all over the place. "I need to know where he was staying, how to contact him— anything you can give me."

"Um. Okay." She sounded flustered, which was not surprising. "I have an old number for him, but I haven't talked to him in six months."

"Where are you?" I asked.

"Los Angeles," she said. "I'll get on the next flight."

"You're half a world away," I said.

"I don't care," she said, and there was iron in her words. "I'm coming over there."

"I can't stop you," I said, "but you ought to know that the entire European Union has made it pretty clear that they're not letting any metas past customs at this point, and I'm pretty sure you're on the no-entry list." She was definitely one of my known associates. If she used her own passport, she'd get ejected from the country in about twelve seconds.

"Well, how are you there, then?" This was tinged with bitterness.

"I got asked to come over. Official channels. State Department called me," I said. "I don't know if you remember them, but Maxwell Llewelyn is dead and we're pretty sure Angus Waterman is, too."

"Sienna, you can't expect me to stay out of this," she said.

"I'm not keeping you out," I said, "the laws of the United Kingdom and the European Union are. Hash it out with them."

"Damn Reed and his Italian screw-up," Kat said, closer to a curse than anything I'd heard from her so far.

"That wasn't his fault," I said, a tad defensive. You can't expect me not to have my brother's back; he was the only one who had mine, after all.

There was a long silence. "Sienna… you have to find him."

"I'm working on it," I said. I could feel the chill through my coat, the April air laced with moisture and cold. "I need whatever you can give me."

"I'll send you his number and the last address I have for him," she said quietly. "But he moved around a lot. He didn't want to run afoul of the authorities. Sienna… I never got to say… he and I left it badly—"

"Kat," I cut her off. "This isn't the end, okay? He could very well still be out there, one way or another. This is just a thread. A possibility. He may be clear of this whole thing, sitting on the Dover shore staring across the channel. I just need to be certain. The guy we're up against… he knows me. He's mad about something. He's leaving pieces of people all over the place. And that's the only trail he's giving us."

"I'll text you what I have," she said, and I heard her voice crack. "Just… do what you can, okay? I know you can beat this guy, whoever he is. Find Janus."

The last word she spoke was like a dagger in my gut. "Please."

Chapter 24

Philip watched Sienna Nealon sprint out the front door and vomit in the grass to the side of the walk. It elicited a chuckle out of Antonio. Philip showed his amusement with a smile as he watched the grainy, pixelated surveillance camera picture. That detective inspector followed predictably behind her, tamed house cat that he was, and they exchanged words for a few minutes before she walked to the curb and stood among all the police vehicles crowding the street.

"She doesn't look so tough," Antonio said, his burned fingers running over his black goatee.

"Appearances are deceptive," Philip said. "She nearly shot me earlier."

"Heh," Antonio said. "But you showed her."

"I hurt her," Philip said. "That's all."

"You could have killed her."

"I could have. Possibly." He stared at the picture of her on the monitor. The video quality was too poor to make out any detail of her face, but he knew her by her clothes, by her height, by the squat shape of her hips. "The odds were against it, though. Besides, she should rightly be last. Keep her busy, don't tangle with her until the end."

"I don't care for that idea," Antonio said. "If she's formidable, we should kill her now and be done with it."

"It will get done when the moment is appropriate," Philip said. "This is all about timing. We're building to a necessary crescendo, and she may be the final note we need to complete the masterpiece."

"Or she could be the sour note that ends the whole thing," Antonio said.

Philip gave him the steady gaze. "You don't think I'd see that coming?"

Antonio seemed to withdraw into the shadows, the color of the computer's monitor leaving him barely lit. "She could be in your blind spot."

Philip leaned forward, staring at her on the grainy picture. "I've planned this for years, every step, every movement. I didn't expect her to waltz into the middle of it, but now that she's here, I have a place in the plan for her as well." He gave Antonio a smile that made the big man cover his mouth with a hand. "Don't fear. Your future is assured."

Antonio relaxed instantly, stroking his goatee. "How do you mean to do it, then?"

"The same as we always planned to," Philip said. "Liliana is still working with Janus, softening him up. Once the possibilities say that he's… malleable enough to do what we want him to, we'll retrieve our business and be gone." He reached a finger out and touched Sienna Nealon on the screen. He almost felt like he could reach through the camera and touch her. He could certainly feel her, the same way he could feel everyone else he looked at.

And didn't she have an interesting road ahead.

"What about the gallery?" Antonio said. Philip could feel him watching without even looking.

"Tomorrow," Philip said without looking away from the monitor. "We can manage it and stir up more of the hornets at the same time."

"Stirring up hornets tends to make them angrier," Antonio said. "Makes them want to sting you."

"They can't sting what they can't see," Philip said. He truly needed a cup of tea, but it was so late. "After tomorrow they'll be all impotent rage, furious and blinded by it. As methodical as they want to be, even putting the entire army into London couldn't stop us. We'll make them afraid. They'll flinch. Hesitate. They won't know what they're looking for. And we'll do the last few deeds that need doing and be gone before they even realize what we've done."

Antonio ran his burned fingers over the surface of the desk in front of them, and Philip caught the scent of gunpowder, wafting off the bomb maker in strong waves. "And the girl?"

"She has to sleep sometime," Philip said, staring at the picture on the monitor. "I would guess soon." He looked to Antonio, gave him a smile. "Why don't you follow her? Find out where she's laying her head tonight."

Antonio smiled in return. "This I can do." Something in the way he said it, his accent or perhaps the quiver of enthusiasm in his voice… well, to Philip's ear, it almost sounded malevolent.

Chapter 25

We were back on the road a few minutes later, heading toward Marjorie Webster's house once more. We'd settled things with Wexford and Marshwin, to no real result, and the crime scene investigators hadn't turned up anything of note, so we were left hanging around outside of a fancy building with a bunch of other cops, yawning into the midnight air. Webster suggested the sensible idea of leaving and getting some sleep, and me, levelheaded and careful-thinking individual that I was, agreed immediately.

I was practically hallucinating from the lack of sleep by this point, everything around me taking on a blurry quality. I pride myself on my endurance, but after spending the night before flying over the Atlantic Ocean instead of sleeping, I was exhausted. Fighting gravity and the laws of physics for hours at a time really takes a toll on me.

"So we've got a last-known address that's vacant," Webster said as the car thrummed along, "and a mobile number that appears to be disconnected." He neatly summed up the results of what I'd gotten from Kat. I'd called Janus immediately, of course, as soon as I got the number, but it had been out of service. Webster had sent a couple of his boys over to the knock on the door of the apartment Kat had given us; the only people home had moved in three weeks ago.

"He was pretty good at staying off the grid," I said, leaning my head against the cold window. "Probably from all those years he spent with Omega."

"I keep hearing you talk about Omega like I should know what it is," Webster said, guiding the car into a turn. "I mean, other than a bloody horseshoe."

Right. Sometimes I forget these things. "Omega was the old gods. Zeus and Poseidon and all them. Operated around the world from behind the scenes since a little before the fall of the Roman Empire."

Webster blinked at that. "That… seems like the sort of information that would have come out when your people were revealed to the public two years ago."

"Omega's dead," I said, succinctly. "They got wiped out in the British Museum by one of Sovereign's flunkies. At least, the last remains of them. They'd already lost their Primus, the guy who led them, a few weeks before that."

"So was that Zeus, then?" Webster's question held an aura of disbelief. "Like, the real one?"

"No, he's long dead," I said. "The last one was a guy named Rick." I kept a straight face. "He was a nobody. I doubt you would have heard of him. Point is, sometime after Zeus but before two years ago, Omega became a front for organized crime. They stopped ruling nations and started putting the squeeze on, using their powers for racketeering, drug smuggling, gun running… hell, you name an illegal activity that could make a buck, they had a finger in it."

"The Smokes," Webster said, like it would mean something to me. He must have seen the look on my face, because he clarified quickly. "Organized crime syndicate that essentially disappeared a couple years ago. They had tentacles like you're describing in everything. We'd get close, get a hand on 'em, and they'd turn to dust in our grip. You'd catch a bloke, think he's ready to roll on his mates, and he'd just disappear from custody. Or we'd have a raid scheduled, show up, and there'd be nothing there. Even though an informant had sworn up and down that there would be a whole shipment of drugs or guns. They were like bloody magic. We called them 'The Smokes' because every time we got close they went up in it."

"Clever," I said without enthusiasm.

"Your friends Janus and Karthik were part of this?" Webster said, cocking his head at me. "Involved in it?"

"On the administrative side," I said, probably sounding more defensive than I needed to be. "Janus was more interested in preventing the coming cataclysm than dealing with their day-to-day bullshit."

"So what happened to all their riches?" Webster asked, thumping a hand against the wheel.

"Who knows?" I asked. "Hell, who cares? This serial killer is clearly targeting them, though." I thought about something. "Omega had a building here in London. We should check it out tomorrow, see if we can find anything. They used to have computer servers underground; they might be able to give us some kind of membership list if we can get into them."

"Have a lot of experience with computer hacking, do you?" he asked, eyeing me warily.

"No," I said, yawning, "I pay other people to be good at it for me. They should be able to access the Omega database. We had it set up so we could get into it from across the pond." I tapped out a text message to J.J. back at headquarters and checked the time at the top of the display: 1:05 A.M. local. Minneapolis was six hours behind. That meant it was seven o'clock back at home. J.J. was probably sitting down to dinner with his cats or something.

"Why did you involve yourself with them?" Webster said, and I was so close to drooling from fatigue that it took me a few seconds to figure out what he meant. "Omega, I mean."

"Because they were all that was left," I said, trying to blink the tiredness out of my eyes. "Everything else got ripped away—friends, family, boyfriend. I lost it all."

"They helped you win the war?" he asked. I could tell he was battling his skepticism.

"Most of them didn't," I said. "They caused me more problems than I could count, in fact, especially when I was first starting out." They'd sent a revolving door of psychos after me, like they were daring me to kill them one at a time. I had killed a couple of them, too, before others started stepping in and doing my dirty work for me. That had been fine by me; killing had been an issue of conscience for me back then.

Now it was an inconvenience of my position.

Or so it had been explained to me, over and over, by people in the executive branch of the U.S. government that oversaw my every move. Having me, an agency head, kill a meta criminal or even a regular one would cause public relations nightmares for them. I'd seen the reason in that after a few go-rounds with the House Oversight Committee following the battle with Sovereign. They'd sifted the ashes of my actions after that conflict and found more than a few embers to burn me with.

The job was important. So I'd conceded that I wouldn't kill quite as quickly as I might have wanted to. It had been two years since I'd racked up my last body count—Sovereign being the last tally mark on my belt—and I'd been all peaceable since.

"So this Omega group," Webster said, drawing me back to the matter at hand, "what's left of them?"

"Janus," I said, ticking them off in my head, "Karthik. Waterman, Max and a few of the others." I waved a hand at him. "The people on your list, basically."

He nodded slowly. "Is that all?"

"Yeah," I said. "I mean, all the ones I know about. The rest are pretty much dead."

He took his foot off the petal and we subtly decelerated into a slow, curving turn. I was used to freeways running through the middle of cities, delivering you to your destination in minutes. Minneapolis was good like that; 35W and 94 ran right through the heart of it, branching into other offshoots as needed. On a clear night at one in the morning, I could be from one side of Minneapolis to the other side of St. Paul in half an hour by car. I had no idea where in London we were or where we were going, geographically speaking, but I got the feeling that I was wasting buckets of time by not flying.

We parked in front of his mother's house a few minutes later. There was still a window lit in the second story, shining out over the red brick facade. "You going home?" I asked him.

"I'd stay here, but my old room feels small now that I'm used to my own flat," he said, getting out of the car. The dome light flashed on, shaking me out of whatever reverie I'd been in. I got out, too.

He produced a keychain from his pocket and unlocked the door, opening it for me in his gentlemanly way. "There you go," he said, his motions a little slowed. "Don't forget to lock the door once you're inside." The way he said it, his voice shot through with fatigue, I got the feeling he was going to be crashing the moment he got home, too.

"Thanks," I said and slid inside. I started to close the door and stopped an inch short of doing so. "Webster?" I called out into the night, and he stopped his trudge back to the car so he could look back at me, profile slumped with weariness, hands stuck in his trench coat's pockets. "Thanks for the vacation," I said, with a half-smile. I shut the door on his grin.

Chapter 26

Philip could see Antonio's car from a camera on a bank six blocks away. It was small, but it was there, and Antonio's voice fuzzed through the speaker of the cell phone. "She's there," he said. "The detective inspector walked her up to the front door and then left."

"Good," Philip said, nodding as he stared at the monitor. "You're sure they didn't see you?"

"I only picked them up on the last few blocks, like you told me to," Antonio said. "I kept far enough away before that. There's no way even she could have seen me, assuming she knew I was there."

"Right," Philip said. "Address reads as belonging to a Marjorie Webster." He cracked a smile. "Looks like the good detective inspector's mother."

"You want me to take the DI out of the game?" Antonio asked.

Philip thought about that one. Thought about it long and hard. "Follow him for now. I…" This sort of uncertainty wasn't quite like him. "It might not be a bad idea to plant a little something for him. Just in case we have to send Ms. Nealon's world crashing down around her."

Chapter 27

I woke to sunbeams streaming in, to the sound of faint movement on the floor below, and the aroma of some kind of breakfast cooking. I blinked the bleariness out of my eyes, then remembered as I thumbed the faceplate of my phone alight that I had not only forgotten to bring a charger with me, but even if I had, American chargers didn't work in British sockets.

Everything was not exactly coming up Sienna. Or maybe it was, in a color sense.

I rubbed at my eyes and sniffed, the enticing scent stirring my interest. Eggs. Ham. No, wait. British bacon? Yeah, that was it. Salty. Toast. And beans?

I shook my head at the peculiarities of the British breakfast palate as I dressed myself in the same clothes I'd worn yesterday. There was a streak on the blouse that I suspected had come from my midnight emptying of the stomach at the Russian diplomat's apartment. I took a breath as I remembered that scene. Part of me didn't want breakfast anymore.

Whatever they'd done to the Russian, it hadn't been quick or pretty. I wouldn't have wanted to go that way, that was for sure. The fact that the commissioner was there for a murder was probably not a good sign. The fact that they'd had the foreign minister himself out there?

Yeah. It was a mess, all right.

"Good morning!" Marjorie singsonged as I stepped into the kitchen, already dressed and as ready for my day as I was going to get without a five-gallon drum of coffee. "I've got some tea ready, dear, and breakfast will be done shortly." She was frying eggs at the stove, one of the older models with the coiled electrical burner. It glowed red like a brand, and I could feel the very subtle heat across the room. That was all Gavrikov, that sense of fire. I caught her humming something as she worked, and I noticed there were at least half a dozen eggs in the skillet.

"Morning," I replied, turning my attention to the bacon that was already on the table. It wasn't the glory that was American bacon, but it was pretty good, I reflected as I snatched a piece up and started to nibble on it. The pot of beans looked to be nearing finished on the stove as well, and I heard the toaster ding and throw up a couple slices.

Marjorie spun as she worked, going from breakfast item to breakfast item in a frenetic dance of activity. She hummed the entire time, and I got the feeling that she'd been bereft of company for so long now that she wasn't going to miss the opportunity to do what she apparently did best while she had the chance.

"Did you sleep well, dear?" she asked as she flipped two eggs. I wondered how she knew to flip just those two, because she left the rest to keep cooking. She seemed a little tentative asking, and I suspected I knew why.

"As well as I could, given the limited time I had to sleep," I said, and she broke from the stove with a teapot in hand to pour me a cup. Cuppa, I think they call it over here. I could smell the strong blend, not quite the coffee I was looking for, but good enough.

"I didn't even hear you come in," she said as she whirled back toward the stove. "Fell asleep with the light on, can you believe it? I tried waiting, but I just couldn't keep my eyes open."

"It's okay," I said. "I found the bed, and I was probably out about five seconds after I hit the sheets." I'd had horrible dreams, too, ones that had involved the souls in my head intervening at various times to wake me before I thrashed out of control. It wasn't the most fun thing to have Wolfe, the cause of so many peoples' nightmares in his life, trying to calm me after having my own. It was actually surreal.

Surreality is more fun than vanilla reality, Sienna, Wolfe said.

I sighed.

"I expect Matthew will be along shortly," Marjorie said, scooping the eggs out of the pan. "He never was one to have a lie-in, even after a late night."

It took me a minute to work out what a "lie-in" was, but I got it. "He's an early bird, huh?"

"Crack of dawn," she said, dishing all six eggs onto my plate with so much gusto that I didn't feel I could tell her to keep some for herself. Next came the beans—half the pot and I was surprised she stopped at that. She dumped four slices of toast next, and I realized now I had enough carbs on my plate to take my already sturdy hips to a new level. "Eat up, dear." She turned away, leaving me to wonder how I was supposed to fit any of the slabs of bacon in the middle of the table onto my plate.

I did what the Brits call "tucking in" and started working my way through my plate. It wasn't much of a struggle, since I'd lost my dinner around midnight and hadn't had anything to replace it since. After a few quiet minutes, Marjorie must have run out of things to do, because she finally sat down across from me with a single slice of toast, a spoonful of baked beans, a half-slice of bacon, and maybe a fifth of a fried egg, probably the corner of one of mine that I hadn't even noticed had been missing a piece.

"So, dear," she said after she'd spent a long minute chewing a bite of food the size of my pinky finger but about a third of the volume, "about what we were discussing last night…"

I cocked an eyebrow at her. I didn't remember much of what we'd talked about. Call it the travel fatigue. "What?"

"You said you hadn't had a holiday in a long time?" She cut a piece of bacon the approximate size of a pencil eraser and positioned it closer to her mouth on her fork. "It sounds like you desperately need a holiday."

I paused, letting my beans drip onto my plate. "I agree. Maybe someday."

"I don't understand," she said, shaking her head, that lone little piece of bacon still poised on the end of her fork. Watching her eat next to nothing and take forever to do it was making me feel extremely self-conscious about my own desire to devour everything, not just on my plate, but in the world. "Why not just take a couple of weeks?"

"Because I'm behind," I said. "Because I have ten thousand idiots who don't know what a meta actually is trying to get my attention every single day. I get calls from the police across the country, from New York City to Los Angeles and all points in between, who've seen something wild or weird, and they automatically ascribe it to metas. And I have to check out almost all of those reports, once they get to a certain point of escalation."

"It sounds like you get about a bit, then," she said and finally—finally, thank the heavens—put that piece of bacon in her mouth and started to chew it.

"Yeah, I do," I said. "Half the time I have to fly commercial or on military transports to get there because I'm not awake enough to fly myself, but yeah. I get around."

"And you can't take a break in any of those places?" she asked innocently enough. Now she had—I swear—one fricking bean on her fork. Just one.

"I got to spend a Saturday in Arizona a few weeks ago," I said with a shrug. "I had a hotel room with a view and everything." I felt a little embarrassed. "But, I, uh… I kind of fell asleep at six o'clock at night. And I had a flight out at four the next morning. It's always something like that."

"Well, surely you get to take some time for yourself on weekends…?" Her voice trailed off expectantly.

I looked down at my plate. "Not really, no."

"Why are you here, dear?" she asked, and I looked up to find her staring at me. "Surely this murderer can't be that bad."

"It is. Your son needs my help." I felt full, now. Appetite gone, back to business. "He's up against something—someone—that he doesn't understand."

"But you do?" She seemed skeptical.

"I don't know if I understand them, at least not on a personal level." I felt my face harden. "But there's no one better than me to fight them."

"Ah," she said and looked away a little pointedly. "I see."

I felt my blood cool a little. Something about the way she said it made me feel uncomfortable, like I'd said something to lose some of her respect. "What?"

"Why your… your young man didn't stick around. The one who walked you out of your house after—" She looked up at me, and her eyelashes fluttered. "Oh, listen to me. I'm so sorry. That came out all wrong!" She reached a hand out as if to reassure me, but I pulled my arm back where she couldn't get to it, and I saw her blanch at the motion. "I mean to say…"

"It's okay," I said. I felt a lump in my throat. "I can see you didn't mean anything by it. And… you're right, for what it's worth. This—this addiction to the job—is exactly why Scott and I broke it off."

Her lips were pursed, and they gave a little twitch. "Something you said, though, dear… it bothers me."

Now I felt my blood really chill. "What was that?"

"You said he wouldn't remember your time together?" She was watching me shrewdly. "Anyone else, I might assume they were being humble or self-deprecatory, perhaps just down-playing themselves." She did not take her eyes off of mine. "Why do I get the feeling that you weren't being any of those things?"

The lump in my throat felt like I'd swallowed Stonehenge. "I—"

Saved by the bell. The front door lock clicked and opened, and I turned to see Webster enter with his coat flapping and swaying as he shut it behind him. I pushed the plate slightly away from me, just enough to signal I was done, and looked back to see Marjorie chewing delicately on a bite of something I hadn't seen her put into her mouth.

"Ready to go?" Webster asked, crossing the sitting room to enter the kitchen.

"Yeah, I'm done," I said, and my voice sounded a little hoarse.

"But dear, you've hardly eaten a bite," she said, then turned her attention to Webster. "And you—"

"No time this morning, Mum," Webster said, cutting her off but not rudely. "Got a call from Dylan, said he's going to stop by the office with something for us to take a look at."

"If it's pics the crime scene photographer took of me with my pants shredded, I'm not going to be surprised," I said.

"If it's that, I'm giving him twenty quid for the lot," Webster said with a grin as he grabbed a piece of toast from the table.

"Matthew!" his mother called him out, though I wasn't sure if it was for grabbing the toast or what he'd said. He kissed her on the cheek, and her moment of ire dissolved into a blushing smile.

"Got to go, Mum," he said, gesturing at me. I was up and on the way out quicker than he could follow. I didn't realize until later I hadn't even thought to thank Marjorie for breakfast.

Chapter 28

"Did I interrupt something?" he asked once we were in the car and moving.

"Breakfast," I said. "It's the most important meal of the day, don't you know."

He let out a chuckle. "I like the way you say that."

I looked over at him as red brick houses passed outside his window one by one. The skies were grey again, and he had the heat going, filling the car with the smell of the hot air ducts. The tangy barbecue from the beans lingered on my tongue. "The way I say what?"

"Dontcha know," he said, chuckling again. "It sounds like that one movie, the one with all the snow and murders—"

"*Fargo*," I said. "It's interesting to hear it described that way, but… that's Minnesota. Snow and murders." At least it had been in my experience.

"Does everybody talk like that there?" He looked over at me as he hit the blinker to signal his turn.

"Some worse than others." I frowned. "I don't really sound like Frances McDormand, do I?"

He let a guffaw. "Just a bit. And you looked a little like her, too, pulling that gun. Smoother, though. Like you'd done it more."

"Hm," I said, noncommittal. I could see him looking at me out of the corner of his eye. The gun comment was his way of fishing, I knew that much.

He waited a few minutes before he made a move to set the hook. "So… you can burst into flame, can't you?" I nodded without looking at him. "Throw fireballs at people? I saw that on the telly." I nodded again, waiting for him to get to it. It took him a minute, but he followed up in just the way I was expecting. "So… why do you need a gun?"

"Because I don't always want to burn everything down," I quipped. That was sort of true. I could throw fire, but it was not the cleanest experience. My nets of light, they were a lot more precise.

"That's a cheap answer," he said, turning back to the wheel. Now he sounded sullen, or at least, just a little bit.

"It was a cheap question." That got a little flare of anger to his eyes. "You know what you are, alone and unarmed, in a room with me?" I looked over at him, waiting for the answer, waiting to see if this would just make him madder. "You know what I'd call it?"

Those little embers of fury cooled, turning into a twinkle. "A damned lovely Saturday night?"

I blushed at that. A lot. Because that was true. But I stayed on point. "Prey. Victim. Easy pickings."

That took him back a step. "You see everyone like that?"

"I don't," I said. "I mean, I always keep my eyes open for threats, but I don't see the balance of humanity that way. But make no mistake about it—in a fight, an unarmed human is nothing but a speed bump between me and whatever I want." I thought about doing something to demonstrate, but damaging his car or personal property seemed pointless; he'd already seen me turn into a dragon and regrow my foot. "Weapons are what my military friends call 'force equalizers' for humans. Without them, you're always at the mercy of someone stronger than you."

"With them, we're all just targets for each other," he said, a little too glibly. "Would you want to do your job knowing that anyone, anytime, could have a gun on you?"

"I always do my job assuming that," I said, shrugging it off. "You're a fool if you don't."

He shuddered. "That's bloody mad."

"What about you?" I kept my voice calm and level. "You can't tell me there aren't criminals out there with guns in London? Metas with powers that could outmatch you? Bad guys who have you outnumbered who would love to see you defenseless?"

"I can tell you this—" he said, and his voice was rising, just a little, to match the intensity of our growing argument. He stopped when my phone rang, though.

"Hello?" I said, answering without even looking at the caller ID.

"Blimey," came my brother Reed's voice in the worst—the single worst, bar none—English accent I've ever heard. "'ow's the weather over there, Guv'nor?"

"You're a jackass," I replied.

"Me?" Webster asked, and I realized I was still looking right at him.

"Not you," I said.

"Not me?" Reed asked, and I made an exasperated noise. "Sorry. I wanted to check in on you."

"I'm fine," I said, keeping my tone carefully neutral. "How's everything back at the ranch?"

"Well, the cows ran away," Reed said dryly, "and there's a fearful drought." He'd switched into some sort of terrible Western accent that made me want to reach through the phone and bonk him on the head, Three-Stooges-style. "Reckon we'll turn to cannibalism when the winter comes…"

"You missed your calling as the first course for the Donner party," I said, mirthless. "Anything going on?"

"SSDD," he said. "Got a call from Atlanta. Local PD ran across something they couldn't handle. I'm having them send me some footage, but so far it sounds like NBD."

"If you don't stop speaking in acronyms—"

"Sorry," he said, and he did sound a little contrite. "NBD is 'No big deal.' You should spend more time on Reddit. That and Whedon movies are where all the cool twists of English phrase are coming from nowadays." He paused for a second, and a little levity crept into his voice. "Need me to explain what SSDD means, too?"

"Some Stupid Damned Dumbass," I said, twisting the generally accepted meaning of SSDD. "What are you doing about the Atlanta thing?"

"I'll hop a plane if I need to," he said. "Until I get any kind of confirmation, I'm not getting off my well-sculpted, happy ass. Details are pretty sketchy yet, anyway. How's London treating you?"

"Well, we've already got a climbing body count," I said. "And I lost a leg."

I could hear the wince. "A leg? Are you going to be walking around saying 'Arrrrr'?"

I shook my head then realized he couldn't see me. "SSDD."

There was a pause. "You meant that in the way you quoted earlier, not what it really is, didn't you?"

"You're pretty smart for a stupid damned dumbass."

"Uh huh," Reed said. "Are you still playing ride-along with that detective inspector?"

"Yep," I said, turning my body to look out the front windshield. I didn't even realize I'd been staring at Webster throughout my conversation until he brought it up. "You'd like him. He and I were just having a conversation that sounds very similar to one you and I have had over the years."

"He's cute, isn't he?" Reed asked, and I heard the teasing through the phone.

I felt my lips pucker. "Mmmhmmm."

"I'm no meta, but your volume's turned loud enough that I can hear him," Webster said with a tight smile.

"Gotta go," I said to Reed, "unless you need anything else?"

"Want me to hop a plane and come over?" Reed asked. "Or would that be a total cockbloc—"

"We're fine, okay, see you later," I said hurriedly and hung up on him before he had a chance to finish his sentence. I could feel my face, flaming red, and I stared out the front window.

"Your brother, right?" Webster asked after an appropriate interval of time. Like, at least twenty seconds.

"Yeah," I said, feeling the heat gradually fade from my cheeks. "He's worried. Clearly."

"Right," Webster said, nodding. "Clearly concerned." His lips twisted in a grin. "About blocking my—"

"Shut up and drive, Detective Inspector," I said, all that redness back in my cheeks. "Because in case you haven't heard, I can still kill a man with a touch."

He was quiet for about two point five seconds this time. "I've heard of worse ways to go."

Chapter 29

The streets were still crowded, but it was dying down. Philip was in the back of the van, one of the larger models, with seats stripped out to carry cargo. He was kneeling behind the front seats on the hard, metal floor, taking breaths every ten seconds or so, trying to control his breathing. Concentration was going to be key for what he needed to do next, and that wasn't going to happen if he couldn't get his anger under control.

The old bastard still hadn't broken. Still. There was a lot of pain in his future, Philip knew, but the possibilities were drawing nearer to the right conclusion. He would break. He would shatter. And then, once it was all but certain, Janus would do everything he asked.

But before that time came—and because the old bastard had been so reticent to surrender—there were other concerns.

"Two minutes," Liliana said from the driver's seat.

"Yes, I know," Philip said from the back. Antonio was waiting on the street ahead, having already completed his work. He'd been out all night doing it with help from Liliana, but now he was finished with his last task. That much, Philip could see. Liliana slowed the van and Antonio hopped in, slamming the door shut as Liliana accelerated again.

"Ready and go," Antonio said, pulling off his black leather gloves to reveal the burned hands. Philip hadn't bothered to ask him how those had happened. Bomb maker with scarred hands; the answer seemed fairly evident.

"One minute to the back of the building," Liliana said, voice calm. It grated on Philip's nerves, but that was her lifetime of training from the Cold War, surely. Either that or she was being intentionally irritating.

This plan was perfectly timed. Every possibility was covered. Every eventuality would be dealt with.

They came out from under trees that hung over the road as they passed the church on the left. Philip looked out the window at the ivory bell tower and saw the dumpster pushed against the facade of the church. It was green, stained with refuse, and didn't look out of place even pushed against the white stone wall. It sat in the shadow of the bell tower, as much a part of the urban scenery as anything else.

The gallery was ahead. It had such a sophisticated name—The Hartsford Gallery—and contained a priceless collection of art the like of which Philip would have gladly spent untold hours surveying.

Unfortunately, they did not have hours.

The gallery sat perfectly positioned on a triangular cross street where five separate thoroughfares met. It was quintessential old London; poor city design for a place with automobiles passing through because it had been built in an age of wagons and horses, oxen and yokes. It was a remnant of the old world, like much of London was, like the narrow alleys and the clock in Westminster. Part of the city that had seen the sun rise and set on its empire.

In spite of all that, to Philip, it had never lost its charm, even in the waning days.

They drove straight ahead, taking a slight right turn to follow the triangular edge of the Hartsford Gallery. It was a tall building, five stories. The fact that it had once been a private mansion was of particular interest to Philip. The Hartsford family had only opened the home—and their exquisite collection—to tourists because the family had fallen on lean times. The thought of the old world decaying came back to Philip, and he sighed as the van pulled around the back of the gallery.

He opened the side door and got out, straightening his suit as he put the black ski mask on and replaced his glasses. "Remember—we don't hurt the people in the gallery unless we have to. One particularly brutal display ought to quell any resistance, if even that is needed. But for the police—" He smiled. "Do your worst."

Liliana gave a smile that was visible under her mask. She had not opted for the simple ski approach, preferring instead to go with something pink and garish. It was one of the more peculiar choices she had made since Philip had first approached her, but every now and again she seemed to take actions that emphasized the femininity that she rarely showed.

Antonio was pulling his gloves back on, mask already placed on his face. "Thank you for this," he said simply.

Philip forced a smile. "You wanted it. I will deliver it for you."

Antonio bowed his head, and Philip swept forward, past the both of them and to the back door of the gallery. He opened it with one good pull, ripping apart the lock that was barely adequate to keep it closed on its own. A poor choice, but as this neighborhood was not particularly dangerous, Philip supposed the proprietors had never bothered to invest in something more durable.

Liliana brushed past him, both knives drawn as they stepped into a storage room. Pallets of water and food, probably for the Gallery's cafeteria, lined the sides of the room. When this had been a house, the room in which they stood had doubtless been part of the servants' quarters.

Ten steps. Philip knew the blueprints of the house by heart. He'd studied them, memorized them, and made Antonio and Liliana do the same. He knew his limitations, and preparation simply opened up all the possibilities to him.

The entrance to the main gallery was just ahead, ten steps, and through that door the game would truly begin. Once they crossed that particular Rubicon, they were committed to this until the end.

And what a glorious end it would be.

With a breath, Philip took the last steps and placed his hand on the door handle. So far, all they'd done was spit in the face of the Metropolitan police. This… well…

"Let's go," Philip said, and he smiled as he tugged on the handle. "I think it's time that New Scotland Yard loses an eye."

Chapter 30

We walked into the bullpen. It was buzzing with activity once more. The faded quiet that had hung in the place close to the fall of night yesterday was gone, replaced with a healthy hum of people talking, yet to start their paperwork for the day. It was a companionable chatter, detectives standing around and talking over cups of that vile coffee, brewed in an old cistern and seasoned with sewer water. The aroma was not pleasant. I followed in Webster's wake as he made his way to his desk, shedding his trench coat as he walked and giving me a view of his backside that I—once again—did not completely ignore.

Any elation I might have felt was stripped away by the sight of Dylan waiting in Webster's chair. The piggish man was spinning idly, moving his hips left and right as though it was the grandest game he'd ever played.

"They don't normally make spinning chairs in your weight class, huh?" I asked as we approached.

"Wha—?" Dylan spun to see us, and his expression darkened at the sight of me. "Oh, it's you." He nodded at Webster. "Webbo."

I blinked and looked to Webster, whose lips had folded in on each other. "Webbo?"

"It's a—" He stopped himself and I realized that he was embarrassed.

"It's what we call him at the pub," Dylan said, grinning broadly. "It's what his mates call him."

"I didn't realize you two were mating," I said. "Awkward." Sarcasm. It's more of a best friend to me than any diamond.

"What have you got, Dylan?" Webster sauntered over to the desk, but I could see the pained expression. "I know you didn't drive out here from Hounslow for the coffee."

"Maybe he came for the insults," I said. "Let's not rule that out. He could just be a glutton for punishment." I looked him up and down. "Because he's clearly already a glutton of the garden variety."

"I've got something for you," Dylan said with a sour look, "though I wouldn't say no to a cuppa. Ours in Hounslow tastes like someone's been pissing in the kettle again."

"Was it you?" I asked. "Be honest. Quicker than hauling your fat ass to the toilet, I'd guess—"

"Will you piss off already?" Dylan said, raising his voice so loud that it brought a hush over the bullpen. My mission of irritation accomplished, I dialed back a little in order to let the bastard speak. The look that Webbo shot me only contributed a little to it.

Oh, the fun I was going to have with that nickname later.

"What is it?" Webster asked, leaning over his desk. Dylan had brought a manila folder with him, something a few centimeters thick.

"Maybe nuffink," he said, just like that, like "nuffink" was a real word. "Maybe something." He opened the file with a flourish to reveal a murder scene in photos. It was messy. Really messy.

"That's a bit sprayed with blood," Webster said, looking up.

"Killer used a knife. Shallow gashes. Forensics said it was a short blade," Dylan said, not looking up from the photos. He seemed kind of stuck on them, his head trapped in the pictures. His face didn't paint him as a very happy guy; more like he'd been seeing these pictures for a while in his sleep.

"Preliminary said something similar about Maxwell Llewelyn," Webster said, gesturing to his computer. He looked back to Dylan. "Still, short-blade knife isn't much to go on. That might not be any link at all."

"This lad's practically flayed," Dylan said. "I mean, look at this, then look at what you had. You telling me you run across this sort of mess every day? I mean, we deal with a lot of shit, but people missing the balance of their epidermis is not the normal run-of-the-mill murder."

I gave him points for use of the word "epidermis" in a sentence. "Is that true?" I asked Webster. "Is it unusual for you to see this sort of... mess?"

"It's uncommon," Webster admitted after a moment. "In spite of what you see on the telly, there truly aren't that many serial killers out there. Most of the time, motives for killings are a hell of a lot more mundane, which means they're not going to take the time to completely skin the victim."

"That's rage you don't see very often," Dylan agreed, a cringe on his pudgy face. "Maybe this was personal, maybe it wasn't, but whoever did it had a bloody madness creeping through their brain."

"Who was he?" I asked, looking at the body in the pictures. It was barely recognizable as a he.

"Elijah Collins," Dylan said, looking down. "Poor bastard worked for the government."

I blinked. "What did he do?"

"Something technical," Dylan said, pushing pictures out of the way in the file to get to a piece of paper. "Something to do with integration of surveillance camera systems in the Greater London area."

I felt a little chill creep down my spine and turned to face Webster. He looked back at me, alarm growing in his eyes. "Doesn't London have like a bajillion surveillance cameras?"

"They're not all linked together," Webster said, stricken with uncertainty. "A lot of them are private and all—"

"Did you ever pull the footage from the ones around Angus's house?" I asked. "Or the Russian's apartment?"

"They were out," Webster said, reaching for his desk phone and dialing numbers furiously. "Dammit. I need to speak with the commissioner immediately." He pulled the mouthpiece away from his face and covered it. "This is not a department we'll be able to have access to without help. Pray the commissioner is in—" He stopped midsentence as I heard a voice break onto the line. "Out of the office? Out of the office where?" He paused. "No, I haven't heard—"

He listened for a moment as his eyes widened, and then he slammed down the phone and looked straight at me.

"What?" I got out before he managed to say anything.

"Three people just stormed the Hartsford Gallery," he said. "They took hostages, but a few people were able to escape."

"Another day in lovely London," Dylan said. "Think I'll flee back to Hounslow."

"All three of the hostage takers were wearing masks," Webster continued, undeterred, "and one of them was carrying—and using—two knives." He wore a look of grim satisfaction. "One of the witnesses who escaped said she hit one of the gallery patrons so hard that they flew across a twenty-foot room like they'd been struck by a car."

Chapter 31

Philip watched Liliana make a messy example of a man— a tourist, probably—who was a little slow to pay heed to her shouts. It was a long flight for the gent and came to an abrupt stop against a far wall. She had the knives out, now. There didn't seem to be much doubt that she would use them, and the screams of the patrons signaled a certain amount of submission.

"Your attention, please," Philip announced in a voice loud enough to gain, well, their attention. There were screams, but they died as Liliana circled with her blades, like a shark in the waters. She cut off the exit of the balance of the gallery patrons, and stood there, pink mask screaming against the deep crimson walls. It was an odd choice, in Philip's mind, but apparently the original owners of the Hartsford Gallery had decided it was majestic or some such silliness. Now it was surely tradition, and thus forever rooted in the stale air of this place.

"Your attention," Philip called again. "I am your captor today. In order to make our stay as brief and as bloodless as possible, I'll need your cooperation on a few things." He held up a hand as if to calm them. He very much doubted it had any such effect. "First of all, get down on your knees and place your heads against the floor. Keep your hands flush against that lovely hardwood. Yes, thank you." The compliance was nearly immediate, prompted by a poke to the back for the slowest mover in the room. This was from Liliana, and she even held back, keeping from penetrating the skin on the poor bastard.

"We have a very specific objective today," Philip said. "Keep your hands to yourselves and your heads on the ground, and you won't be harmed. This is a robbery; it's not meant to be a mass homicide. Every single painting in this gallery is insured, and the owners will be financially compensated by the company who takes their money for just such a possibility as this. Should you oppose us, there will be no one to make your family whole. Your death will be bloody and will come at the edge of a knife. Do not be foolish; you have no reason to try any heroics. In twenty minutes we will leave, and you will have the rest of your life to live. Or, alternatively, you can die now, and spend the last moments screaming as you bleed to death over a piece of canvas covered in oils that doesn't even belong to you." He scanned the small crowd, saw not a single head looking up at him, and smiled. "All right, then, let's begin."

Chapter 32

"You're thinking metas?" I asked as we rolled up on a vacant lot that the police had commandeered into a command post.

"It's a possibility," he said. "But we're just observers in all this, keeping an eye out unless asked for more."

I could see the Hartsford Gallery from where I stood as I got out of the car. It was a pretty tall building, constructed in that London style with the columns and stonework. The roof was sloped, and the building was practically a whole block unto itself. A short, triangular block, right at the joining point of five different roads, but still. I could see an alley leading down the back of the building from here, but it looked narrow.

The front of the building faced us; we were at the point of its triangle, staring across the street at the glorious grand entrance, with its massive steps and impressive arches leading to the main door.

There were buildings of a similar height across the alley, to the left of the building, and also beyond to the right. The avenue on that side was covered with tall trees that looked like they'd been growing for a few centuries. Immediately across the street to my right, past the blockades the police were setting up, was a massive white church with a bell tower that stretched into the air higher than the gallery.

"Snipers already positioned," Webster said, leaning against the open door of his car. He wasn't exactly springing into action or heading for the command post. "Armed response team ready, probably about to storm in before the terrorists get too comfortable."

"You assume they're terrorists?" I asked.

"They're causing terror, that's for sure," he said, still not moving.

"What are we doing here?" I asked. I thought I knew, but I wanted to hear it from him.

"Staring straight ahead and watching what happens," he said and gave me a significant look. "It's not like I'm far enough up the ladder to be involved, but they like to have as many of us on scene as they can for these sorts of things."

"Because staring at the exterior of an art gallery is a productive use of your time, Detective Inspector?" I wasn't razzing him, really. Just probing.

"It's the department's time," he said, just a little tense. "I do what they tell me when I'm on it."

"I could help," I suggested, sending him a sidelong glance.

"Or you could sit right here and stay out of trouble," he said. It wasn't an argument, really. I wasn't in charge here and neither was he.

I stared at the gallery across the way. He was right, the British equivalent of a SWAT team was moving into position up the steps. There was really nothing else for us to do but watch.

Chapter 33

"What the bloody hell are you doing?" Philip asked. The air smelled of richness, of culture, of a history and tradition that he had always found so appealing. And, of course, it smelled of fear.

Liliana was running one of her blades in a broad stroke down some of the shorter canvases that lingered near face level. The room they had occupied was a large one, an enormous... well, gallery... that reached two stories at least. Paintings filled the room from floor to ceiling over the deep crimson walls. Paintings that were hundreds of years old, representative of the crowning achievements in the art of western civilization...

And Liliana... that savage, silly little bitch... was slashing them one by one.

"I'm striking out against the bourgeois tastes of the thieves who have taken so much of the world's wealth for themselves," she said, running her blade down a landscape of a lake done in bold colors.

"Stop immediately," he said, flushed. Philip could feel his hands shake. "That is priceless cultural heritage, regardless of who owns it."

"These should be in a public museum for all the people to see," Liliana said with a flash of crimson rage. "Not here in a place where only those who are willing to pay can come in." She spat on one of the shredded canvases, and Philip felt a twitch at the corner of his eye as he contemplated killing her right there. He'd killed for less.

But she had other work to do, work he couldn't take her away from.

"Don't you have somewhere to be?" he asked, barely restraining his rage. She was truly a vicious piece of work, a product of her upbringing. She needed to be reined in, kept on a tight leash.

He caught a flash of anger in her eyes that faded quickly, and she nodded once in acknowledgment. She slunk toward the open archway that led into the main entrance to the gallery.

Once she had gone, Philip felt his hand unclench. That Philistine had torn eight paintings before he'd gotten her back in line. He ran a hand over his mask, straightening it, and looked up at Antonio, who was still on a ladder they'd retrieved from the storage room, working on freeing a painting from the wall. "Are you nearly done?"

"Nearly," Antonio answered.

Philip ran his fingers over his masked face. This job could not be over quickly enough for his tastes. But once it was, then he could get back to the business of breaking the old man. Accomplish that, and he'd have no need for any more of these foolish errands, or the pests that pulled him into them. It would be a happy day, that one. And that day could not come swiftly enough for his tastes.

Chapter 34

I could see the SWAT team making their way up the grey steps, their black uniforms dark and stark against the plain background. The gallery was an impressive piece of architecture that commanded attention, centered as it was in the middle of the thoroughfare. I wondered if that was a statement about the place itself, like a cry for some sort of attention through the building's placement and manner of construction.

There was a dull smell in the city air: the stink of car exhaust. Birds cawed somewhere in the distance, and I could taste the breakfast I'd had still lingering on my tongue. I wanted coffee, and lots of it, but the likelihood I'd find a Starbucks anywhere nearby was low, I figured.

"Are we still on the sitting and watching?" I asked. "Because that's boring. And also a misuse of my talents."

"You can go if you want," Webster said, tense. "Perhaps apply your talents for mayhem somewhere else while I sit and wait." He didn't look any happier to be here than I was. He was just standing there, leaning against his door. He hadn't even checked in with whoever was in charge of the scene, so I guessed his presence was minimally important.

Besides, he looked good in that pose. Commanding. Even though he wasn't really commanding anything.

"You think I could get a cup of coffee anywhere around here?" I asked. "No mayhem needed."

"Sure," he said and pointed to his left without looking away from the SWAT team, which was now at the top of the steps and stacked up outside the main entrance to the gallery. I could have given them some pointers, maybe, because I'd been in that situation more times than I could count. "There's a Starbucks just up that road," Webster said, drawing my attention back to him.

"Wow, they really are everywhere." I considered it for just a moment and then paused, remembering that I didn't have any money. I sighed, taking a breath of the exhaust that filled the air. I realized several of the police cars were still running. "What are they doing to control the scene?"

"Snipers," he said, nodding to the buildings to our left, to the bell tower of the church to our right, and then pointing at the building beyond. That had the gallery surrounded on three sides, with coverage of the thin alley around back from the buildings on either side. "SO19 goes in, sorts them out."

Tactically, it was sound. If you were dealing with humans. "If this is a meta, you're going to have a mess," I said.

"The response team is heavily armed," he said, brushing me off.

"Heavily armed does not equal well prepared," I said, gritting my teeth in annoyance.

"Yeah, well," he said, not without a little annoyance of his own, "I'm not in charge, am I? You're more than welcome to talk to the Commissioner about that, if you'd like—"

I felt the air around me compress with the strength of a shockwave the moment before I heard the explosions. Webster was thrown against his car from the force, and I barely managed to steady myself using my power of flight as a cloud of dust rushed over me, covering the police command post with debris from the buildings on either side of us as they exploded.

Chapter 35

Philip was only peeking around the corner, but he got to witness the entire exchange with the SO19 team. The explosions came right on schedule, of course, the facades of the buildings on either side of the gallery and the church directly opposite disappearing in a blast of flame and force. Antonio had spent the whole night planting and preparing, seeding the explosives in places they would not be immediately obvious to the police, who would quickly canvas the area with bomb-sniffing dogs as they formed their perimeter.

The bomb maker had taken great care sealing each bomb well enough to fool a cursory sniff by a dog. Philip had watched some of it, impressed with the effort it took.

Worth it, now, though, he reckoned, seeing the places where the police had placed their snipers falling to the ground in a cascade of debris.

The front door to the gallery was open, the response team already entering when the bombs started to go off. Philip popped his head out just as they were turning, instinctively, toward the thunderous sound of the buildings collapsing outside.

They did not see Liliana sweep into their midst.

She had buried her blades into the first member of the team before he even knew what was coming at him. A fountain of blood splattered on a canvas placed just inside the hallway, causing Philip to cringe in horror. The black-clad policeman dropped his weapon and clutched at his neck fruitlessly as the blood continued to spurt from his carotid artery.

Liliana did not wait for his body to reach the conclusion that it was dead, though. She had already moved on, spinning and twirling with a grace that would not have been out of place in a ballet—sans the knives, of course. She hit the next two team members and placed the daggers directly in their hearts, piercing their black vests and lifting them off the ground with the force of her impact. She threw them off the tips of her blades as though they were mere refuse bags being thrown upon the pile, heaving them onto the next men in line behind them. They all fell in a jumble and she struck the fallen, blades in their necks before they fired so much as a shot.

There had been noise and chaos as a distraction when she'd begun, but it started to fade even as the cloud of dust from the church across the street blasted into the gallery in a sheer wave. Philip strained, ducking around the corner as a billow of white and brown rushed past him. He closed his eyes and heard the sound of gunshots for the first time. Sharp, barking, earsplitting. A second's fire, if that, and then they ceased abruptly with the sound of a scream. Another series of shots that came to a quick end, and a gurgling noise.

The noise went on, just for a little while longer, and Philip stood there, back against the wall, listening to the angel of death do her work on the Metropolitan Police. Their finest against his, blood against blood—and he smiled as heard his own cut them apart in triumph, knowing that what she was doing here was a mere fraction of the death he'd just seeded out there.

Maybe even enough to completely destroy the Metropolitan Police Service completely.

Chapter 36

The explosion was loud, was long, was furious and destructive, with force and fire to spare. Most explosions weren't exactly like those you see in the movies, with the orange flames. That's movie magic for you, special effects. Most explosions were force and power. If you've ever seen a building demolished, you know what I'm talking about. You may see some fire, but it's behind the cloud of smoke and debris.

This explosion brought the damned fire like it was a volcano. Someone had put some serious pyro into this, like napalm or another combustible designed to wash over the police presence.

Designed to burn a hell of a lot of people to death.

I didn't even think before I started to react, and all I had was the space of a second. *Gavrikov*, I called into my head, slowing time as I withdrew into my mind, summoning forth the Russian master of fire whom I had made my ally years before.

I felt myself rise into the air, born not by conscious thought but by impulse, my mind carrying me up where I could best help. I stretched out both hands and called to the flames, the rich, burning heat that coursed toward me from the church on one side and the office building on the other.

I called it forth, and it changed its very course like a stream blocked in the bed. The fire twisted and drew off the ground like it was composed of snakes of ember. I ripped it from its path and brought it toward me like a magnet pulling metal. It writhed like a living thing as it surged to my hands and I pulled it in, devoured it.

I don't know how you could measure a volume of flame like that, but there was a hell of a lot of it.

I pulled it in, all of it, hovering ten feet off the ground like a demon of fire, like a flaming angel taking it into my hands. I could feel the heat but only barely, like I was sitting around a campfire somewhere about to tell a ghost story and roast a marshmallow with chocolate and graham crackers.

The smoke remained as I took in the last of the heat, and I sank to the ground. The blood felt like it drained out of my brain, and I sagged against the car. I looked down and the sleeves of my blouse and coat were singed and blackened, flaking off as the smoke closed in around me.

"What the actual eff?" Webster said, his head buried in the car. I looked back to see him fallen to a knee.

"Bombs," I said, panting. What I'd just done was more control of flame than I'd ever exercised. It was like trying to take in a breath that was far, far too big for me. I felt like I'd lost all control of my limbs, I was weak, my head telling me I needed to pass out. My hands just burned and throbbed like they were ready to explode, and I could feel my pulse racing, fire threatening to fountain out of me with every beat of my heart. "Someone meant to wipe out the Met."

Chapter 37

The flames were not as bright as Philip had thought they'd be. He frowned as he stared out the front door, the clouds of smoke and dust obscuring everything. He thought he'd seen flames, the pyrotechnics that Antonio had specially designed and placed to burn alive the police springing into action. It had been meant to shower them with a fire hot enough to reduce their vehicles to flaming wrecks, to leave their bones scorched and their flesh turned to ash.

He stared into the cloud and supposed he might have missed it. He had been stuck inside because of the response team, after all, while the explosions were going off. Still, there should have been fires burning...

"We need to move," Liliana said from beside him. He looked back and saw her blades dripping with blood. She hadn't bothered to clean them, apparently. A quick look over her prey found several pieces missing that hadn't been part of her original attack—ears, noses. His eyes tipped downward and saw a bloody cloth bag on her belt, dripping on the floor.

"What the hell is that?" He pointed to it.

She had a thin smile of satisfaction as she bumped it with her fist. "Trophies."

Philip shuddered as he brushed past her. The woman was a psychopath, but she had her uses. For now, that necessitated keeping her around.

Still, he knew what her future held, in all probability, and he had a sense that when it came time for her to exit the plan, she would go in a messy fashion. A fitting end for her, he thought.

"Time to go," he said as he breezed back into the gallery's main room and looked up to see Antonio descending the ladder with a rolled cylinder. Presumably the painting he'd wanted more than anything in the world was inside, since that had been his price when Philip had come to him to acquire his services. "Are we ready?"

"I have it," Antonio said with a smile that was uncharacteristic of the bomb maker, a sense of deep-seated satisfaction that went far below the surface-level brutality he had been so quick to exhibit in the past. "Finally, I have it."

"Our exit, then," Philip said and gestured toward the storage room. The gallery was filled with dust, the air looking smoky. Philip wanted to squint through the mask but kept from doing so. "Two police, just outside the door on either side. They'll attack the moment we step through. Well within range of your toys."

"No problem," Antonio said, fingering a small remote that looked like a car key fob. It hung from his belt, dangling like a lucky rabbit's foot. He pressed one of the buttons, and there was a popping noise just ahead, outside. Twin screams followed, higher pitched.

Philip breezed out the door with a sense of relief. The dust was thicker here, a heavy veil that closed the air around them, made it impossible to see very far. Screams and cries echoed down the alley, and Philip gave only a perfunctory look to the downed police officers on either side of the door. They'd been waiting in ambush, not noticing the improvised explosive devices that Antonio had left in the form of a wine bottle and a discarded coffee cup on either side of the door. After all, who would care about trash when they were waiting to ensure that criminal terrorists didn't escape out the back of the gallery?

"That it?" Antonio asked as they headed toward the van. The dust was so thick it was nearly impossible to see more than a few feet.

"Follow the course and we'll be fine," he said. The police had been counting entirely too much on their snipers—overwatch, they were called. Well, that and the helicopter that was now blinded somewhere above them. "Straight down the alleys to the escape car. Five more minutes and we'll be clear of these fools." He smiled. "Or at least what remains of them."

Chapter 38

I fought my way to my feet, struggling against the sweet pull of gravity. It would have felt so good to just drop into the passenger seat of Webster's car and stay there, letting sleep take over. Using the powers at my command was exhausting, and doing what I'd just done, swallowing a sky's worth of fire, had run through all the stamina I had left. I felt like curling up for a nap was the single best idea I'd ever had, and I wanted it more than I'd ever wanted anything.

Except to put a hurting on whoever was pulling the strings here. A rage flared in me, heating my stomach, and it had nothing to do with the fire I'd just absorbed.

Yeah. I wanted to do violence to the person who'd set those explosives more than I wanted to sleep. It was close, but for now, sleep lost.

I felt like I'd taken a shot of adrenaline right to the heart, and my blood was pumping hotly as I stared into the smoke and dust that swirled around the police encampment. I couldn't see the gallery in the distance, but I knew it was there. I took off at a run, not chancing my power of flight both out of respect for the pact I'd struck with the commissioner and also out of fear that I'd drain myself even drier of whatever energy I had left in the process.

I had a nasty feeling about what I was up against here, and I didn't want to be powerless when I came face to face with the big bad.

I ran pretty quickly, though, and had sprinted across the street in seconds. I took the stairs in front of the gallery a few at a time, hurtling up them like I was vaulting nothing of consequence. I saw the bodies inside the door just before I entered and leapt to avoid them. My jump carried me over them and into the smoky entry to the gallery. I squinted in the dust and looked for tripwires. Fool me once, shame on you. Fool me twice, and I'll put a whole magazine of bullets in your skull.

I had my pistol drawn and slid my back along the wall as I moved down the main hallway in the gallery. I could see an enormous arch to my left and a massive room beyond. I slid right to the edge and entered the room with my pistol outstretched, ready to fire.

There were people everywhere, on their knees, heads turned away. I could see them in the haze, and at least a few of them saw me. It took me less than a second to assess them and realize that none of them was a threat. Their faces glowed with pure, visceral fear, and the one guy who had gotten to his knees threw his hands in the air in a blatant display of surrender.

I scanned the gallery quickly and saw a ladder on the wall behind me, a frame emptied of its contents hanging up above it. I frowned. One painting? Someone created a hostage situation and a freaking ambush outside that had caused the death of a SWAT team and who knew how many snipers and spotters for *one damned painting?*

No.

Not just the painting, I realized.

It wasn't even half the goal.

"Where'd they go?" I asked the guy who was waving his hands like white flags at me.

"Out the back," he said in a breathless British accent, nodding his head like he could use it to push me in that direction by sheer force of fearful will. "Just a minute ago."

I studied him quickly, just to be sure in my own mind that he wasn't lying, that he wasn't actually the enemy in some sort of disguise. If he was, Matthew McConaughey had nothing on this guy in terms of acting ability. I made for the back of the building.

I flew through a storage room (not literally—this time) at high speed and exited out the open doors into an alley. Two cops were on the ground to either side of the door; one writhing in pain, one as still as a corpse.

I reached down and grabbed the shoulder-mounted mike on the nearest and shouted into it. "Officer down at the rear of the gallery!"

"We got officers down all over the bloody scene!" a voice came in return, masculine but high and edged with panic.

"Hell," I breathed, realizing he was right. I looked down the far end of the alley and saw the back of a white panel van disappearing into the haze. The terrorists.

I didn't even give a thought to anything as I felt the anger surge through me, revitalizing me. I felt like I could have run for a hundred miles.

I started by heading full speed toward the end of the alley.

The brake lights flared a halo of red in the white smog as the van slowed. I was after it, closing the distance as it eased across the road at the side of the gallery. It crossed the empty street and detoured around a pile of rubble caused by the collapse of the building across the street as it darted into an alley. They were taking their time, watching for obstacles in the road.

I did not waste any time with such precautions.

I came up on a pile of broken stone and glass and leapt over it in one bound. I landed in the alley across the street, forty or fifty yards behind the van. It was going faster now that it had cleared the bomb damage, speeding up as it shot down the narrow, dim space between the two buildings.

My legs pumped as I came after them, pouring on the speed. I was probably going forty or so miles per hour myself, keeping to the ground and drawing on my stamina to keep me going. My breath came in shallow bursts, my lungs taxed by my efforts. It had been a couple years since I'd had to work very hard at this. A very long couple years in which I was either stuck at the office or away on a hunting trip for work. I hadn't even realized how complacent I'd gotten. At first I'd worked out every day, honing my skills, keeping my edge sharp. That had been the first six months, before everything had hit the fan and I'd realized...

I'd realized that there was no one out there who could really match me.

Stupid.

Oh, so stupid.

Somewhere in the exhausted haze of the job I'd lost sight of the fact that training was a way of life. Preparation for moments like this *was* my life—or at least it had been until I'd gotten so frigging tired that I spent the few spare moments I had left splayed out on the couch watching Netflix or sleeping.

Dumb. I was kicking myself for being so dumb.

I caught the van because it slowed down in a parking lot just beyond the mouth of another alley. It was a triangular space surrounded by buildings on all sides, the narrow passages set up to allow cars to come and go. The van slammed on the brakes and came to a halt in two seconds.

I came to a halt just slightly more slowly.

I ricocheted off the back of the van, fortunately unhurt but a little dazed. I rolled back to my feet, breath coming and going in gasps. I was a little slumped, too, back hunched as I stood there, waiting for someone to emerge so I could kick their ass.

Then the back doors opened, the front door opened. I saw two people coming toward me, and for the first time in a long while, I felt a pang of concern.

Chapter 39

The person who came out the back of the van was a woman, there was little doubt about that. She had on a pink ski mask, some sort of abomination that didn't go very well with her black tactical vest and...

It took me a second to realize that she was wearing the black tactical vest over normal clothes, and another second to put together that it had come from one of the downed SWAT team members. It was unzipped and a white tank top was visible beneath, as was an extremely flat chest and stomach. She wasn't small, but damn she was in shape. Military-style conditioning, at least it looked like to me.

And she had two knives in her hands.

Bingo.

I didn't get much of a look at the guy getting out of the front of the van before knife-lady came at me. She wasn't that fast, but I was feeling pretty damned slow at the moment. I didn't even get a chance to squeeze off a shot before she was on me. She had some training with those weapons; that much was sure by her motions, which were confident and practiced. A couple years earlier, I could have dusted her in seconds. Now I felt slow, not only from my recent lack of practice but also from the drain I'd experienced from absorbing the fire. I was faster than she was but punchy at the moment, and she pressed on me harder than I would have expected someone to come at an unknown quantity like me.

I turned her aside, but just barely. She drifted out of my sight every time I tried to get the gun barrel lined up for a shot. She took a chunk of my elbow, and I felt a thin slice of the blade cut through my coat and draw a paper's width of blood from me. It stung, but it got my brain working a little faster. She came back at me again, and this time I knocked one of her hands aside with a pistol whip and lifted a knee to strike her in the gut. I heard nothing more than a grunt, and she kept coming, so I pushed her out of the way to give myself space to maneuver.

"Stop," came a proper British accent from behind, and I turned in time to see the man in the black ski mask. I recognized the eyes, of course hiding as they were behind the wire-framed glasses. I backed up to put myself at the bottom of a triangle of knife lady and the man in the glasses. He wasn't making any offensive moves, but I didn't expect that to last. I had my pistol back at low rest, but my elbow was burning, interfering with my aim. I started to summon Wolfe to fix it, but I couldn't muster the will to do it. Bad sign.

"So, it is you," I said, keeping my hands up defensively and trying to focus on all three of the threats before me. The guy who'd gotten out of the front of the van was just standing there, a rolled-up cardboard cylinder tucked under his arm. The stolen painting, I presumed. Now our murderer—murderers, I should say—had branched out into art theft and the wanton killing of police officers. I thought about firing a shot at Mr. Ski Mask, the leader, but I didn't exactly have a great backstop here and he'd already proven adept at dodging bullets.

"'Tis I," he said gamely. "And it's you, as well. Sienna Nealon, look at you. The girl herself. The face of metahumans everywhere." He stared at me, and cocked his head. "I didn't really notice this when we were staring at each other across the kitchen, but you look taller on the telly."

I wanted to grind my teeth. I was average height for a woman, dammit. "So, you know my face. Why don't you show me yours? We can be on a first-name basis." I asked, just playing him for time. His knife-wielding flunky was keeping her distance, hovering just out of reach, which suited me fine. I wasn't super enthused about my chances of taking her, because at the moment I just wanted to go back to bed. I didn't like my odds, not feeling as weakened as I did. If she came at me, I was definitely going to have to take a shot at her, backstop be damned.

"I don't think so," he said with a light chuckle. "You wouldn't know my face anyway. My power lies in anonymity. Let's just say I'm one of countless people you've had some influence on. Though probably not in the way you intended it."

"Is Angus dead?" I asked. I watched him carefully, but he looked utterly composed. And utterly unsurprised at the question.

"He did meet a bitter end," the man in the mask said with a glee he didn't bother very hard to hide. "I was trying to decide whether it was even worth it to leave him for your friends at the Met to try and put together. See, he's in so many pieces that it'll take you a while to sort him out, and I rather suspect New Scotland Yard is going to be a bit busy for the near future."

"What about Janus?" I asked. "And Karthik?"

I caught a hint of something in the way he answered. "You'll just have to wait and see what turns up, I'm afraid." There was a glimmer of triumph in his eye. "Though I expect the capacity of the police to deal with all I'm about to throw in their path is going to be rather limited, what with the stunning casualties they just took—"

"That SWAT team was a real loss," I said, managing to break into a taunting smile of my own. "The snipers, too. But that's all they lost."

He hid his outrage well; it cropped up in a twitch of his brows for less than a quarter of a second before he blunted it, covering his slip with an amused grunt and smile that didn't feel at all real. "So... ever the hero, everywhere you go."

"I do what I can," I said.

"What you can do is so limited that it falls easily into the category of 'pathetic,'" he said with a barely concealed hiss of anger. "I've seen your interview; your arrogance is astounding given your utter lack of true ability. You strut around the world as if you were some being of high accomplishment." His face hardened, the smile turning into a sneer. "As though you didn't preside over the massacre of some eighty percent of our kind."

"I didn't preside over anything," I said tautly. "I did everything I could to stop it—"

"Oh, yes, you did everything you could," he said in smug, cool fury. "You turned to the very devil of our world himself looking for succor in the heart of conflict. Your high-minded rhetoric, your moral fortitude? You threw it all away when you were going after Sovereign, didn't you?"

"I don't know what you're talking about," I said. I genuinely didn't, but he was clearly pissed about something.

"Of course you don't," he said, somehow even more smug. "Everyone thinks you're the hero, don't they? They saw what they saw, the end of the fight. The last battle. Do you think they'd canonize you if they knew what you did before that?" He took a step toward me, menacing. "If they knew the lines you crossed? The enemies you embraced in your mad dash to stop Sovereign? How many serpents did you clutch close to your breast and give succor to in your struggle to survive?"

I narrowed my eyes at him. "Is that a metaphor? Because if so, you lost me—"

He launched at me, stepping closer in a move that was more fury than direct action. I recoiled a step, defensively, and he moved to counter so fast I would have sworn he knew what was coming. If I'd been at full capacity, I might have been able to block him effectively; as it was, I barely bounced off a hard punch thrown at the side of my head.

I staggered back a step, lurching. His hit hurt; even though it was a glancing blow it still caused my vision to shift from the impact. I sidestepped—

And ran right into a blade that penetrated into my kidney.

The pain was staggering, and it was followed by another knife to the ribs that was withdrawn so quickly it took a second for it to register exactly how badly I'd been hurt. I stayed on my feet, turning away from the woman with the knives. I turned to shoot her, but my gun was gone from my grasp. Her smile showed through the pink ski mask's mouth opening, and it made her look all the more demented. My pistol was in her hand, clutched with one of the blades.

"I admired you, you know," the man in the ski mask said. "When I first heard about you. When I first saw you. I thought you might be the sort of person who could help me. Who could aid me in getting the satisfaction I was due."

I felt the blades hit me again, and I looked to the left in time to see that the woman had swooped in again while I was distracted. Stupid mistakes. Amateur mistakes, really. I felt the shock of pain, the screaming of nerves as she twisted the knives in my side. I cried out to Wolfe, somewhere deep inside, to help me, but his voice was near-faded, the over-exertion from controlling the fire coming back on me now and stopping me from healing as fast as I needed.

I called on another soul to help me, reaching out for Eve Kappler, and the answer was nearly non-existent. I shot a faint web of light out my left hand that pushed the knife-wielding woman away from me only a few feet before it disintegrated like dust in the breeze.

"Gavrikov," I muttered under my breath. I needed to fly or needed to burn.

Neither came to me.

My legs folded beneath me, and I looked up into the masked face of my enemy, his cold eyes staring down at me. "I admired you until I found out what you really were," he said, taking another step toward me. I took a clumsy swipe at him, but he dodged with ease. I saw motion out of the corner of my eye and there was suddenly a blade at my throat. The woman had me by the arm, holding me up. Hell, she was the only thing holding me up; without her, I would have pitched forward onto the alley floor. The blade dug into the skin of my throat, and I could feel it breaking the flesh, the trickle of blood running down the front of my blouse. She did not even bother to hold my own gun at my head; she didn't need to.

"I know who you are now," the man said, squatting down in front of me. I reached out for him but felt the blade dig in and the woman's strong hands pull me back. "What kind of person you are when you're cornered. What sort of options appear to you, the ideas you'll embrace, the desperate gambits you'll attempt to save yourself." He slapped my hand down, breaking my wrist in the process, a perfect hit that even I might not have been able to pull off at the height of my training. "I know your past as well as your future." At this, he smiled. "You'll be the last of them to die, because you were the last of them to join."

I wanted to cry out, to ask him what the hell he was talking about, but I couldn't. I felt the knife slash across my throat, opening it up, and the warm flood ran down my chest like I'd spilled a cup of water down my shirt. I felt lightheaded, but the pain was already fading, along with the light. My eyes fluttered as I stared at him, my mouth moving futilely.

"You'll probably survive this," he said as I hit the ground, no longer supported by the woman. "If you do, I know we'll meet again."

I heard his words as I faded into the darkness. "Sienna Nealon—the last head of Omega."

Chapter 40

Philip watched her bleed with a strange sense of detachment. It was supposed to be joyful, but it wasn't, really. She would survive this, he was certain. That was both a relief and a curse. A relief because in spite of what he'd said, she really could be useful as a last stopgap. Beating her would be easy. Containing her for very long, though? That would be nearly impossible.

"Shall we go?" Antonio called. He had moved over to the parked BMW that was waiting for them here. The smell of drifting smoke from the wreckage around the gallery was heavy, though not as heavy as it had been in the immediate area around the destruction.

"Just a moment," Philip said. His mind ran through the probabilities. She was wounded but not critically; left on the street she'd be found in a matter of minutes. Too soon. "Move her to the bin," he said, pointing at a rubbish bin against a dull grey wall.

Liliana did it with glee, stabbing the girl under the armpits, burying her knives between the ribs as she dragged her along. It left a clear trail of blood that caused Philip to sigh in sheer annoyance. He said nothing, though; there was no point.

Liliana tossed the girl into the bin as if she weighed nothing at all. Philip held the top for her, barely, his thumb and forefinger tingling at the thought of all the bacteria surely covering the thing. He kept from making a grimacing face, but only just. "Antonio?" he called, and the bomb maker came round the BMW to give him a look of curiosity. "Give her a little something extra for her trouble."

Antonio smiled, his dark goatee pushed back around the edges to make room for the fearsome expression. Keeping the painting cylinder tight under one arm, he pulled something off his belt, slipped a pin out of it and tossed it, perfectly, into the open bin.

Philip let the lid slam shut and he started toward the car. He didn't bother to count out loud, and he'd lost track by the time he slipped into the back seat of the BMW and removed his mask.

They had reached the turn outside the alley when it went off, a faint pop that sounded like a gunshot in the distance. He did not turn around to look as they made the left onto the crowded road, quite secure in the knowledge that everything was in perfect placement. When she woke—if she woke up—even she could not stop him now.

Chapter 41

I drifted along like I was riding a tide. I floated, suspended on a calm ocean, the sound of the waves crashing in my ears and a salty, metallic taste on my tongue that wasn't at all like water. It was so bright, the day shining down on me, and my breaths came slowly, one after another, my body utterly relaxed.

I blinked at the bright sunshine, and realized I wasn't actually on a beach. It felt like a beach, water and all, but it wasn't.

It was all in my head.

The sand was there, gritty, sticking to my shoulders. I didn't feel like I was wearing much, probably just enough to be considered beach legal. It was peaceful, though, even though I knew it wasn't real, and I was quite content to just sit there and feel the heat radiating down on my skin.

At least, until a voice with a thick German accent interrupted my bliss. "We need to talk."

I opened an eye to find Eve Kappler standing over me. Bitch was stealing my sunshine. I could see her face, knotted into an unpleasant expression. Her arms were folded, and she was wearing a black tactical vest, black pants, and high boots. She was the picture of a soldier, the picture of her I saw in my head every time I thought about her.

Of course, she also looked very much alive, which she wasn't and hadn't been for a couple years.

"Not now, Eve," I said, waving her off. "I'm enjoying my imaginary day in the sun."

"Nothing wrong with taking a break every now and again," came the voice of Roberto Bastian, causing me to crack my eye open. He was dressed almost exactly like Eve except he was taller, and instead of short blond hair, his was dark and cut close to the scalp, military-style. "But this is not a great time for it."

I sighed and tried to roll over. I failed, and the two of them continued to block my sun. "I disagree. It feels like a great time for it."

"Your life hangs in the balance," came a heavier voice, deeper. I recognized Bjorn, one of Odin's—yes, that Odin—sons. He was a big son of a bitch in life, and I could tell just by peeking out at him for a split second that this hadn't changed in death. He was still big. And stealing my sunshine, too.

"You are at risk," came the cool yet strained voice of Aleksandr Gavrikov. He still sounded Russian in my head. Of course, he—and the others—actually *were* in my head, their full personalities. However happy I'd been for their recent silence, they were destroying all that goodwill here in one fell swoop.

"I'll deal with it later," I said, brushing them off.

"Sienna," Wolfe's husky voice said, causing my eyes to pop open. He used to call me Little Doll with alarming regularity, but hadn't done that in a couple years. I was starting to feel surrounded, the sun blotted out by their shadows. "Do you know where you are?"

"On a beach," I sighed. "A beautiful place with mild temperatures and pleasant winds and an ocean that will feel wonderful on my skin when I go to take a dip in a few minutes."

"You're in a back alley in London," came the voice of Zack Davis, causing my eyes to snap open, "your throat has been cut, your internal organs have been shredded by a bomb, and you're less than a minute from dying."

I caught a flash of something beyond the beach. There was a faint tapping of something like rain on metal, sirens echoing in the distance, and I saw a dark that was only penetrated by light seeping in from half a hundred holes in a wall of blackness. There was pain everywhere, everything that I could feel was agony, and I let it go—

And I was back on the beach, back in the sand, legs pulled close to me, the heat on my skin feeling oh-so-good. I could feel the lapping of the tide at my toes, and it felt like it might be time to go up the beach a little further or maybe just let the water wash over me—

"Sienna," Zack said again, and I saw him there next to me, a snow falling down around his pale cheeks, all the life gone out of his face. "I don't want you to end up like this." His mouth moved unnaturally for the voice that spoke, stiff and dead, his jaw creaking open and closed barely in time with the speech.

I felt a swell of sickness in my stomach. "Zack, I'm not... I'm not..."

"You're getting closer," he said, all the color washed out of his features. His blond hair, usually a handsome contrast to his tanned face, looked dark and dull against his white skin. "You need to go back to the world. You need to fight."

"Yes," Eve Kappler said, her pixie haircut flashing in front of my eyes as I glimpsed her dead body on a snowy tarmac at night, lights shining down on her in the darkness, "you need to start putting up a fight again."

I felt the heat of resentment burn through me. "I don't know if you've just been on vacation yourselves, but I've been fighting for a couple years now."

"No," Roberto Bastian said, dead eyes staring at me in judgment, "you've been going through the motions for a couple of years."

"Or at least one year," Bjorn said with a darkness in his face. I saw him as he had looked when he died, body lit by the flames of burning buildings all around him..

"I've done what was required of me," I said.

"And nothing more," Gavrikov spoke, and I saw him on the top of a building—the IDS Tower in Minneapolis—home—the sun rising behind him, his skin glowing like it was about to burst into flames.

"That's not living, Sienna," Wolfe said, and the darkness surrounded us completely. I looked around, trying to peer into the infinite black, and saw a single light in the dark. An incandescent bulb pitched a soft glow from above me, lighting a concrete floor beneath my feet. I could smell sweat, fear, and other things. Wolfe's face peered at me from out of the dark where he lay on my basement floor. "That is little more than surviving."

"What is this?" I asked, turning about in the darkness. "An intervention? Because the six of you are the last people in the world who should be lecturing me about—"

"We're not in the world, are we?" Zack said, stepping out of the dark. He looked alive again, healthy, that confidence he'd always carried with him evident in the smile on his face. He was wearing a suit, and he looked good in it. His cheeks had a dash of rose.

Like they had before I'd killed him.

"No," I said, staring at him, my voice low and near to cracking. "No, you're not."

"You've always been a girl who did what she had to do," Zack said, and the bulb swayed gently above him, casting a spotlight on his handsome features.

"You've been someone who fought the long odds." I turned to see Bastian staring at me, his skin flush with life again as well.

"Who fought the hard fights that no one else would take," Eve said, stepping into her own little lit circle to my left.

"No matter what... you fought," Bjorn said, his massive, tattooed chest on display as he stepped into his place.

"You beat one hundred of the strongest people on the planet," Gavrikov said, his skin wreathed in flame.

"Mercy was a concept for lesser mortals," Wolfe said, his dark hair looking like menacing fur on his body.

"Whatever it took," Zack said.

"No matter what," Gavrikov said.

"No mercy," Eve said.

"No fear," Bastian said.

"No stopping," Bjorn said.

"Until the job was done," Wolfe said.

I stood quietly at the center of the circle, not even bothering to turn to face my accusers, because the world spun so I didn't have to. As each of them spoke, the circle rotated to bring them right in front of my face, edging ever closer the longer this wore on. At the present rate of acceleration, I realized I'd be tasting Wolfe's most recent dinner in a couple more minutes. He was a cannibal, so that prospect held little appeal for me. "What do you want?" I asked.

"For you to be you," Zack said, hands buried in his pants pockets. He shrugged and did it with a boyish smile. "For you to go back to being you, the you that fought for the whole world. For you to turn back the clock a couple years, shake off the weariness, dig deep, and get after this man in the ski mask like you're out for his blood."

"I can't do it like that anymore," I said, looking away. "Guys, there are rules. Perfectly reasonable rules. We have a society here that doesn't respond well to the level of destruction that—"

There was a chorus of crosstalk that felt like it burned my ears. I recoiled away, and the world spun around me.

"Don't be a fool—"

"—can't keep doing this—"

"—better as you were—"

"—world burning around you—"

"—going to die—"

"STOP!" I said, and they did. The world slowed, the spin reduced, and I stared at each of them in turn as they stood in the quiet darkness, the light bulbs above each of their heads shining down on them. "I'm not the same person I was back then. I have a job and a responsibility. I'm not some rogue agent flying under the radar who can just do whatever she wants without fear of the consequences. I blew up a resort, in case you forgot. I haven't forgotten because it landed me in about a hundred and fifty hours of disciplinary hearings that never got aired on C-Span. I have a job to do. I'm very good at it. No one else can do it. And in order to keep doing it, I have rules to play by—"

"Rules will get you killed," Wolfe said.

"Rules limit your freedom of action," Bjorn said.

"Freedom comes with responsibility," I said. "This is a civilized society—"

"So called," Gavrikov said with a dismissive snort.

"—and you don't just roll around killing people," I said. "This isn't me, being outmatched, outgunned, and in danger of losing everything and getting everyone killed. This isn't war any longer."

Bastian chucked a thumb over his shoulder. "I don't know if you just weren't paying attention when that guy in the mask blew up those buildings, but that looked like a declaration of war to me."

"Not the same," I said. "He's got like, three people."

"How many do you have?" Eve asked, a little snottily.

"I've got me, and that's always been enough," I said.

"You're dying, Sienna," Zack said.

"I'll fix that in a minute," I said. "One thing at a time, because right now I'm arguing with the people in my head, apparently."

"What are you willing to do to stop this man?" Wolfe asked, and the world grew still around me. His black eyes stared at me and I stared back.

"What I have to do," I said.

"Whatever it takes?" Wolfe asked, staring back at me, hard.

"Within limits," I said, folding my arms and staring right back.

"Those limits will be his best weapon," Zack said. "And once he figures out where you won't go, that's where he'll stay."

"You don't even know who this is," I said.

"But we know what he just did," Bastian said. "He killed a lot of people for a painting."

"To prove a point," Gavrikov said.

"Oh, yeah?" I wheeled on him. "And what was the point? Chaos for the sake of chaos?"

"To show anyone watching that this is a man who has no limits to what he'll do in order to get what he wants," Wolfe said.

I stared at the big, hairy bastard. "You'd know a little something about that, I suppose."

His eyes were blacker than the darkness around him. "Wolfe knows everything about it."

"Thanks for the advice," I said, and waved them off. "I could use a little help pulling my guts back in, if you're done with the sermon."

"Sienna—" Their voices were in a chorus, concern and fear and a ripple of anger all together.

"I will take care of it," I said, and my tone was all ice, all the way down, a whole shelf of it. "Thank you for your opinions."

With that, I stepped through the sunlight blue into the darkness and re-entered that world of pain, of agony that encompassed my whole body, and of sirens in the distance under the bleak and stormy sky.

Chapter 42

I pulled myself out of the dumpster a few minutes later, my skin bloody, my clothing tattered and shredded. I was wearier than I could ever recall having been. Drawing the power of Wolfe to heal my body nearly drained whatever stamina I had left. He'd been right when he'd said I was close to dying. There had been a heavy layer of blood in the dumpster from more lacerations than I could rightly count, and even as I pushed the lid up and hooked my upper body over the edge to come tumbling out to the pavement below, I was still so weak that I couldn't immediately stand.

"My God," came a voice from down the alley. Footsteps pounded toward me as drops of rain fell on my face. I could smell everything, and it smelled like I'd gone dumpster diving in a medical waste bin. Webster's face came into view above me, and he halted before kneeling next to me. "Are you there, Sienna?"

"I am right here, yes," I said in a nearly normal tone of voice. "Trust your eyes on that one."

"Where are you hurt?" he asked, urgently running his fingers over my shredded clothes. In any other situation, it might have been considered copping a feel, but since he looked utterly panicked and I'd been bleeding out from the places his fingers were treading, there was really nothing erotic about it. Unfortunately.

"Mostly on my pride," I said, brushing his hands away gently. "Although there's a hell of a metaphorical bruise on my ass where it just got kicked."

He blinked at me, then blinked again. "You're—you're all right, then?" He didn't look like he believed me. Like he hadn't seen me regrow a foot yesterday.

"I'm more or less fine," I said, gingerly sitting up. "How's the count back at the gallery?"

His face paled, which took some doing since he'd already been white as a blank canvas when he'd shown up and seen me. "Not good, though I think it would have been a great deal worse if you hadn't dissolved that bomb's effects."

"These people are some nasty customers," I said, my voice hoarse and cracking. "It's the guy."

"The guy?" Webster said, sheathing the baton he was carrying in his hand like an afterthought. "What guy?"

"That guy from Angus Waterman's house," I said, suppressing a coughing fit that was threatening to consume me if I didn't get a drink of water soon. "Our guy. The one we're hunting."

"This is him?" Webster asked, a little disbelieving. "That seems a bit farfetched." He paused then glanced down at my ragged appearance. "Are you quite sure you're all right?"

"It's him," I said firmly. "Think about it—a serial killer using bombs? He had a woman with them who used two knives to dispatch your SWAT team, another guy lurking in the background that was probably our bomb maker, and the man himself taunted the hell out of me." I thought back to what he'd said. "He mentioned Omega. This is about Omega somehow."

"Bloody hell," Webster said. "Are you sure?"

"Oh, I'm sure," I said. I was pretty certain I hadn't been hallucinating that. I ran a scraping, ripped-up boot across the pavement as I drew my leg closer to me. "He was pretty blatant about it."

Webster looked like he was trying to decide whether to believe me or not. "Hell, hell and more hell," he said finally. "Can you walk?"

I pushed against the ground and failed to rise. "Give me a minute," I said.

I saw motion above and looked up to see his hand extended, reaching down to me. I took it, and he pulled me to my feet. With maybe a little help from my own strength. "Thanks," I said.

"We need to get everything he said to you down on paper," Webster said, starting back down the alley toward the gallery. "Every word, every gesture, a description of the people you saw—everything. Any part of it might be a clue that could lead us to him."

"Agreed," I said, following behind him with just a little bit of a limp. It wasn't because I was hurt, it was because once more my boot had been damaged so badly that I was walking with an uneven gait. "I just need to make one stop first."

"Oh?" He slowed to let me catch up. "Where's that?"

"A clothing store," I said, matching his shortened strides with my wobbly walk. I gestured toward my shredded outfit, sweeping over the bloodied flesh exposed by the bomb damage. "Can I borrow a few dollars—err, pounds?"

Webster just looked me over once quickly and turned his head again, like he was trying his best not to gaze on anything that might maybe have been exposed. "Of course," he said, but I could see the blush on his cheeks even under the dirt from the explosion.

Chapter 43

"Murder, murder, murder," I said, standing in the middle of the bullpen in New Scotland Yard. "Why kill the guy out in Hounslow other than to somehow penetrate the city's surveillance grid?"

"I told you that's not all linked," Webster said. It was depressingly quiet in here, the bitter smell of stale coffee left un-drunk filling the air.

"I read there are like two hundred thousand cameras in London," I said, pacing around in my new jeans and blouse. I'd gone more practical and less dressy this time. Also, cheaper. Webster didn't dress impressively enough for me to blow his clothing budget with impunity, so I'd gone as practical and low-cost as I could. "You can't tell me that someone doesn't have the ability to run through each of them."

"I don't know," he said with a shake of his head. "Some of them are private, some of them belong to individual towns—"

"Wonderful," I snarled into the empty air. The bullpen was pretty well abandoned save for the two of us. "So someone is watching, maybe. They've at least got the ability to black out certain cameras that could give us a hint of where they are, but apparently there's no central location we could go to... I dunno, watch where the cameras started to go dark so we might have a hint of where this guy is going next?"

"Well," Webster said, "that's how I understand it, yes."

"Gahhhh," I said, letting out a slow breath. "Okay. So. We need to get access to the systems one by one—"

"I can try to do that," he said, making a note on a pad. "Though I have my doubts whether the commissioner will believe that the bloke who did the gallery heist is the same one we've been after."

"We need to figure out how they got to this guy that worked the system. If they're doing this, there has to be more network in place than you know about."

"I don't even know who we'd speak to about that," he said.

"And I need something to eat, desperately," I said, feeling at least some of my current state of crabbiness being brought on by the angry rumble in my belly. Healing always drained me, especially my stomach.

He blinked at me. "Well, I suspect I can do something about that, at least."

"Good," I said, feeling a little embarrassed, "because I'm still broke." I didn't have an ATM card to my name, and it was a few miles past embarrassing.

"How's your phone?" he asked.

"Not so good," I said, holding up the debris that I'd retrieved from my pocket before I'd discarded my old clothes. The faceplate was shattered, a spider web of cracks spreading out from the upper right hand corner. A piece the size of my thumb had been broken cleanly away, revealing a speaker and some other little electronic doodads beneath. "I don't think it's salvageable."

"I bet the mobile insurance people see you coming and close the shop straightaway."

I stared at the broken phone. "Honestly, this doesn't happen to me anymore. This is like... a throwback to the way things were a couple years ago, when I couldn't own anything nice without it getting destroyed."

"Back in time," Webster said with a single nod. "Right, so. Fancy a curry? Fish and chips? You Americans like hamburgers, right?"

"This American fancies whatever the hell she can put in her mouth at the moment," I said, and it took a second for my brain to catch up on that one. "I mean, whatever you're hungry for is fine." I knew I blushed on that one.

He chuckled, but not too much. "Fish and chips?"

"Sure," I said and grabbed the cheap plastic poncho I'd bought for a pound instead of spending Webster's money on an actual coat. It did a billowing thing of its own as I pulled it on over my head, but this was way less cool than what his trench coat did.

"Very nice," Webster said, staring at me and my clear plastic poncho.

"I kind of doubt that, but you're sweet."

"It doesn't obstruct the view," he said and turned to head for the door, smile on his face.

We were almost out when he stopped in the middle of the aisle. I didn't run into him, but only because I was paying attention. "What?" I asked. His attention was fixed on the TV in the corner, and it took me only a second to see what he was looking at.

TV news is TV news, whether it's in America or Britain, I realized. Constantly reporting on the same recycled shit, with the same breathless vomiting of regurgitated "news" every few minutes until the air becomes so saturated with it that they're forced to find some new tidbit or angle lest their viewers tune out. Or pass out, possibly.

The footage of the explosion had doubtless been on all morning, dissected panel-style, with subtle glee by journalists of all stripes. I could have sworn I'd seen that at least a few times in my endless pacing of the bullpen while we'd talked. I'd figured it would have been on all day and night, as surely as the sky was blue and politicians were hard or wet at the thought of a crisis to manage.

This, though… this, I hadn't quite predicted.

I knew Parliament when I saw it, and this was a full shot of it. Big Ben to one side of the frame, the view looking across the Thames quite picturesque even with a hint of haze and fog with the grey sky as background. That was normal.

No, it was the caption on the giant bar at the bottom of the screen that drew my attention. Because that was a cause for worry and concern.

It read, "Metahuman attack spurs Parliamentary response; emergency legislation and vote planned for tonight."

Aw, hell.

Even in England, this couldn't be good.

Chapter 44

"Ah, politicians," I said as we walked down the street toward our lunch. "Always just one or two laws away from fixing everything that ails you. Utopia is just a few bills away, ladies and gents."

"People are scared," Webster said, the rain dripping down the bridge of his nose and gathering there like an unfallen tear. "They want a response."

"How about an intelligent response?" I asked, gathering my poncho around me. "I suppose that would be too much of a stretch."

"You think that passing some laws in response to this situation is a bad idea?" He gave me that cocked-eyebrow look.

"Well," I said, "let's see. They tried to kill your police. They murdered civilians. They stole a painting and took hostages. They set off a series of bombs in the middle of London." I ticked the points off on my finger as I enumerated them, talking over the rain dripping against the hood of my poncho. "Seems to me that if we actually catch them, you've got a great basis for charging them with enough shit to keep them in jail for the rest of their lives. So what's another law going to do for you?"

He looked deeply uncomfortable. "Perhaps fund training for dealing with these sorts of situations—"

"I'm sure that'll come, and I don't think it's a bad idea," I said. "But you know they're not talking about that. Mostly they're talking about passing laws that seek to control the situation while failing to acknowledge that sometimes the things that evil men do are just beyond their control." I felt my expression darken. "Or they're talking about putting those of us who didn't have anything to do with the so-called bad guys and their craziness into jail or detention or deportation."

Webster looked like his cheeks were burning, but he was almost contrite. "I honestly can't blame them." He took hold of a door to a nondescript pub, opening it and holding it for me. That was a nice touch, I thought, even as we argued about how best to treat my kind.

"I can't blame them for being scared, either," I said, pulling the hood down as I stepped into the pub. It had a bar straight in front and a lot of wooden tables dotting the room. A long plate-glass window overlooked the sodden street. There was a smell of something fried in the air. Smelled like home to me. "But again, there's a difference between taking intelligent action when you're afraid and just taking action. One can get you out of trouble; the other does nothing or makes it worse. It's the difference between being in a hole and continuing to dig down versus starting to shovel sideways and up."

"I can't see how passing a law is going to make it worse," he said with a shrug as he led the way over to a wooden, circular table in the corner of the pub. There were only a few patrons here, scattered around, and having conversations as hushed as ours was.

I stared at him. "And I can't see how a law making something already illegal even more illegal is going to do anything but put a bunch of words on a page that someone will sign for no purpose."

He extended a hand to offer me a seat, and I sat down as he pulled off his coat and headed for the bar, ostensibly to order, since the placard on our table said that there was no waitstaff and the bar was the place to do that sort of thing. I sat there in silence, pondering what to say to him next while I waited for him to come back.

He spoke first when he returned, surprising me. "My mum called while you were in the toilets earlier." It took me a second to realize he must have been talking about before we'd left New Scotland Yard. "She was worried."

"I don't blame her," I said with a shake of the head. "What happened this morning was scary. She probably saw it on the news. I'm surprised it didn't give her a heart attack or something."

"She asked if you were all right," he said, sitting down next to me instead of across. He placed a menu, retrieved from the bar and covered in a smooth, faux leather binding, in front of me.

I took a second before grasping at it. "I hope you told her I'm fine."

"I left out a full description of what happened, yes," he said, browsing the faded, yellow-tinged pages of his menu. Mine smelled faintly of old cigars. I wondered how long this pub had had these menus. "I decided it would be better if she thought we weren't anywhere near the goings-on."

I stared evenly at him. "Probably for the best," I agreed and turned my attention to the menu.

He ordered for us a few minutes later, ever the gentleman—fish and chips times two. While he was placing the order, standing at the bar with his suit pants creased and one foot up on the actual, metal bar that rested underneath the—well, the bar, he was the very model of an English gentleman.

But I wasn't thinking about him at the moment.

His mother had asked if I was all right. That was... uncommon.

My mother had died a couple years earlier, and while we'd been on good terms toward the end, it hadn't exactly been the warmest relationship of my life. Not that I'd had a great many warm relationships. She and I had butted heads in my adolescence because I wanted to be my own person, grow and explore the world, and she wanted to keep me safe from monsters that would have used me for their own purposes. It was a long-running series of arguments that always culminated in her imprisoning me in a metal box she kept in the basement in order to keep me in line. And it worked. It was a beautiful limiter of my desire to rebel.

It had also cast something of a sour pall over our relationship once I had escaped said house and wasn't subject to her authority anymore. Stunted our ability to get along as adults. Not that I was much of an adult, still, now twenty-one.

My phone rang, a harsh, discordant noise that sounded more than a little off-key compared to the ringtone I'd had yesterday. I pulled my broken phone out of my pocket and stared at the cracked faceplate, trying to read the caller ID through the shattered glass. I slid a finger across the screen and prayed it would answer. It did.

"Sienna?" the high, near-panicked female voice came from the other end of the line before I'd even said anything. "Are you there?"

"I'm here, Ariadne," I said. Ariadne Fraser was the head of the administrative side of my little agency, putatively my co-head. We worked together and had for years. It was a relatively easy familiarity, though her hair had greyed more over the last few years than I would have believed possible. Or maybe she just hadn't had time to dye it with all we had going on. She damned sure hadn't had time for much of a life.

"Should only be a few minutes," Webster said as he came back. I pointed to my phone and gave him that tight expression that you're federally mandated to give when someone finds you on the phone and you don't want to interrupt your conversation to tell them to shut it. "Oh. Right."

"I saw the news," she said, sounding a little more urgent than usual. "What's going on over there?"

"Things are blowing up," I said, nonchalant.

"I know, that's why I called," she said.

"It's all right," I said. "I'm fine."

"You're not fine. Things are blowing up."

"Yeah, but—wait, why would you assume I'm not fine?"

She spoke slowly because apparently I'm an idiot. "Because things are blowing up."

"It's a big city, London," I said, a little defensive. "How do you know I was even anywhere near that—" I just stopped. "Right. It's me."

"It's you."

"Well, I *am* fine," I said. "Now."

"What happened?" she asked. "Start at the beginning."

"Some guy is hunting down old Omega, the folks we gave shelter to during the war," I said. "He's got a couple of accomplices, a bomb maker and a lady with knives. Seems like he's got a personal problem with Omega and anyone associated with it."

There was a pause. "Does that include you? What with your own fleeting association with them in the war?"

"Apparently," I said tightly. "He says I'm last, though." Webster looked a little alarmed at that but said nothing. I'd told him while he was taking my statement on the whole ordeal, and he hadn't looked any happier about it then, either.

"What can you tell me about him?" she asked, all business again.

"Not much," I said. "White guy, looked from the edge of his mouth and his eyes like he was twenties or thirties, but since he's a meta he could be hundreds of years old and still look like that."

"Any idea what his power is?" she asked. "Our database isn't that impressive at this point, but it might be able to turn up something."

"I won't go holding my breath," I said. "As for powers? Not a clue. He's fast, though. Fast enough to dodge bullets."

"That's not normal," Ariadne said, sounding like she was giving it some thought.

"I'm supposed to be at the top of the speed and power scale and I can't dodge bullets," I said. "Ever heard of anything like that?"

"No, sorry," she said. "What about his accomplices? Anything on them?"

"The woman is pretty fast, but not as fast as I am," I said. "She's mean, though. Ruthless and efficient. Probably the one who's cutting up the victims." I snapped my fingers at Webster and he got it, picking up his phone and tapping on the keys. I assumed he was making up a note to check on this for later.

"I'll run the government databases for a similar modus operandi," Ariadne said, sounding like someone taking my order at a drive-through. "The FBI might have something on that. As for the bomb maker…"

"I'll get you a copy of the report as soon as it comes through," I said. "I'm assuming whoever's in charge of the investigation over here will want all the help they can get." Webster nodded absently. "Interpol might have some record of him if he's been playing the game for a while."

"Bomb makers tend to stick close to their preferred explosives," she said. "Odds are good if he's been active before, we'll be able to at least trace him, and if not, maybe we can get an idea of who trained him."

"Cool," I said, and realized how out of place that probably sounded. "Did Reed tell you about Janus?"

"Yeah," Ariadne said. "Obviously I don't know him as well as you do—"

"Who does, really?" I asked dryly. "When I spoke to this guy last time, he pretty much admitted to having Janus. Seemed to indicate he might still be alive. There's some pattern in the way he's doing things. First he kidnaps and kills a couple Omega expats, then murders a Russian spy in his own home. He pulls an art heist this morning but creates more havoc in the escape than he has with the murders he's been spending his time on. This has the feel of unfocused rage, but he's disciplined in his approach to everything, covers his escape by blotting out London's surveillance." I said this all while looking solidly at Webster, who was nodding along and tapping occasionally on his phone as I spoke. "It'd be nice to know what his grievances are."

"We don't have much on Omega," Ariadne said. "As soon as Reed got off the phone with you yesterday, he tasked J.J. to access the old Omega database in London. We have a copy on our local servers from a couple years ago, but the higher-level stuff is encrypted. J.J. is working on it, but he says to brute force it he'd need about a decade and a lot bigger team to do the grunt work."

"What about local access over here?" I asked. "Me at Omega HQ, giving him an in at the servers themselves. Would it be easier if he could work on the original instead of the copy?"

"Based on his analysis of the encryption, he's not hopeful," Ariadne said. "But he did mention in his initial report that it might be worth a look. If Janus or Karthik had been anywhere near the computers on that side, it's possible they opened them up for local work while using the firewall to block outside access. He said there's been a definite change since last time we accessed it with Karthik's help and downloaded what we have. Someone's been in there."

"I guess that leaves me with my next destination planned," I said. "Thanks, Ariadne."

"You're welcome," she said, with none of the frost I might once have expected from her. "I'll call you if I have something."

"So where are we going?" Webster asked, standing as the barman beckoned him over. A couple of baskets of fish and chips were waiting on the long, wooden bar, steam coming off them. I could smell them from here, a deep-fried slice of heaven.

"You're going to get our food," I said slyly. "Then we're going to eat it."

"I see," he said with amusement. "And then, after that?"

"To the belly of the beast," I said with a smile, as I pocketed the wreckage of my phone. "Right to the heart of where it all began. Omega Headquarters. Right here in London."

Chapter 45

Philip was sitting in the darkness when she came in. He did not bother to open his eyes, because that would have necessitated looking at her, and he couldn't quite stomach the thought of that. Not yet.

It was an odd thing, the nature of his sensibilities, and he would be the first to admit it. He could sit and gladly watch Omega operatives get their skin pulled off in fine strips all day long, with all the requisite screaming. But to watch her drag one of her knives across priceless pieces of cultural heritage...

It made him ill to think about it.

"Antonio is in his bunk, cradling the painting's tube as though he's ready to make love to it," Liliana said, her low voice coming steady, completely unamused. "I think now he would follow you into the bowels of hell if you asked."

"I don't plan to go there anytime soon," Philip said, leaning his head against the leather seat. "But it's excellent to hear that if I needed to cross the Styx, I'd be assured of at least some company."

"You would have worlds of company," Liliana said. "All the souls of the capitalist swine would be with you in any such world." She let out a little scoffing noise. "Of course it does not exist, so there is little to fear, but if it did... all the swine would be there. You would not lack for playmates."

"You truly hate them, don't you?" Philip asked, cracking an eye. "Do you still long for the good old days?"

She sniffed, and her eye twitched just barely in the dark. "I long for the days when men believed in the cause. When they were strong and willing to do what it took. Before the KGB and the Politburo all sold their souls so they could drive BMWs to work every day and listen to iPods filled with Western corruption in their dachas. For the days when the worker was—"

"All right, then," Philip said, keeping his smile carefully concealed. "Are you ready for our next target?"

"And the one after and the one after," she said, deftly switching gears. He had heard her on such ideological rants before. It was a fascinating dichotomy, really, to be fueled by such rage for a system that she felt had betrayed her, yet to be open to what he offered, well...

It was more than a little delicious, that irony.

"All right, then," Philip said, and he pulled the felt-lined bag out from beneath the desk. He knew what he was looking for and his hand groped in the semi-dark until he found it. The light necklace chain was at the bottom of the bag, and as he pulled it out, it snagged on one of the other objects in the pouch. He tugged it free carefully, not wanting to break it. He laid it out on the desk before him and ran a palm over it, gently, letting his skin brush it.

The flood of images cut loose in his mind, and he could see the owner. She was out there, hiding, quivering, mewling in the dark. Her future looked painful, there was no doubt. Angela Tewksbury. An old name for a young lady. He knew her past by her file, knew she'd been just a secretary at old Omega, sitting in the middle of the most grossly criminal underworld organization man had ever seen. Right in the middle, rivers of filth and corruption passing all around her.

Even a lowly secretary could not help but get dirty in the midst of all that.

Philip focused his mind. He'd gotten quite good at this, the discipline part of it. It wasn't terribly difficult, focusing in. He could see what he needed to see by looking past the fears, the terrors. Success lay in slowing it down through the lulls. The unemotional parts, the lowlights were never as exciting as the highs. It was easy to skip over them given how mundane most of what he saw was.

He did not skip over them this time, though, and was rewarded with a view of a street sign as the car carrying her to her destination rounded its last corner in the vision in his mind. He saw her dark hair as she looked around her before ducking inside, and over her shoulder was the house number.

"I've got it," he said with a faint smile. Liliana was there when he opened his eyes, her own hungry at the thought of what came next.

Not many more now, he knew. Janus's ability to resist was waning by the day. Soon, he'd have it all—a plan fulfilled, in spite of a thousand obstacles in his path.

Soon. He looked at Liliana's uncultured face as he rose and met her smile with one of his own.

Chapter 46

I found Omega HQ right where I'd left it, down a back alley I was surprised I knew how to get to after all this time. It had taken a little work on Webbo's version of Google maps, but I did it. I would have been happy with a congratulatory hug—or something—but he gave me a grunt and that was about it.

The place looked run-down, which wasn't a huge surprise given it had been well over two years since I'd last been here and the building had (presumably) been unoccupied for most of that. Omega had owned it, I thought, probably through shell corporations and the like, and I wouldn't have been surprised to find it completely undisturbed.

Well, it wasn't undisturbed.

"Someone's been here," Webster said, drawing his baton. I gave him a shake of the head and pulled my pistol. I stared at the side of the barrel and cursed at the indentation in the smooth, shiny metal. "What?" he asked.

"My gun got damaged in the explosion," I said, frowning at the Walther. "I really liked this weapon." Not as much as I liked the Sig Sauer I carried as my primary, but still. I hadn't noticed the damage when I'd reholstered it under my arm, which was probably a good indication of how tired I was.

"Looks like a ding," he opined.

"On the slide," I said. "Might have impinged the barrel."

"Looks superficial," he said with a shake of the head. Like he knew anything about guns.

"Here," I said and spun it around to offer him the grip. "Try firing it and let me know how it works. Of course, if the barrel is damaged, it could blow up in your face, but you're right, it's probably superficial."

"Ah… maybe try your backup," he said, looking away from me.

"This is my backup," I said.

His face creased. "Where's your main one?" He stared at the silver, palm-sized piece in my hand. "That big, black beast of a gun."

"The knife lady took it away from me," I said, sliding the Walther back in my holster. It hung loosely in the leather casing meant for the bigger Sig.

He looked apoplectic for a second, probably pondering the thought of our enemies with another destructive weapon at their disposal. I wasn't happy about it, either, and I had no one to blame but myself for chasing after them when I was plainly not in a good state for fighting. I wished—not for the first time in the last couple years—that I wasn't damned near completely on my own in this.

But I pretty much was, other than Reed.

"Right," he said, his anger diffusing. "I guess you'll just have to get by on your natural charm. And the ability to throw balls of fire at people."

I pulled Eve Kappler and her nets of light to the forefront of my mind. "I told you I don't like to burn things to the ground." I slid ahead of Webster and his collapsible baton before he could answer me. I could have used one of those for myself; in my hands it would have been lethal. In his, it was probably just enough to get him killed. He held it awkwardly, over his shoulder, like he hadn't deployed it in years. I started to wonder if he'd ever used it in battle and then I remembered: normal people don't get into battles.

Casual, everyday warfare was the province of the military or lunatics like me.

I slipped into the hallway under the Omega parking garage. The place had cars that had been here for years, their tires looking like they were rotting beneath the vehicles. I figured them for company cars, moldering here because their masters had all died or run away.

I slipped into the entry hallway. A plastic cage where a security guard had once sat was to the right, spiderwebs crossing inside as if Shelob and her closest friends had taken up residence within. I shuddered and Webster caught me.

"Don't fancy spiders?" he asked.

"No, I don't," I said. "They creep me out."

"You can get your innards shredded, get thrown into a dumpster and crawl out under your own power, but an arachnid puts the fear in you?" He shook his head. "You're a mite peculiar, Sienna Nealon."

"Thanks," I said with sarcasm.

"It's not an insult," he said.

"Well, it wasn't exactly a compliment." I thumbed the elevator switch at the end of the hall and was surprised by the sound of electricity thrumming through the installation. I *shouldn't* have been surprised; the servers may have been offline, but it was a fair guess that Omega would have had backups for everything, including the power.

The elevator dinged and opened, spilling light out into the hall and nearly blinding me for a second. I flinched against it and forced my eyes open to find the elevator car empty. I sighed. That had been dumb, closing my eyes, but the overwhelming light had been... well, overwhelming.

"Where do we go?" Webster asked as we got in the elevator.

"Top floor," I said, pushing the button tentatively with my index finger. The doors closed slowly, and I prepared myself. "Right to the place with the answers."

"All right, then," Webster said and adjusted his feet like he was ready for an attack. I glanced at him. He did look a bit ridiculous, but it was best to be prepared for anything in this situation.

The elevator door dinged to indicate our arrival at the top floor, and I prepared myself. The doors started to slide open—

And something hissed, a cloud spraying in before the doors even had a chance to finish opening.

It was a thick fog, blinding my senses, shrouding the light from above. I could see no more than shadows moving around within it, as it increased in volume, and I felt myself start to cough as an accidental breath entered my lungs and I began to choke.

Chapter 47

I fought through the fog, trying to expel the poison out of my lungs even as I stormed forward. I saw a shadow in the cloud and beelined toward it, hitting it straight in the middle as I charged—

And flew right out the other side without making contact with anything.

I slammed into a desk on the far side, though it took me a second to recognize what it was. It was set upright, on its side, like a barricade forming a perfect channel, a defensible position in what had been a giant, open-air room when last I'd been here. Clearly someone had done some rearranging since I'd left. And not for the better. At least not for me.

I hit the desk and caromed off, my shoulder aching where it had hit after missing the shadow in the cloud. I blinked my eyes and fought to keep them open in spite of what I'd just been sprayed with. It didn't feel chemical, there was no burning, just a feeling that something was in my eyes and lungs that wasn't meant to be there. I coughed and sucked in a breath of oxygen, felt the stars begin to disappear from my vision.

That's when I got hit, something smashing into me from the blind side like a kick to the head.

I hit the ground and rolled, coming back to my feet even though my head was swimming. I shook it to try and clear it (that never worked) and didn't even have time to recover before something hit me full on, tackling me around the midsection.

I hit the ground with a hard thump, my head smacking against the wood floor. It sent an echo through my ears, a skull-splitting noise that wasn't quite bone cracking but resonated like it. I was so stunned I barely had the instinct to fight back.

But I did fight back. Of course.

I caught my assailant with a punch to the side that did break bones. I heard them. I pressed my advantage (okay, it wasn't so much of an advantage as it was a lucky shot) with another hammering blow to the same spot, and this time I got a cry of pain for my troubles. Whoever I was up against was a tough son of a bitch to take a hit like that and not even yell about it the first time.

I decided to test their strength by raising my knee to their groin, but he twisted out of it with a grunt as I landed my attack on his inner thigh. I could tell by the noise he made that it was a dude, and while he was distracted trying to keep me from turning his balls into a pudding, I slammed my fist into his ribs a third time and sent the bastard flying through the air with the force of the blow.

"Okay," I said, wobbling to my feet, still blinking the cloud of out of my eyes, "now you've got me pissed off, Mystery Man. There are only so many sucker punches I will accept before I start hitting back without gloves, and you've just earned your way onto my shit list—"

"Sienna?" came a familiar voice. The cloud and the dark together had left me near-blind. I blinked, three times in rapid succession and my vision started to clear a bit.

"Yes, congratulations," I said, narrowing my focus onto the shadowy figure leering at me from out of the dark, "you've successfully identified the person who's about to lay the most heinous damned beating of your life upon you—"

"Sienna, it's me," came the thickly accented voice. I blinked again and I could barely see his figure as he stepped out of the shadows, hands up. He wore a dark beard over his dark skin, and he looked worlds rougher than the clean-shaven man I'd known who dressed habitually either in tactical vests or suits, depending on what he was doing that day. Now he looked like he'd last shaved a hundred years ago.

"Karthik?" I asked, squinting into the dark. "Karthik, is that you?"

"It's me," he said, dropping his hands to his side. "It's me. And I have to say… thank the deity it's you." He let out a sigh that left me in no doubt of his sincerity.

"What the hell is going on here?" Webster said, stepping out of the cloud around the elevator. There were tears down his cheeks, and he looked a little askew, like someone had sidelined him.

"That's a really good question," I said and looked at Karthik, who was deflating before my eyes, looking for all the world like a man who was weary from running for entirely too long, "and I have a feeling we're about to get an answer to it."

Chapter 48

Philip saw her come out of the flat. She was nervous, like a cat that had been beaten around by a larger predator for entirely too long. He saw her emerge at a distance, moving tentatively, as if she knew it was possible she was being watched at all times.

It was a quiet street in a quiet neighborhood of London. Not a bad place to hide, Philip would have conceded, even for an ex-Omega rat. But this was her, foolishly stepping outside her hole. Outside her safe place.

And she didn't even know what the predator that was after her looked like.

They followed her at a distance, walking side by side like a couple. Liliana was wearing jeans and trainers, for once, convinced of the import of this mission. Antonio was waiting in the van. Circling the block slowly, in the opposite direction each time.

Angela Tewkesbury was shorter than Philip had pictured her. It was an imprecise thing, what he saw when he'd touched the necklace chain that had once been hers. His ability gave him a misperceived image of the height of things, sometimes. Hazard of the power, he supposed, but it wouldn't have been very interesting if he'd just known it all.

On second thought, who cared about interesting when you have the all-knowing power of God at your fingertips?

He feigned a laugh at something Liliana didn't even say; she was practiced enough in this fieldcraft to go along with it. He didn't even have to say anything.

The street traffic was sparse; one car every two minutes, by his reckoning. Pedestrians darting here and there, heading for the corner shop, heading back their homes, a few scattered children on bicycles on their way to the park just down the road.

Angela Tewkesbury was alone in the middle of all of them. She looked alone, apart. Scared. Philip felt the thrill of following after her. Being the breath on the back of her neck that she felt but could not see the source of. It was his teeth that descended on her even now—metaphorically speaking, of course. His teeth were Liliana's blades.

The teeth of the tiger.

They closed the distance slowly, letting her aimless shuffle gradually get overtaken by their steady forward progress. The girl was trying to take her time. She probably only allowed herself to go out once per day, and this was her time to see life, something she probably wasn't getting much of a view of, being stuck inside all the time.

There was weakness in people. Everyone had their blind spots, their points of vulnerability. He knew this Angela, had looked into her future and seen the bare basics. She was in for pain, which meant that their efforts would surely succeed. Now all he had to do... was make it happen.

Their pace was such that they would surely catch her in just a few seconds. Philip laughed again, just slightly, and Liliana echoed it, pitch perfect save for its empty quality. He doubted she could laugh, at least not truly, all the way to the depths of the heart, reaching up from a soul she didn't have. This small detail didn't matter, though. Not here. If timing was everything, he was the master of it. He'd seen this, studied it, planned it out.

Now it was just a matter of execution.

He gave a nod to Liliana as his eyes swept the street. It was clear, everyone looking in different directions. He could hear the van easing up behind them. He looked back and saw Antonio in the driver's seat slowing the vehicle.

Liliana took two long steps forward and punched Angela Tewkesbury in the back of her head with vicious force. Philip admired the strength of it. He stood motionless and watched the girl crumple. Liliana caught her, of course. Caught her the way a spider catches an insect, delicate and predatory all at once. A morsel saved for later.

Philip kept his lookout as he made his way through the cars parked on either side of the street to the back of the van. He opened one door as Liliana dragged the girl past. They watched carefully for any sign of trouble. Philip knew there wasn't any; all the probabilities were against it. Still he watched. It was habit more than anything.

As soon as the girl was loaded, he hopped in himself and slammed the back door of the van. There was not a sound, not a scream, not a hint that anything untoward had just happened on this quiet London street.

Philip looked at the girl on the floor of the van as Antonio accelerated—not ridiculously, just enough to get them going and avoid the suspicion of the police. He felt the sway of his weight as the van went round a corner.

The screaming would start soon. Back at the warehouse, as soon as she woke up. Or maybe she'd wake up before the warehouse. Soon, though. The path of vengeance he'd begun was like a train rolling out of the station. It was certainly picking up speed now, and soon it would be roaring so quickly and loudly that anyone in the path would be forced to move out of its way—

Or perhaps not even have the chance. He thought of Sienna Nealon again, another dark contemplation, and let his gaze drift back to the girl on the floor of the van.

Helpless.

They were all so very helpless.

Chapter 49

"It's good to see you, Sienna," Karthik said, wiping sweat off his dark brow. He spoke with a British accent that was inflected by his native Indian, a resonant voice that I'd always thought was attractive and soothing.

I wasn't feeling very soothed at the moment, though. "What the hell did you spray in my face?"

"Ah." He looked a little embarrassed. "Fire extinguisher. It's non-toxic, I just wanted to provide maximum distraction for whoever was coming up. I didn't expect it would be you."

"Who did you think it would be?" I asked coyly.

"I'm not sure," he said, annoying me with his lack of specificity. "Why are you here?"

"Why are *you* here?" I asked, tossing that one right back at him.

He sighed. "This is not going to go anywhere fast, I see."

"Last time I saw you," I said, brushing the white powder residue from the extinguisher off my sleeves, "you bugged out back to England when things got a little too heavy in the war. And here I find you, two years later, still hiding?"

"I've only been here for a few weeks," he said, sweeping a hand to indicate the massive, open-air room of Omega's headquarters. "But yes, I've been hiding."

"Why?" I asked.

"Because someone is kidnapping former Omega members," Karthik said. "And I don't wish to be among them."

"Well, I knew that much," I said. "This is Detective Inspector Matthew Webster." I threw a gesture at Webbo. "He summoned me over here to look into this mess you're up to your neck in."

"Detective Inspector," Karthik said with a courteous nod. "Young for the title, if I'm not mistaken."

"I have a good case record," Webster said, still coughing.

"I'm sure you're a veritable Nicholas Angel," Karthik said.

"So you're Karthik?" Webster asked. "I guess we can scratch off one of those disappearances as self-inflicted."

"Kind of an obvious place to hide, don't you think?" I asked, looking around the room. A series of offices ringed the place, glass windows obstructed by blinds. When this was Omega HQ, the peons worked in the big room and the muckety-mucks in the offices, closing the blinds when they didn't want to be seen.

Actually, that was kind of how my agency worked, too, so I probably shouldn't be quite so down on them.

"It has kept me quite sheltered thus far," Karthik said. "Most of the time I stay in the underground chambers and keep the doors closed."

"But today you're out to greet us," I said. "Why?"

"I needed to go outside," he said. "I need to try and find some of our people. Let them know they're in danger—"

"Some of them already know it," Webster said, dabbing at his face with a handkerchief. "And some of them are past caring."

"They're turning up dead," I said, drawing Karthik's gaze to me.

"Who?" he asked, and I could see the element of anticipation as he waited for the axe to fall.

"Maxwell Llewelyn," I said. "Angus Waterman, too, I think."

"Damnation," Karthik said. "I've been trying to get in touch with all the old crowd, but some are harder to reach than others. They were two of the ones I'd not been able to get ahold of."

"Should have tried a letter to their last known addresses," Webster muttered, face behind the hanky.

"Who have you gotten in touch with?" I asked. "And how?"

"We have an old communication protocol," Karthik said, looking a little dazed. "An email system in a hidden part of the internet. Janus and I reactivated it shortly after your brother got into that spot of bother in Italy." He looked up at me. "We decided to plumb the depths of Omega's remains, see what was still out there."

"What did you find?" I asked.

"More than we expected, that's for certain," Karthik said. "There are a lot of survivors out there. Many of them saw the direction of the coming wind and sought shelter. Now that Omega is dead, they've stepped out on their own."

"I've heard that story somewhere before," I said dryly.

"Well, you can't blame them," Karthik said with a shrug. "They were running rackets for Omega. It shouldn't be an utter surprise that they've stepped into their own rackets after emerging from hiding."

"No, it shouldn't come as any surprise," I said. "Criminals always return to the scene of the crime, right?"

"When the scene of the crime has as much lucre as old Omega was bringing in?" Karthik said with a shrug. "I can't entirely blame them."

I narrowed my eyes at him. "You and Janus were going to restart Omega, weren't you?"

He looked a little caught off guard. "We had *discussed* the possibility. It wasn't anything concrete. I think he felt a bit... useless. Aimless, perhaps."

"This guy," I said, measuring my words to keep from snapping off some hostile ones at Karthik, "your enemy, the one who's targeting old Omega faces. He's a got a real anger management problem stemming from you lot. Any idea why?"

Karthik shrugged, looking sincerely mystified. "Omega was certainly not without enemies, as well you know."

"As well I know," I said. "Who else is missing?"

"Janus," Karthik said. "Janus and Rory Kilmeade. Those are the two I knew about before I went into hiding."

"Rory Kilmeade is the one that reported you missing." Webster was finally done mopping his face. He still looked like he'd been wearing Joker makeup, though. "Who's left that you've talked to?"

"Angela Tewkesbury, Ryan Mortenson—" Karthik paused. "Are we just talking about London?"

"For now," I said.

"Those are the only others," Karthik said. "Everyone else left the city after the war. Too many bad memories, I suppose."

I clicked my tongue against my teeth. "But you don't know anything about the guy doing this? Or his bomb maker accomplice?" Karthik shook his head. "Lady with the knives?" Another shake. "Well, what the hell good are you?"

"I have access to some of Omega's databases," Karthik said. "Janus has opened things up for me. Other than that, I'm well aware of my lack of utility. It's why I'm hiding rather than waiting to get snatched. If they can capture Janus, they can certainly take me. I'm even more sure of it now that you're telling me there are three of them working in concert."

"Show us your databases," I said, waving a hand at him. The relief was evident on his face, and I turned away rather than look at it. I didn't hate Karthik, but he'd left me in the middle of the war to come back here and hide with a group of metas who couldn't do much in the way of fighting. "I need you to open up what you've got to J.J. back at the Agency."

I saw him straighten at that, almost bristling. I could see the conflict in his motions, like he'd frozen for just a moment at the mere suggestion of cooperating with us. Which I thought was interesting, considering that a couple years ago, Karthik had contorted himself into a pretzel shape trying to help me out in the early days of the war.

Now, a couple years later, he was considering resisting. I doubted he actually would, but it was interesting to watch him struggle with it. It suggested that he'd changed since last we'd met, and not for the better.

Or maybe it suggested that he'd thought I'd changed. In either case, I didn't like it because it had the overtures of a very "us versus them" mentality. I don't like it when people oppose me. It makes me want to crush the life out of them.

"The servers are still downstairs," Karthik said, leading us into the wood-paneled office that had once been the seat of Omega's Primus, their grand poobah. The room looked incredibly dusty, like the quality maid service had lit out of the place decades ago. I guess Karthik and Janus hadn't tidied up since their return, which made me wonder exactly what they *had* been up to.

The wall to our left was fitted with long bookshelves, covered in a layer of dust that would have made Pompeii look clean by comparison. One of them was noticeably cleaner than the others, and I brushed past Karthik to grab the spine of a copy of Charles Dickens's *Hard Times* and pull it.

The bookcase slid back like something out of a Bond movie, and Webster made a subtle noise of surprise. "What the eff?"

"They were proper villains, Omega," I said, looking into the darkness beyond as fluorescent lights struggled on. "It wouldn't surprise me if Ian Fleming knew them, because they really did it right, embracing all the tropes like a Bond girl getting on Connery after he'd just saved her life."

"You sound as if you might have had a fantasy or two about a proper British gentleman who handles himself well in life-threatening situations," Webster said to me with a grin that was hardly impaired at all by the white powder still plastering his face.

I batted my eyelashes at him playfully. "Maybe once or twice." So sue me, I'm bad at flirting.

"Down here," Karthik said, interrupting our back and forth.

"I remember the way," I shot back. I followed him into a concrete staircase that descended into the depths of Omega HQ. I hadn't been kidding when I said they were proper villains. They had a secret underground lair and everything. Well, sort of.

It was really more like a concrete bunker in the sub-basement, but it certainly looked a little sinister. It had a corner filled with treasure that looked a lot less shiny and large since I'd last seen it. There was a kitchenette area and what looked—bizarrely—a little like a science lab. Something had been welded to the floor there, once, but it was gone now and had left a gaping space where the coloration of the concrete clearly denoted the absence of something. A series of beat-up, seventies-vintage filing cabinets had once rested along one wall, but they were gone now, replaced by servers giving off a prodigious amount of heat. I walked by one and felt like I was going to start sweating, even in the cool subterranean basement.

"I see you've brought Omega into the twenty-first century," I said, running a hand over the warm casing of one of the servers. "Does this mean you're Primus now?"

"Janus and I haven't discussed the formalities," he said with a hint of bitterness. "Seemed a bit like putting the cart before the horse, since it was only the two of us with no operations of our own to supervise."

"I don't get it." I gestured at the treasure trove in the corner, and Webster turned around. It was cute. His jaw dropped and everything. "Why not just sell that stuff and retire? That's got to be millions in gold right there."

"It's not about the money," Karthik said with a frown. "It's about the exercise of vital powers."

I just stared at him. "The what?"

"Classic Greek definition of a good life," Webster said, peeling his eyes off the gold in the corner. "'The exercise of vital powers along lines of excellence in a life affording them scope.' I think your own President Kennedy might have quoted that once."

"Did you steal that from Janus?" I asked Karthik as he made his way toward a computer set up on a folding table.

"I didn't steal it," he said. "We've had many discussions about philosophy, about our place—metahumans' place—in the world now that the secret is out. He mentioned it at one point, and I thought it was a fantastic answer. Selling off your baubles," he made a dismissive gesture of his own toward the treasure trove in the corner, "would certainly afford me a retirement. But it would not result in the exercise of vital powers, there'd be no lines of excellence, and I think the scope would be somewhat limited."

"I could sell a few of them," I mumbled as he started tapping keys, "maybe afford to take a beach vacation that I'd never come back from."

"Help yourself," Karthik said. "I don't want them and neither does Janus."

"Let me get a shovel," Webster said, grinning at me. "We'll split it and both be rich."

"Find your own stash of bullion and goods, copper," I said. "According to our villain, I'm the last Primus of Omega, so technically that is mine, all mine."

"Because recognizing the fiat handed down by a murderous madman is good practice," Webster said with a cocked eyebrow.

"When in Rome…" I said with a sly grin.

It took him a second to get it. "Hey! That's my country you're talking about."

"Mostly kidding," I said, leaning over Karthik's shoulder. "Just a little friendly, across-the-pond trash talk."

"I'm in the database," Karthik said, looking up at me. "I need search parameters."

"Can you search for a woman who kills with dual knives?" I asked.

Karthik blinked a couple times. "I can certainly try." He tapped some things on the keyboard and a minute later something popped up. "I only have one active in the file. Liliana Negrescu. Romanian born, KGB trained. Emigrated to England under an alias following the fall of the Iron Curtain. Looks like the British government granted her citizenship in '95. She's worked a lot of off-the-books jobs, freelance. Omega tried recruiting her once…" His eyes skimmed across the monitor. "She spat in their faces, called them the worst sort of capitalist pigs."

"She sounds bloody charming," Webster said.

"And then she proceeded to eviscerate the recruiters and spread their body parts around the city," Karthik said, "along with a note expressing the aforementioned sentiments."

"Ding, ding, ding," I said. "We have a winner. Omega let her get away with that?"

"Looks like she skipped town afterward," Karthik said. "Our trackers couldn't get a location. Tried and failed."

"But they can find a shut-in in Minnesota without any trouble," I muttered.

"Actually, I read your file," Karthik said, looking up, "when I was bored, a few months ago. Omega was completely unaware of your existence until—"

"Story for another time," I said. "This chick got any known associates?"

Karthik went back to the computer, his dark skin illuminated white by the monitor. "Nothing here. Solo operator since she left the KGB."

I made a sucking noise, pulling in air between my front teeth. "How about bomb makers? I'm guessing Omega has tons of them on file."

"Without doubt," Karthik said. "Can you give me any more?"

"Olive complexion," I said, thinking about it. My brain searched around for something, anything. I remembered the guy clutching the tube close to him, and remembered the way his hands gripped—

His hands.

"Burn scars on his hands," I said, leaning over again.

"Probably fairly common for a bomb maker, but let's see if it narrows down—" Karthik rolled his head back like he was surprised. "Here's one. Antonio Ruelle. Looks like he's a bit of a mystery until he showed up in…" Karthik leaned forward and squinted. "… in…" He sighed, and sat back. "I don't know how to say that."

I leaned forward and read the monitor to where he'd left off. The name of the town was Cwmbran. I stared and read it again to see if I had it right. "That's a town? What the hell does that say?"

"That the Welsh have hilarious notions about the utility and placement of vowels," Webster said with more than a little mirth.

"Anyway, he shows up in our records at… Cwumbran," Karthik said, probably maiming the name of the town but doing at least as well as I would have, "and nothing before. He learned his craft from a former member of the IRA who decided to leave the isle before his luck ran out. Took on Ruelle as a pupil and passed on his trade. Ruelle has been active in bombing for hire, according to our info, taking on contracting work from dozens of terrorist cells." He pursed his lips. "But never here in the UK. Apparently he prefers to keep his backyard clean of his own mess."

"Well, he broke that rule today in rather spectacular fashion," Webster said.

"Oh?" Karthik asked. "What did he do?"

"Blew up three buildings around the Hartsford Gallery and killed nearly a hundred cops," Webster said.

Karthik's eyes widened. "What's that American expression? 'Go big or go home'?"

"Known associates?" I asked, bringing us back on point before I was forced to come up with something to rebut that quote. Given my track record of late, it would probably backfire in yet another hilarious double entendre.

Karthik scrolled, then held up his hands. "I have nothing for you there. His mentor has been dead for a decade. I can give you a list of groups that have hired him—" He froze. "Well, that's interesting."

I felt a tickle down the back of my neck. "Let me guess: Omega has tried to hire him in the past."

"He made the bombs that we destroyed your Directorate with," Karthik said in surprise. "Went to America and built them himself, showed our people where to place them based on maps of the targets—"

I felt a twitch in my eyelid. That was just another reason for me to lay a beatdown on Antonio. For a group of people I hadn't even formally met until a few hours ago, this bunch of assholes had a lot of personal ties to me in some way or another. "Last known address?" I asked.

"Still in Cwumbran," Karthik said.

"Oh, for—" Webster said, exasperated. "It's pronounced Cumbran."

"What the hell?" I felt my whole face scrunch at him. "What law of English allows for a silent W?"

"Who cares?" Webster asked, throwing his hands up. "So, if this bloke is from Cwmbran, I can have the constabulary up there knock down his door."

"Send the local police to kick in the door of a bomb maker who created a booby trap that blew my foot off," I said, not bothering to hide my disbelief. "You might want to reconsider that one, Ace."

"Bomb squad, then," Webster said, looking a bit sheepish.

"Good call." I turned back to Karthik. "I need the contact info you have for those other two people you mentioned that were still here in London." I racked my brain. "Um... I already forgot their names."

Karthik looked a little steely-eyed at me. "You didn't remember them when they were under your protection in America either, so why would you recall them now?" He let that little dagger of guilt twist in for a moment. "Angela Tewkesbury and Ryan Mortenson. I'll find you their last known addresses, but I believe Ryan has left the city by now, and Angela has bolted if she knows what is good for her."

I gave him a slow nod. "Best we check up on them anyway," I said. "Because sometimes people just don't know when to leave." I caught him looking away, unable to meet my eyes as he went about the business of looking up the files I'd asked for.

Chapter 50

I waited for Webster to get off the phone before speaking to him on our drive back to Scotland Yard. He'd made a call, got some cops dispatched to take a look at Mortenson and Tewkesbury's last known addresses. He'd taken one look at them and informed me that they were across the city, which was apparently not easily reachable for us at this time of day, late in the afternoon.

Staring at the cars ahead of us as we eased onto a roundabout, I bowed to his wisdom on the matter of London traffic.

"How long do you think it'll take the police to get to them?" I asked. The car smelled a little like fish and chips because one of us—okay, it was me—had wrapped up a bit of fish in a paper napkin and brought it along two stops ago. What? I was hungry.

"Couple of hours, I'd imagine," he said, nodding as he took us out of the roundabout on the other side. I had to admit, I preferred intersections with stop signs or stop lights to traffic circles, but part of that was because I'd traveled through a Wisconsin town last year that had gone nuts with the damned things, slowing down what otherwise might have been a pretty fast trip into a slow, painful crawl. The town only had a thousand people, tops. Just spring for the traffic lights, you damned cheapskates.

"Hopefully we'll catch up to them alive," I said, just putting that thought out there. Webster seemed a little distant, like he was running through a few thoughts of his own after sending out his orders.

"Hopefully," he said by way of agreement. I could tell he was working up to something, and then he said, "Can I ask you about the war?"

Not exactly the question I'd been thinking he'd ask. "Okay," I said.

"How many people did you kill?"

I was taken completely aback. I shouldn't have been; I got asked this question all the time, usually by starry-eyed girls and hormone-propelled guys. From the guys it was the ultimate macho question; from the girls it was usually a quiet indictment. It didn't always work that way, of course. I'd had a guy ask me once in a bar in Minneapolis and then spit on me when I'd given him the honest answer. Letting him walk away with both of his lungs still in his chest may have been the hardest thing I've ever done, and I'm including the day that I turned into a flaming dragon and shredded a man with my jaws.

Needless to say, I wasn't thrilled to find out what Webster's reaction was going to be, because he didn't seem like the macho, hormone-driven type that would punch me on the shoulder and call me "Bro" as a compliment once he heard.

Still, I answered honestly. "I don't know."

He blinked at the wheel in near disbelief. "You don't know? You're not sure how many people you killed?"

"I didn't exactly keep a pad with hash marks, you know? I didn't have a cockpit where I could paint the tally as I went." I squeezed my arms tightly across my chest. "It was war. Toward the end, especially, they weren't human beings to me. They were numbers. I had a hundred of them to wipe out and I damned well did it."

"So…" he didn't sound like he wanted to let it go, "… a hundred?"

I felt my eyes burn in the most curious way. "More than that."

"Two hundred?"

I felt a scratch in my throat and attempted to clear it to no avail. "Probably somewhere between a hundred and two hundred."

"Were they all part of that band that was exterminating your people?"

I felt a shiver unrelated to the air conditioner. "Mostly. Them or the mercenaries they hired to do some of their dirty work." Or the enemies I made even before Century and their extermination scheme fell into my crosshairs.

"Ever kill any civilians?" he asked.

"No," I snapped.

"Just curious," he said, shrugging. "It's war, I know sometimes accidents happen."

"Not to me," I said. "I didn't have any accidents. I was very focused when I was… doing what I was doing." For a person who said the first part with such certainty, I sure did let the second part of that sentence trail off.

"I would say it's probably best you're out of it now," he said, tentatively, "but I suppose these last few days it probably seems like you're right back in the thick of it again."

I grunted. What could I say to that? This time the body count was all at the feet of the other side. Well, so far it had been.

"Why did you stay on?" Webster asked. He must have caught my cockeyed look at him. "After the war, I mean. The way you said it, you'd seen that pile of gold in the Omega base, and you had access to it. It was all yours."

"Honestly," I said, looking out the window, "I totally forgot about it until just now."

"You forgot about a pile of gold that could make you as rich as Harry Potter, at least?" Webster chuckled. "I notice you didn't bring any of it with you."

I held up my hands. "I don't have a purse to carry it in."

He gave that half-shrug again. "Still, it seems like to me a lady just looking to do a job might have jumped all over that pile of gold like—"

I felt the dam that was my patience break open, and I leaned over to him. "Just get to the point and say what you mean to say already."

"I was just wondering," he said, choosing his words carefully, "why someone would choose to keep doing a job that—by your own admission—gives you no time off, has you running 'round the world like your arse is on fire and you're in a perpetual race to put it out. I was wondering why someone would do all that when they had riches beyond most measures right at their fingertips."

I stared straight ahead. "Why do you think?"

"Because you want to be a force for good, I reckon."

I felt a light cackle build until it burst forth from my lips. "You say 'be a force for good' like it's something easy to choose. Like it doesn't require sacrifices that eat the whole heart out of you."

He turned his head, almost apologetic. "There are other jobs—"

"You think this is a job?" I snapped. "Clock in at nine, punch out at five? It's not. It's my life. Twenty-four hours a day, seven a week, three-sixty-five." I felt my speech deteriorate as the sentence tailed off, like I was so beyond caring that it didn't even matter to me that I was missing words.

"Then why don't you quit?" he asked simply.

I stayed speechless for about a minute, and my mind snapped back to the multitude of people who had died in the days after I left my house for the first time. "Because once upon a time I sat back and let a lot of people die while I felt completely powerless to stop them. And now I've got power enough to stop anyone who threatens to do the same."

"So it's like a debt, then?" His eyes were dark, his manner quiet.

"One I can never pay back." I swallowed hard. "Never."

His cell phone beeped and he held it up, a text message lighting the faceplate. He frowned, a look of distaste marring his handsome face. "What?" I asked.

"Commissioner Marshwin wishes to see us back at the station immediately," he said, looking up at me. "It would appear that Parliament has come to some decisions… and none of them sound very good."

Chapter 51

Angela Tewkesbury screamed and screamed, and Philip enjoyed every note of it. He couldn't decide if it was his imagination or if Liliana was going even rougher on her because she was a girl. Either way, this delicious pain felt likely to go on for some time, and that rather pleased Philip.

The only problem was one that there was simply no escaping. He covered his hand with a sleeve as he yawned, the day's labors having wearied him terribly.

Liliana noticed, halting her routine of slow cutting, as Tewkesbury made a strangled, crying noise beneath her. "Is this boring you, boss?"

"Not at all," Philip said, stifling another yawn into his hand. "I'm afraid I've just reached the end of my stamina for the day. A good night's sleep, perhaps a bit of a lie-in, and I'll be quite fresh and ready to continue tomorrow."

She looked straight at him, and he could see her assessing, judging, trying to weigh what he had said. "It has been a long day," she finally said. It sounded like a very reluctant concession.

"Exactly," Philip said with another yawn. "Let's adjourn for the night. Give her time to stew in her juices. Give her a chance to look into her future," he nodded toward Janus, who was stripped and hanging upside down, still dripping blood from Liliana's previous efforts. "Approaching this again in the morning should offer a fresh perspective, perhaps some new pain." He kept down another yawn, but only barely. "Or at least a newfound appreciation given that my eyes will actually be open."

"Perhaps." Liliana slung her knives downward as she stood from the squat she'd been in. Blood flicked from the blades of her knives and spattered into the puddle on the floor. Philip watched it in a daze, watched the droplets rejoin the sea below, and wondered exactly how much more he'd see spilled before he got everything he wanted.

Chapter 52

Commissioner Marshwin was in her office, in a snit, and—for all I knew—experiencing the worst day of her professional career. The air felt stale as she filled it with heavy words. I tried to pay attention, but it was hard. Mainly because she was talking at a comically elevated level and her accent seemed to go Deep Scottish, something I did not have any experience with.

"And what do you have to say about that?" she asked, presumably noticing the glazed-over look in my eyes at last. She slowed down for this, making herself understood in the process.

"Sorry for your losses," I said, shrugging. I actually did mean it. It was never easy to be the boss when you lost people in the line of duty. I knew from experience.

"That it?" This with an air of disbelief. It was just her and me in the office, though I wished Webster were here to experience this joyous occasion as well. I didn't usually take a lot of crap, but today it was coming from all sides, and I didn't feel quite as predisposed to putting her face in the carpeting as I had the ambassador.

"I'm not sure what else you want me to say."

"How about an explanation for all this?" She was looking at me with straight-on irritation.

"Some guy is pissed off about something," I said. "He decided to steal a painting and punch your department in the

208

face in the process. He's also murdering people by having a knife-wielding psycho beast carve them up like Easter ham."

"I know this much already from DI Webster's reports," she said, more than a little agitated. "You're telling me you can't give me any sort of explanation as to who this is causing my problems or why it's happening?"

"It's all a mystery to me," I said. "But hey, I got you a couple names for this guy's accomplices. Which is more than you'd have without me."

"This is precisely the sort of madness that has Parliament pondering a law even now to remove your kind from the United Kingdom," Marshwin said with something between disgust and self-satisfaction.

"Good luck with that," I said, slapping my hand on my knee and rising to leave.

"Where do you think you're going?"

"To go find this guy, truss him up, and hang him on that coat rack in your corner," I said, gesturing at the wooden monstrosity that took up three square feet of floor space. "I know the UK doesn't have the death penalty anymore, but I figure if I leave him there long enough, you'll drown him in sanctimony and speechifying."

"Och, you're a smug thing, aren't you." Not even a whiff of suggestion, just a flat statement. "Do you have any idea how many officers I lost today?"

"Less than you would have lost if I hadn't been here," I said, no sugar added. "Do you have any idea how many pints of blood and pounds of flesh I've parted with since *I've* been here?"

"Well, then walk away, why don't you?" she sneered. It fit the moment.

"I don't cut and run," I said, "and I damned sure don't *get* cut and then run."

"I don't want you anywhere near this case," she said.

"Well, that's brilliant," I said. "Got anyone else who stands a chance against these maniacs? Or is your strategy to just keep overwhelming this guy with dead cops until he cracks under the strain of stepping over their bodies?"

Her relative calm shattered and her mask deteriorated into shock as her jaw fell. She said nothing for ten seconds, then twenty. After a minute I stopped counting, and she just continued to stare at me in mute shock.

"Well, shit," I said, "looks like I broke her."

"I'm not broken," she said, voice back at normal volume, though slightly brittle. "Though it occurs to me to make mention of the fact that you've yet to make much of a dent in these conspirators yourself when you've gone up against them. Why do you think that would change if you were to face them again? Perhaps this time they'd actually finish the job proper and leave you dead—and me explaining to your ambassador how I got you killed."

"Try and pretend he wouldn't be overjoyed at the news," I said and thumped my knuckles down on her desk. "If they can do that to me, imagine what they'll do to all those poor, unarmed police officers you've got out on the streets."

"We have armed response teams standing by," she said, a little iron in her spine causing her to straighten, "they're ready and eager to get their own back."

"I hope they kill this guy, I truly do," I said. "But trust me when I tell you that I'm a better than fair shot with a pistol and he sidestepped my bullets like I'd lobbed a slow, underhand softball at him. Whoever he is, your villain is not playing by amateur rules. He's a pro. He's big league, not bush league. He's shown you that he's serious and willing, and I would submit to you that the only thing scarier than a man like that is the fact that he's got two accomplices that seem to cover his every weakness." He had to have weaknesses. Everyone did.

She walked to the window behind her. It looked like she was dragging her way over, she moved so slowly. "Wexford came in before you got back to explain the political situation to me." She glanced over her shoulder. "They're going to vote metahumans right out of the country in line with the rest of the European Union. After what happened today, we have no enforcement, and the politicians have no tolerance. They're going to start expelling every one of you within the next few days." Her expression softened.

"Well, I hope your bad guy follows that law," I said dryly, "but his past history leads me to believe that much like every other bad guy, he's going to continue to hang around until he either gets what he wants or you catch him."

"Or kill him?" Marshwin asked.

"Or kill him," I said, but I did not meet her eyes.

She started to say something else, but the door burst open to reveal Webster standing there, hanging on the knob. I could see Marshwin ready to unload on him but she held back long enough for him to silence her burgeoning critique. "Someone just called 999 claiming they'd escaped a captor that was torturing them."

I straightened, my knuckles coming off the desk so fast they left indentations in the wood. "Janus?"

Webster shook his head slowly. "It's a she. Said her name is Angela Tewkesbury."

Chapter 53

We rolled up next to a warehouse in South London, the red brick crumbling and fading. There were other cop cars filling the street, their lights off and their sirens silent. I counted three SWAT vans, and I knew they weren't empty just by looking at how low they rested on the shocks. There was another warehouse behind us, deep blue corrugated sides showing in the light of a dim street lamp. It was the only one working in view.

I took one look at Angela Tewkesbury and knew she was the real deal. I suck with names but I'm pretty decent with faces, and I knew her right off. Brunette, scared, one of the secretarial pool at old Omega in the days when they'd been the only game in town for protecting metas. She'd been a secretary at the Agency back home for a few months, too, and done some decent work if I recalled correctly.

Now she was missing chunks of flesh. She had a hand raised, pointing down a nearby street, and her fingers were shaking as she made the gesture.

I've been told it doesn't take much to piss me off, but something about seeing Angela Tewkesbury partially skinned alive, sitting in front of me… well… it just put me right into the red zone.

I didn't remember opening the door and getting out, but I was standing in front of her before I knew it, and she let out a low gasp. "Ms. Nealon!"

"Angela," I said. I looked down at her arm and saw one-inch squares of skin missing up and down both arms. She should have been in shock. "You're going to be all right."

"They've got Janus," she said, nearly breathless. "They're... they're torturing him." Her lips became a thin line and her eyes scrunched up. "It's terrible."

"We're going to get him back," I promised. We were. I was going to do what was colloquially referred to as "laying an ass whooping" on this scheming, torturing clown. "How far?"

"Three blocks, big warehouse windows up high," she said, her lip quivering. "I just ran when I got out." Her hand landed on my sleeve, tugging it like a weight. "He helped me get out—Janus did. My powers are... they're weak. He boosted my emotion, helped me use my luck to sway my odds to unlock the chains they had me in..."

"Janus did that?" I stared down at her.

"He told me to just go when I tried to unlock his." She wasn't crying, but I suspected it was only because she'd probably lost every tear in her body while she'd been screaming in pain. "I had nothing left, and he knew it. He told me to get out, and I did."

"Smart move," I said, gently tugging my hand free of hers. "You did the right thing, getting the police here." I felt the lines of my face harden. "Now it's time for me to do what I do best."

She blinked at me. "What's that?"

I stared down at her arm. "Make these bastards bleed a gallon for every drop they cost you."

Chapter 54

Philip was having such a pleasant dream. He knew it was a dream, of course, by that all-too-pleasant way that dreams have of commanding your attention through the most unusual things. It surely wouldn't hang together in any logical way once he was awake, but he was enjoying it while he was in it, submerged like it was a bath of warm feelings.

Then, rather unexpectedly, he was shaken awake.

"She's gone," Liliana announced as Philip tried and failed to fight off the bleary feelings that clouded his mind.

"Who—?" Philip asked, his head in a fog. He was dimly aware that Liliana was still shaking him, damn the woman, and if she didn't stop soon he'd feel compelled to slap her damned head right off her shoulders. The irritation rose.

"The girl," Liliana said in her hard, flat way. "Angela. She's gone."

Philip felt the stirs of the world's pieces falling back together around him. Some of what she said had started to make sense. "Gone where? She was bound in chains and hung from the ceiling."

"She's *gone*," Liliana said with a final shake that jolted Philip into full consciousness. "Not in the warehouse."

Philip sprang up from his cot with a rattle of the metal links that kept the light mattress in the frame. He walked past Liliana to the door and opened it, looking out. He reached out and got a sense of the place, felt for what lay out there, sure that it was the same, dull, boring future that had existed for this place the last time he'd felt for it, just as he was about to go to bed—

A feeling slammed into his gut like a spear and jabbed right into his middle. Cold and sharp, it bled him of his warmth. How—?

"As I said, she's gone," Liliana said. "Antonio is preparing to go after her—"

"The police are already on their way," Philip said. "So is Sienna Nealon." He could see the spectral figure of her drifting through the warehouse. The ghost of Christmas future. "She'll be here in moments."

"Fight or flight?" Liliana asked. She had a way of boiling it down.

"Flight," Philip said in an instant. He could see the police response even now, and it involved dozens of men with weapons, firing happily into the dark of the warehouse and filling the air with far too many bullets for even him to dodge. Assuming he could have seen his own future in there anywhere.

Liliana bristled. "We've hurt them once today already."

"And we shall again," Philip said and touched her shoulder just briefly. "But we're not going to do it by standing toe to toe with them in some crass, pugilistic contest. Our encounters must be neatly structured to our advantage." He met her eyes, those soulless pools, and repressed his shudder. "Antonio!" he called. "We're leaving. Now."

He heard the movement of the bomb maker in the darkness near the torture room. "I can be ready in less than five."

Philip mentally blessed a man who lived his life so much like a rolling stone. "Exit plan one." He looked from the darkness where the bomb maker stood to the darkness that filled Liliana's eyes. "No reason not to give them a few rounded slaps to the face while we're fleeing, is there?"

Chapter 55

The bomb squad was on the scene, trying to help by planning things out, but after about twenty minutes of listening to all the various jurisdictions whipping their junk out and peeing for distance and to mark territory, I got bored of it and went smashing through the upper windows of the warehouse.

Yes, it was probably dumb. I did not care.

At home, backed by the power and support of my own agency, I would have waited and planned out an assault that hit all the appropriate entrances while minimizing the risk to everyone involved.

The problem was that I was on foreign soil, the people I was working with didn't realize how powerless they were, and the bomb squad was intelligently tentative but insanely slow. I could read the writing on the wall for this one, and I predicted that Mr. Ski Mask and his crazy cohorts were going to have plenty of time to wake up to a nice, leisurely breakfast of bacon and beans—in North London, if they were so disposed, with enough time to wander back and take a luxuriant afternoon nap followed by a late dinner downtown before the boys in blue were comfortable with moving.

It wasn't like I could blame them; they'd lost their sniper teams to explosives they hadn't even seen. Being cautious was prudent.

As I went crashing through the spray-painted windows at the top of the warehouse, I had to concede that prudence was a suit I was extremely short in.

I didn't land on the concrete floor, figuring I'd be safer not wandering anywhere Antonio Ruelle might have placed a tripwire. Once the glass finished shattering and falling, I listened as I hovered in the air.

Not a sound. Not a drip, not the hum of a fluorescent light, not the tick of a ventilation system, nothing.

I almost thought I'd smashed into the wrong warehouse, but then I smelled the blood.

It hit me in a wave, heavy and thick, like the time I'd been with federal agents when they'd raided a slaughterhouse thinking a suspected meta was hiding out among the crew that worked the killing floor. It had turned out to be a guy who'd done a little too much cocaine and made a few errors of judgment while on the stuff. Like parking his car in a fashion that had led an overly jumpy police department to believe he'd thrown it through a local shop's front edifice rather than judiciously applying the handbrake and sliding through the plate glass window sideways. I didn't blame them for that, and I'd even told him how much I'd admired his non-sober driving skills. With a fist to the head. He didn't shake that off, the menace to society.

But I digress. The place smelled of blood, and I followed my nose to a square-shaped room with thick walls. I drifted down and pushed open the steel door that was barely cracked open, almost afraid of what I would find.

It was not pretty, not one little bit of it. There was beauty in the human body, wonder in the blood vessels that pumped oxygenated liquid from the lungs to the heart, down to the extremities and up once more for trip after trip. I had long admired the curves and lines, the muscles and tendons that made us work as we did.

But I admired them when they were all together, in working order.

What I found in that room looked like a jigsaw puzzle that had been taken asunder and would never fit back together, no matter how many medical examiners stood by with their books debating the placement of the pieces that remained.

I heard something, in the far distance, and strained my ears as I drifted out the door of the slaughtering room. There was no reason to remain, no other entrances or exits, and the only thing left to keep me there was a sickening sense of revulsion. I left. Left and closed the door behind me in the faint and foolish hope that I could leave what I'd seen behind the door.

I moved toward the sound. An office was raised above the floor, a series of metal stairs leading up to it. I drifted slowly toward it, as though I was too afraid that rushing would set something off. I could hear police sirens just outside now, and I knew my hasty action had prompted them to move. And probably to curse me. I was pretty sure of that last one, anyway.

I entered the office, its wood door and glass window propped open like it was waiting for me. From within I could see into the other side of the warehouse. There were a few vehicles parked there and little else of note. Garage doors that stretched to the ceiling were closed firm, and I stood there in the silence, waiting for my senses to give me a clue of where to go next.

It came in the form of a scratching, one that still sounded terribly far off. There was a desk in the corner and I flew over it in a slow, wafting, gravity-less arc that let me drift until I stopped.

Below me was a hole cut into the floor. It looked as if the desk had been covering it until very recently. A rope, anchored to one of the desk's legs, flowed down into the darkness below.

I sighed, pondering my course of action. The smart thing to do would be to wait for the police. There could be bombs.

It could be booby-trapped. My enemies could be waiting down there to ambush me; they'd already proved to be surprisingly effective at it.

A flash of hot anger ran through me, and I realized I really didn't care if they were down there waiting or not. I wanted them, wanted to pound them into snot and stuffing, to bleed them the way they'd bled others, and leave their messy smears in a room where someone could find them and wonder if they'd ever formed a full and complete human. In their cases, though, I had the luxury of deciding that no, the piece had never formed a whole human, because an actual and complete human could not casually and happily do what these bastards had done to Maxwell Llewelyn, to Angus Waterman, to Angela Tewkesbury.

The fury filled me and I felt it burn under my skin. "Wolfe. Gavrikov. Eve. Bjorn. Roberto." I stared into the darkness, and I could almost see the eyes of the people in my head staring back at me from within. "Stay close."

I flew down into the blackness below the warehouse, and hoped—just hoped—that I'd soon find the three antagonists who had done so much to make my last few days a hell.

Somewhere, maybe, if I was lucky, I'd find Janus, too, alive and close to well.

If not, I doubted any of the three of these bastards would make it back to the surface alive or well.

Chapter 56

Philip could hear her coming down the tunnel, the clammy air seeping in through his suit. A thousand drips of moisture stained the walls, the filth and the dirt even deeper set in this place than it had been in the warehouse.

All he needed to do was run, taking care to avoid the nearest rail. He wasn't exactly sure which of them was electrified, only that one certainly was and he didn't want to touch it.

Liliana was leading the way, moving ably down the tracks with Janus over her shoulder. He was vital. He was necessary. If he hadn't been, Philip would have been quite content to have her drop him on the electrified rails so they could be done with it and run full speed away from the lurking nuisance that was working her way toward them even now.

This was a disused tunnel, Philip knew, a spur for a line that had been closed a few years earlier. It was a fortunate thing, something he'd known before he bought the warehouse. They'd bored the tunnel shortly after, always planning ahead. He'd learned long ago that no future was certain, only that some were more certain than others. The escape of the Tewkesbury wench had proven that point once more. He had no idea how she'd done it, but she had, and she'd pay for it later in spectacular fashion, if he ever caught up with her again...

"She's coming," Antonio said from behind him, forcing him to instinctively look back. The bomb maker had the cylinder with the painting in it under his arm and was listing a little to the right. Philip knew it wasn't from the weight; it might have been from a previous injury.

"We need time," Philip said. "You have to stop her."

He'd hoped for a smile from Antonio but got nothing of the sort. Instead, the bomb maker held up the cylinder. "I can't drop this. Not now." He eyed the thing with a loving feel, like it was his wife or his mother rather than a piece of canvas with oil paint on it. Philip hadn't even bothered to mention that rolling a painting of that sort would likely have a deleterious effect on the canvas. Why bother? The bomb maker was an unsophisticated sort; he would have been better off with a poster of the damned thing rather than the genuine article.

"I'll take it," Philip said, stopping and holding out a hand. A drip of water from overhead caught him right in the shoulder, but he kept his irritation in check while waiting for Antonio to hand over the painting. "You can do this. Right now you're the only one who can." He did not leave any element of suggestion in his words; better to have the man think he was destined for success than leave any doubt regarding the probabilities.

"You won't drop it?" It figured. The idiot was more worried about the painting than his life. Ah, well, that was probably the effect of having the nearest thing to the faith in a deity without having any actual deities present.

"I will ensure that it comes to no harm," Philip said, taking the cylinder and tucking it under his arm. "Now, quickly, prepare your ambush, stop her, and then catch up with us."

"All right," Antonio said with a sharp nod. Then he spun, heading back into the darkness of the tunnel, running back toward the entry to the warehouse.

Philip waited until he was well out of earshot before tossing away the cylinder into the space between the wall of the tunnel and the closest rail. The police would surely find it there—eventually. And it would, indeed, be safe, being far enough away from Antonio to hopefully avoid his explosives and his idiocy.

Philip turned to see Liliana waiting for him, eyeing him, having watched the whole thing. She said nothing, but her expression said worlds.

"His future is not bright," Philip said by way of explanation. "And neither is yours if we don't keep moving."

That got her in motion once more. Philip sighed. In the kingdom of the blind, the one-eyed man may indeed have been king, but talking to people who had no concept of what you were discussing held frustrations and loneliness entirely of its own.

Chapter 57

I swept slowly down the tunnel as my eyes adjusted to the darkness. I couldn't see in complete darkness, but there were lights mounted on the walls of the tunnel every ten or fifteen yards, glowing just faintly enough that I could see. I could tell I was in what looked like a train tunnel, complete with tracks running beneath me. I could see the darkened metal and hoped like hell it wasn't an active line. Was the underground electric? I was pretty sure it was, since there wasn't any steam or smoke fogging the stations, which meant that somewhere beneath me was a live rail that would shock the living hell out of me if I were to touch it.

Objective number one—don't touch the giant taser.

There was the faint sound of voices somewhere in the distance, but even with the scant light source I couldn't see anyone. I knew they were out there, though, and probably in the direction that the lights led into and that the voices were coming from.

Objective number two—don't get ambushed.

I was checking my back every few minutes just to be sure I wasn't missing someone sneaking up on me. I went relatively slowly, which is to say I wasn't blazing along as fast as the human eye could see. I was still afraid of bombs, still sure they were planning on pulling something else to cover their retreat.

I just didn't know what it was going to be or when it would hit.

I was working on a plan, but that old saying about plans not surviving contact with the enemy was doubly true when your enemy had unpredictable super powers. So far all I had were a series of objectives and a few tools to accomplish the job. One tool was super fast healing, but my enemies had previously showed that they knew how to overwhelm that one. I needed to be extra careful.

Another tool was my ability to throw fire, but I wasn't overly excited about using that one down here. I didn't know exactly how London's utilities were set up, but I was guessing there were gas lines around here somewhere, since people didn't tend to want to run those above ground. One wrongly thrown fireball and I wouldn't be worrying about touching the giant taser or getting ambushed anymore.

I also had the ability to turn into a dragon, which was null in these close quarters, unless I wanted to defeat my enemy by mushing them between my super scaly skin and the block walls. Tempting, but using my dragon power shredded my clothes and left me naked, and also left me covered with their bloodied remains when things were all said and done. That wasn't necessarily a deal breaker by itself, but when combined with the lack of mobility in these tight quarters, it didn't make me super excited about it.

Plus, I'd already gone through like ten sets of clothes in the last day. If I had to borrow money from Webbo again, I'd definitely be in danger of not being able to use his nickname with impunity. Priorities.

That left me with the ability to cast non-lethal nets of light and to project a distractionary measure called the "War Mind" into my enemies' heads. By themselves, neither of those powers sucked. When combined with the ability to punch like a 747 crashing into a field mouse and to heal most of the injuries thrown my way, I like to think most people would have thought my odds were pretty swell.

I am not most people. When I'm playing a game of poker with my brother, bad odds are acceptable. He cheats anyway.

When I'm betting my life, I prefer to stack everything on my side of the table and let it ride with the confidence that when shit goes sideways, I have eighteen aces in the hole. Yes, I know there are only four aces in a deck. I don't care. I want more. Only losers want less.

I could hear something in the middle distance, something lurking in the darkness. I wondered how many of them had hung back, waiting to spring the trap on me. Probably at least one. Three would have been smart but not wholly necessary for a rearguard action. If two of them were out there, there'd be no reason for all three not to stay. So the smart money was on one, probably.

"Probably" was not very reassuring.

There was no doubt that whoever was out there was watching me. I was in motion, they were not, and I was in the warm light from the nearest lamp. Breaking it would leave me just as blind as the person I was trying to ambush, maybe even more so.

I floated a few feet above the ground, tentative, and wished I had a working pistol. Not that it would have necessarily been much use right now, but it would have been encouraging to have it on hand. I drifted forward slowly, at the same pace you'd take if you were taking steps extremely gingerly.

And then something exploded.

It was on the ground when it went off, a flash and flare of force and shrapnel that I reacted to as soon as I heard the click of it starting to arm. I hurled myself backward into the void as it lit the tunnel with a sharp white light, and the roar followed a moment later. My ears echoed from the boom and I felt slivers of metal run over the arm I threw up to protect my face. I felt a half dozen stings running through my flesh and hoped I'd been lucky.

"Wolfe," I said, though I could barely hear myself through the ringing in my ears.

On it, he said. The pain began to subside.

"Antonio Ruelle," I said into the darkness. The explosion had faded, leaving only a hint of embers where the bomb had waited for me. I could see its casing by the fading light. It was round, hollowed-out, a few inches wide, and looked a little like a mine. I knew I hadn't stepped on it, what with the fact I'd been flying at the time, so it must have been remotely triggered. "Mad bomber."

"I'm not mad," he said, breaking the silence. I could still hear a ringing in my ears and the stink of the explosive residue lingered in the air.

"No?" I looked into the darkness and felt something—someone—watching me from its depths. "You helped kill a lot of people this morning, Antonio. That's pretty crazy."

"I did a job which I was paid for," he said, and I could tell he was to the left, just not exactly where he was. He sounded muffled. "That makes a tradesman. Death was incidental."

"That's cold," I said, coming forward again, a little at a time. "I mean, at least your boss has a personal axe to grind to explain why he's so eager to kill. You just do it for the money?"

"Lots of people do things for money," he said, indifferent. "Horrible things. Reasonable things. You do what you have to do to survive."

"A lot of people didn't survive the day because of you, Antonio," I said, drifting closer to the sound of his voice. "What if it had been the other way around?"

"Then I'd be dead and they'd be alive," he said. There was not a trace of emotion in the way he said it, which produced a chill in me. "That's the way of the world."

I knew he was just waiting to set off another bomb. Trying to draw me in, trying to take me down. He'd tried to kill me with the last, though, and it hadn't worked, which meant his reflexes weren't as fast as his boss's.

Not as fast as mine.

I saw the solution immediately and gave myself a five-count to prepare before I started to move. He said nothing in the meanwhile, which gave me hope that if I caught him, I wouldn't have to endure an insufferable monologue on why he did it.

I threw up my hand and called Eve Kappler to the forefront of my mind. She showed up dutifully and with her help I shot eight nets of pure light into the darkness ahead. I only aimed three of them, pointing them in the direction I thought Antonio was. They flashed through the air, illuminating the tunnel brick as they passed, shining off the wet walls and striking ground, tracks and stone with a flash upon impact. The one that hit the electrified rail exploded in a shower of sparks. I can't say I had planned it that way, but I didn't complain when it happened, because it bathed the whole tunnel in a momentary flash of light that exposed Antonio lying prone against the side, sandwiched between the track and the wall.

I shot forward at top speed, going from zero to supersonic in the space of less than a second. I also came right back to a halt and spun, my blood rushing through me so fast I almost blacked out from the intensity. The sound of my body breaking the sound barrier reverberated through the tunnel with a force all its own and I heard three other explosions sound off in my wake.

I ended up a few hundred yards down the tunnel from where I'd begun and I charged back, flying through the air as I shot another spread of light nets toward where I'd seen Antonio only moments earlier. He was still there, getting to his feet clumsily, staggering like he'd been hit by something. Which he had. A sonic boom going off a few feet from your ears was bound to cause some disorientation.

I flew back to him, saw the blood running from his ears as he nearly put a foot on the electrified rail, and I caught him just in time, lifting him off the ground into the air and slamming him into the wall. He looked at me with wide eyes that were still dazed, head bobbing from side to side with his right cheek covered in blood from where he'd smeared it on his face when he'd touched his ear.

"What the hell was that?" I heard from my left and glanced over to see the SWAT team coming down the tunnel, about a hundred yards away and moving swiftly.

I looked back to Antonio and found him fumbling with something at his belt. I reached out and broke his arm, causing him to grunt in pain. For good measure I broke his other arm, because he started to go for his belt with that one, too. Then I ripped his belt off and tossed it down the tunnel, away from the SWAT team.

"We need to have a talk about your boss, Antonio," I said, staring straight into his eyes as I held him firm against the wet tunnel wall.

"What are you going to do, American?" he spoke in an off-tone, teeth gritted in a scowl. By the sound of him I started to suspect I'd ruptured his eardrums. "Waterboard me?" His scowl melted into a smile. "London cops. They'll come and take me away. You've got nothing."

"I wouldn't say 'nothing.'" I lifted one of my hands into his field of view, playing on a hunch about his burns. I lit my arm from fingertips to elbow, letting the power of Aleksandr Gavrikov's flames wash over my skin. I felt the temperature in the tunnel rise by several degrees, and in the orange light of my flickering hand, I watched Antonio Ruelle's grin dissolve into a look of absolute fear. "Waterboard you? I think not." I flexed each of my fingers in turn, flaming joints articulating as the inferno raged over my skin, dancing and creating shadows on the wall. His face was pure terror, mouth open, any pretense of bravery abandoned.

"Waterboarding is for pussies," I said, and let my hand drift closer and closer to his face.

Chapter 58

They found the end of the spur tunnel and hurried along the tracks. Philip knew the area well enough from the maps, but actually being in them was quite a different story. There was enough space to walk, fortunately, between where the train ran and the wall met, and that proved fortunate indeed when a train bearing a lighted sign marked "Jubilee Line" came rushing past.

"The station is ahead," Liliana said, causing Philip to look. Sure enough, she was correct. There was the unmistakable light of a station glowing in the distance, and it prompted him to quicken his pace.

They hurried forward, the tunnel widening before it tightened just ahead of the station. The walking path that they'd found spread wider and veered off the track into a closed, locked door. Probably a safety measure, narrowing things like this, to keep someone from running off down the tunnel.

Liliana broke the knob, ripping out the guts of the lock and tearing the thing off its hinges. They stepped inside, Janus still slung over her shoulder. They found themselves in a maintenance room with dimly lit bulbs and a few storage lockers, all of which began to shake as another train approached.

"How are we going to get him out of here?" Liliana asked, stonefaced.

"Let me look around the station," Philip said. He felt the prickle of a frown as he reached out. In twenty minutes, regardless of any action they took, the station would be flooded with police. In ten minutes, Sienna Nealon would show up, he could feel that without doubt, one hundred percent probability on both events. Which meant that Antonio had already failed.

Philip dodged through the nearest maintenance door and found himself on a nearly empty platform. Dark tiles decorated the floor and ceiling from one side to the other, and Philip stared across the sparsely occupied space. There were only ten people here at most, and one of them—

Oh, wasn't that perfect?

One of them was sitting in a wheelchair, ready for the next train. Philip reached out; it was less than a minute away. He looked up and realized that the sign above said much the same, but those things were slightly less reliable than his own sense of events.

The timing would have to be precise on this one; a second or two off in either direction would accelerate the arrival of the police and also lead to a bloody conflict with the other people on the platform.

But precise timing was exactly what Philip excelled at.

He sauntered over toward the man in the wheelchair, who sat with a magazine across his lap, waiting patiently. He paused a few feet away, taking careful stock of the situation. His opportunity was coming in five... four... three... two...

Philip stepped forward quickly but not absurdly so, bending to flick the left brake on the wheelchair, which had been locked into place to prevent sudden motion by someone other than the occupant. Using his rather substantial speed and his gift for glimpsing what the future held, Philip picked the exact moment that the man in the wheelchair was looking in the other direction to make his move, and by the time he had finished, he was back behind the man, the wheelchair occupant none the wiser to what he'd done.

The next bit would have to happen in three... two... one...

The train began to arrive and every head in the station turned in response. It was coming from the right side of the platform, the low rumble following the rush of air out of the darkness. Philip rested his hands on the handles to the wheelchair's back, lightly, taking advantage of the momentary distraction. One more second now that he was positioned, and then he'd need to—

He pushed the chair forward, hurrying it with his metahuman speed into a ten-mile-per-hour dash. He stopped it just as abruptly, causing the man in the chair to grunt in surprise. Philip followed the halt with a firm slap to the man's back, just enough strength in it to cause him to surge forward—

The man sailed out of the wheelchair and hit the edge of the platform with not so much as a cry before he disappeared onto the tracks below. Philip was already moving, turning the chair about and walking it toward the maintenance door. His next actions were crucial to their escape, and if he made it to the door without interruption in the next six seconds they would be able to escape without incident.

As he dodged into the door five seconds later, he spared only a glimpse back to the edge of the platform, where a small crowd was now huddling around the edge of the track, already in hand-wringing mode. The station would be shut down for hours, but with a wheelchair they could be long gone, halfway to the next station by the time that the police put together even half of what had happened here.

Chapter 59

By the time I got Antonio out of the tunnel and trussed up in enough handcuffs and leg irons to prevent Houdini himself from escaping, I figured Ski Mask had already gotten away. A safe bet, as it turned out, because Webster met me with his police radio in hand and a severe look on his face.

"They did what?" I was in sheer disbelief when he told me the story.

"Dumped a man in a wheelchair in front of the train," Webster said with intense disgust. This was getting personal to him, too, I could tell.

"If they're willing to kill cops and blow up buildings, this shouldn't come as a total surprise, I guess," I said as I watched the SWAT team strip Antonio of all his clothes with the bomb squad's help. He'd had some stuff on his person that had been deeply disconcerting. Bombs, I mean. Get your mind out of the gutter.

"No sign of them, though our people are reviewing the camera footage from the station," Webster said. "I hate to give up too soon, but with the way it looks like they plan things out, I'm going to guess they're clear of this by now."

"Safe bet," I said. "Ski Mask seems to know police responses well enough to know which direction to run in case of emergency."

"That's a bit frustrating, but I tend to agree," Webster said. "By the way, don't know if you'd heard, but they found the painting down the tunnel."

I turned my head to watch Antonio's reaction to that. His neck pivoted ever so slightly in response, and I knew he'd caught what Webster said. "Score one for the good guys, I guess. One bad guy in custody, two more in flight." I folded my arms with a slight sense of satisfaction. "I think we can put that in the victory column."

"Some poor disabled bloke under a train in the next station might find reason to disagree," Webster said ominously, "but I'll take what we can get."

I watched Antonio as the police put him into the back of a prison van just for him. It had those metal grates over the windows, the kind of thing you'd expect from a maximum security prison, and he was being duct-taped across the arms and upper thighs for good measure, supplementing the multiple sets of hand and ankle cuffs. I started to tell them that he wasn't that strong a meta, and then I realized they were better safe than sorry. He hadn't spilled his special talent to me when asked.

Actually, he hadn't said anything. In spite of his blatant and obvious fear of fire, I'd rendered him catatonic in my attempt to get him to talk. Maybe waterboarding would have been a better option, but unfortunately my ex was the one with the water powers.

I pushed my way through the SWAT team, who were all admiring their fine handiwork. "Step aside for a second," I told them, and held out a finger. Summoning Eve to the forefront again, I spun a slow web across Antonio's body where they'd placed the duct tape as their hedge. He had on eight pairs of handcuffs and twelve sets of leg irons. I counted.

I spun him around eight times, weaving that narrow thread of light around him from top to bottom. "It's not exactly a lasso of truth, but it'll hold for about twelve hours, give or take," I said to the officer in charge. "Where are you taking him?"

"Her Majesty's Prison Belmarsh," the SWAT captain said, a hard look on his face. Honestly, when you were someone who'd seen as much shit as a SWAT captain had, was there any other sort of look to wear? "He'll get a lovely stay in a new section they've built for…" The SWAT captain looked me up and down, struggling with the words, "… special prisoners." I admired his attempt at diplomacy. "The CPS is going to make a special example of this one."

I frowned. "What about the other two? Hard to make an example out of people who aren't there." The SWAT captain gave me a grudging nod. "Also, I know it's not exactly in vogue, but can I recommend having his liver eaten by a vicious bird every day? Just a suggestion."

"If only, ma'am," the SWAT captain said with a tip of his helm to me. He said ma'am like "mum." "If only."

Antonio looked over his shoulder at me as they took him by each arm, and I waved at him, sending my hand to flame as I did so. He sucked in a breath of air abruptly, fearfully, as I did so, and I couldn't help but smile at him as they put him in the prison van.

"I'm pretty knackered," Webster said, appearing at my shoulder as I watched them haul Antonio off. "Mum left me a message saying supper is in the fridge. Are you ready to go home?"

"Yes, please," I said, staring at the prison van. If I could have flown, I might have been in a better position to escort them to the prison, but… they'd be fine, right? It'd be nearly impossible to lay on an operation to free Antonio after we'd just cost them their headquarters, right?

A thousand possibilities filled my head, from the idea of a prison break to another attack like the gallery, and I realized that there was absolutely no predicting what the man in the black ski mask was likely to do next. With a sigh, I followed

Webster to his car, and wondered idly if I'd get a full night's sleep before hell started breaking loose again.

Chapter 60

"This is not like any investigation I've ever been on," Webster said with a weary sort of chuckle as he drove us on. The window was cracked and the London night air was coming in just enough to disturb my hair in a good way.

"This is like every investigation I've ever been on," I said, staring at the facades of the buildings as they passed by my window. "The volume is turned up a little on this one, but it's not that different from every meta chase."

"I find it hard to believe you do this daily," Webster said.

"I haven't done it like this in a couple years," I said. "But metas always put up a harder fight than humans. Back when I first started chasing down metas, I had this one case where someone was attacking convenience store clerks and draining their memories of the event—"

"That's possible?" Webster asked in disbelief.

"Yeah," I said. "For a succubus like me, or an incubus—my male counterpart—your mind is like a notebook we can rifle through. Tear out a page here and there, borrow a memory or two that we like. Whatever."

"You didn't do that to Antonio," Webster said, staring at me. "You could have gotten right to his memories about the man in the ski mask?"

I felt a little cold rush over my skin. "I don't... do that anymore. Take memories, I mean. Not to mention that if

237

your government found out, they'd probably be pissed off about it. And my government would—"

"You say you have no limits, but you follow rules as best you can," Webster said, and I was hard pressed to figure out whether he was saying it with scorn or admiration.

"I'm a contradiction in terms, I know."

"You are... truly something," Webster said. "Truly something."

I wanted to ask whether I was truly something bad or truly something good, but I wasn't sure I wanted to know. "I don't know whether that's a compliment or not," I finally said.

"It's a compliment," Webster said with a smile. I liked his smile.

"You're truly something yourself, Detective Inspector."

He eased the car to the curb and I was surprised to see that we'd reached his mother's house without me even realizing it. I blinked, not sure I believed it was really there. "I guess this is my stop."

"I'll walk you up," he said, and got out of the car. He didn't quite get to my side in time to open my door for me, but he closed it after me once I got out. "So... about these powers of yours..."

I gave him a wary eye. "What about them?"

"Does anyone who touches you start to lose their... soul?" He said the last word like it was a bit of a joke.

"Only if they do it for too long." It would sound cheesy to say I felt a thrill of hope at his question, but... well... I hoped it wasn't just idle curiosity that brought it out.

"That's interesting," he said, studying me carefully. "How long is 'too long'?"

"You'd feel it working after about twenty seconds," I said, watching his face as we made our way up the walk.

"I see," he said as we made it to the stoop. "That seems like enough time to be getting along with."

He leaned in and kissed me, and it was like a rush of energy when his lips met mine. I let my hand come to rest in his hair, fingers running through it as he pressed to me. It was like the breath of life came back to me, and when he pulled away I had to resist the urge to pull him closer, keep him there.

We parted and he smiled, that same smile. "I don't feel as if I've lost anything." He adjusted his pant leg. "Maybe might have gained a bit of something—"

I laughed. "Good night, Detective Inspector." He unlocked the door for me.

"One last question," he said, keeping the door held for me as I stepped inside. "You said you had a boyfriend."

I felt that old chill creep into the house after me. "Had, yes."

"When you were together... did you... do things?" There was a sly glint in his eyes.

That warmed me up a bit. "We did... do things. There are ways. Perhaps not the sexiest of... ways to do... things... but there are certainly ways to avoid... soul loss."

"I would really love to hear about them," he said with a disarming smile.

"Tomorrow," I said, savoring the promise. "Tonight I'm just a little too tired."

I closed the door on his smile and stood there with my fingers against the wood as I waited to see what he would do. To my disappointment, I heard him lock it from outside. Then I heard him whistle his way back down the path toward his car, and I thought about tomorrow.

Chapter 61

As I lay down in bed, scraping the carbonized bits of scorched thread from the sleeve I hadn't bothered to roll up before I set my arm on fire, I was still thinking about tomorrow. I thought about Webster, about this whole ordeal I'd let myself get dragged into. Because he was cute.

Also, I'd be lying if I said I didn't feel at least some loyalty to Janus. He and I had been through a few things, and it hadn't been my choice for him to leave after the war to return to England. He'd seemed like a natural fit with what we were doing at the Agency, but he and Kat had left together about three months after the close of the war.

Like most of the departures, it had been quiet, a few words of goodbye and little warning. They hadn't been the first. They certainly weren't the last to leave. But with each departure my world started to feel smaller and smaller, the job seeming bigger and bigger with fewer people to help me get it done. There had been a point about six months after the war's end when Reed had left to settle some business in Italy, where I was the last of the old crew left. Me and Ariadne, I guess, if I'm being totally accurate, but since she had no powers of her own, it was basically down to me.

Janus, though… I owed him. I owed all of them.

I thought about Janus as I lay there, wondering whether he was alive or not. I wished I could have just kept trucking, kept running, kept pursuing every lead every hour of the day.

I needed to chase down the man in the black mask. I needed to know what happened to Janus.

And it was the man in the black mask that I was thinking of when I drifted into sleep.

For a succubus, the power is mostly subtle things. My ex, Scott, could control water, pulling it out of the very air. My brother could control the currents of wind, stirring a roaring gale out of a balmy, still day. Janus could play with your emotions, pushing and pulling you in whatever direction he so chose.

But incubi and succubi had a different playground—the soul.

And for some reason I had never quite figured out, this included being able to visit people in their dreams.

I recognized the alleyway near the gallery as the place where I'd been unceremoniously tossed into a dumpster with a bomb after having my throat slashed. I wasn't sure which part of that was the most disrespectful and invasive, but it was safe to say that the whole thing had added a certain stew of rage to my normally pleasant and docile personality.

Kidding about the pleasant and docile part, of course.

I looked around the alley, and I could almost smell the spent explosive wafting out of the garbage bin. The crumbled brick all ran together as I spun, knowing I was in a dream. This was how it happened; you encountered people you had met by thinking about them as you drifted off to sleep. I'd considered showing Webster how it worked; it could be pretty intensely pleasurable – in a romantic sense – for a guy.

I could also turn it into hell on earth if I so desired. I had a feeling—based on where we were—I was going to so desire, very soon.

"So this is the fabled dreamwalk of a succubus?" came the cultured, unmistakably English voice of the man in the black mask. I was so sick of calling him that in my head. I wanted to give him a more appropriate name, and immediately. "And here is the fabled heroine herself."

"And here is the fabled turdblossom himself," I said, letting my arms fold in front of me. "Or do you prefer something more floridly descriptive, like 'psycho-loser mass murderer'?"

"I think I rather enjoy the simplicity of 'turdblossom,' actually." His smile never dimmed. "Wherever did you come up with such a concise and descriptive phrase?"

I felt a slow boil, wishing I could say I came up with it myself. "In a movie."

"Truly, whoever wrote that one was a wordsmith," Ski Mask said.

"It had a talking raccoon with a machine gun in it, so don't fall over yourself heaping praise."

He took in the surroundings once more and made a subtle, two-handed gesture toward the dumpster. "Since we're here, I suppose we should talk about your impending death."

"Or your rapidly approaching comeuppance," I tossed back.

He smiled, which made me boil again. "I admire your spirit. Of course, that's all you've got, since I've been bludgeoning you from the outset of our little game, but still. I admire it."

"I just took out your headquarters, Smugly McSmuggerson, so I wouldn't get to feeling too untouchable if I were you."

He let out a low, short, breathy laugh. "If you were me, perhaps we wouldn't be in this situation."

"If you weren't dedicated to cutting the skin off people an inch at a time, we wouldn't be in this situation."

The smile faded. "You're a fine choice to lecture me on the art of revenge." He paused, and the smile returned as he took in my reaction. "Oh, yes, I know about that. Four of them, wasn't it? That's how many people you killed in your mad quest for vengeance?"

I felt a little cold. "Yeah. Four people directly responsible for the murder of…" I paused, composing myself.

He leapt right in. "Your first lover, yes? I'm sure it seared your heart, losing someone you'd known all of… what? Six months?"

I blinked my eyes, which were burning. "More like nine, but—"

"But you're the hero," he said, a sort of slick sarcasm slipping out like the blade of a knife. "You've killed more people than I have, but you're the hero."

"We were probably neck and neck until the wheelchair thing."

He grinned. "Well, I needed it more than that fellow did."

"You're a sick bastard."

"So are you, yet you're still the hero of this piece," he said, the smirk not diminishing one bit. "Don't you find that hilarious? You've murdered people. You've killed dozens—"

"In war," I said.

"And in revenge," he interrupted. "It's really a matter of timing. Because if you'd been alive two or three thousand years ago, you truly would have been more than just a hero. You would have been a goddess. The historians of the time, the storytellers, the prophets, they would have treated you with your due respect. They would have sung your praises from every rooftop and in every marketplace, and small children would hear the tale of your murder of M-Squad as a cautionary one. Do not cross the Soul-Tearer, or she shall unmake you."

"'Soul-Tearer' is a little melodramatic, don't you think?"

"And the legend of Hercules is cheerfully understated," he said with that same smile. It was getting infuriating. "Even a hundred years ago, the world was black and white enough that you could have been a true and virtuous heroine if the truth had all come out then. Casualties of war, they'd say. A righteous fight to the death. If they made a movie of your life, even including the dark moments where you wavered and acted in self-interest and in the name of vengeance, you would still be lauded. But now? Someone whispers a few words about certain dead bodies you've left in your wake and your carefully spun lies become the twine in which you strangle."

I listened, strangely riveted and utterly horrified. My past had been buried carefully by the U.S. government, but the fact that there were people out there who still knew the truth was an inescapable fact—and probably the thing I feared the most. "I'm no hero," I said.

"But you are," he went on. "Built up by the talking heads on television—the storytellers of our time—even in spite of that dreadful interview. Lionized by those who were taking their first steps into this new world of metahumans. The fiction has held for two years. And do you know why? Because people are obsessed with heroes."

"I said I'm not a—"

"They love the idea of strength," he said. "Your strength. They're repelled by weakness. No one ever fantasizes about being the victim—"

"Except a lawyer," I tossed in, just to be snarky.

"People hate the weakness they see inside." His smile was twisting into something malevolent. "They despise the pathetic and sad parts of themselves, and rather than try to fix them, they latch on to that weakness in others and disclaim it. Hate it. Shout it from the rooftops. Loathe it in a raging mob." He was angry now, and it was flowing out of him in a low, bubbling rage. "Because even though we love them, we don't believe in heroes anymore, not truly. You were raised up by the storytellers, and you will fall the same way. Once there was a deification of heroes, a belief that they were better people than us. Then we realized they were gods with feet of clay."

"Well, I'm sensing some unresolved anger here," I said. "Daddy issues?"

"I believe you might be projecting," he said coldly. "Though it strikes me as ironic, given the plethora of problems you've had with your mother."

"You're a telepath," I said.

"Wrong," he said with a muted sort of glee. "I can't read your mind. Only your future." His eyes went slack. "And all I see is blood, from now until the end."

It almost felt like something clicked in my mind when he said it. He'd let it spill because he was angry, that was certain; he would have been a lot smarter to keep it to himself. "A Cassandra type," I murmured.

I saw a waver of uncertainty beneath the mask, but it resolved as he realized he was committed. "I can trace my lineage back to the oracle at Delphi. Thousands of years of heritage."

"Family is important to you," I said, trying to work my way through it. There was something else going on here, something driving this whole machine. "You're angry at the UK government."

He made a noise with his lips that conveyed utter disdain. "I am annoyed at the government. It's Omega that I'm aiming to burn."

"Omega is dead," I said. "Over with. Finished."

"Truly?" His eyes caught mine, and for the first time I realized that they were deep brown. It was hard to tell under all that rage. "Are you actually that naïve?"

"Are you really that stupid?" I asked. "They fell in the war. Their Primus died, their ministers were killed, and the chaff got mostly swept away by Century. They're gone."

"I thought they were dead, too," he said. "But it was all a masquerade. You see, the rats are the best at leaving a sinking ship. And that is what Omega was, a nest of rats. They were better prepared than anyone to weather the storm that Century brought, because there was no other lower form of life than them."

"They were the cockroaches in the nuclear apocalypse?" I asked. "All well and good, but metaphors aside, whoever burned you at Omega is probably dead."

His eyes narrowed. "Omega is more than a person. It is an institution, made up of the people who run it. As you stand before me in perfect evidence, the last person to run Omega is still alive and well." He glanced at the dumpster. "At least for now."

"You're down to two people remaining in your little gang," I said. "The entire Metropolitan Police force is looking for you. If you really can see the future, I find it hard to believe that you could think that this is all going to resolve well for you."

There was a hint of uncertainty that wafted off of him. "That's not exactly how it works."

"No?" I asked. "How does it work?"

"That would be telling," he said with that smile. "As much as I wish I could forewarn you, forearm you and let things play out, I prefer to place all the odds on my side."

"Join the club," I muttered.

"And about the Metropolitan Police," he said, putting his lips together. "I don't think you'll be getting much help from them going forward. Parliament is making decisions even now that will put you out in the cold with them."

"I don't really enjoy being out in the cold." I lifted a hand and my fingers blazed to light, flames crackling on them. "But it's not as much of a problem as it used to be."

He smiled. "You should be grateful. I read all about what happened to you in the wake of your Directorate's fall. Seems to me that you never did appreciate the gift of perspective you were given that night." He straightened himself up. "Perhaps you need a repeat of the lesson in order for it to sink in."

I felt my jaw tighten. "I'm going to catch you. I'm going to stop you. Whatever you're planning, I will take you apart one piece at a time until it's just you and me, and I don't care if you can see every second of the future—I will be the punch you cannot stop."

"I'm afraid we'll have to agree to disagree on that one." He straightened his tie. "Because you know what they say." He lowered his voice. "Fortune favors the brave."

"In America we say the bold," I said, "but either way, it doesn't favor the clinically insane who tear the skin off living people and bomb entire blocks in order to kill police officers."

"I will destroy everything I have to," he said with that smile. "Blow up anyone. Tear the flesh from all in my path. I've proven that." He made a motion like he was pushing a wheelchair. "You are the last touched by Omega, which is why you are last in my calculations." Something in the way he said it rang hollow to me. "The fact that you are a hero—yet sullied, dirty—fascinates me to no end and will make your inevitable fall all the more glorious."

He looked at the dumpster and fixed his gaze on it. "No matter what you do, I can see every move you will make. I have plans for you. When it comes to gods, the old ones may have been fallible, but I have a will of iron." He pointed at the dumpster. "So, prepare yourself—hero," he said it with such scorn it dripped, "because that is your past, and your future is dimmer still."

"There's just one thing you forgot," I said, staring at him with a seething fury of my own. "You may be able to see the future, but you don't control it." He actually rolled his eyes at me on that one. "And you definitely don't control the world of dreams we're in right now."

I took two strides toward him before he could move, before he could react, and I tore his mask right off his face like it didn't exist. Because it actually didn't, not in this dream. It dissolved into smoke and he let out a cry of pain at my touch. When the black smoke cleared I was left staring down at a pale man, with long dark hair, a tall forehead and a small, pointed nose.

The face of my enemy.

"Now let me show you what else I can do in a dream," I said and applied my hand to his face. I could feel the burning anger in my touch, and he screamed in absolute pain, his shrieks not manly in the least.

"Philip!" I heard somewhere in the distance and knew that I had only seconds left.

"So long, Philip," I said, and brought my touch of agony back to him for a farewell stab of pain. He screamed again, and then he disappeared as someone woke him, shouting his name again. He looked at me with those hateful, hateful eyes as he disappeared.

I awoke in the bed in Marjorie Webster's house moments later, my breath coming in long, uncomfortable gulps. My skin was covered in a sheen of perspiration and the sheets were tangled around my body.

"Philip," I murmured aloud and stared at the ceiling as my mind prickled at me, filling me with the sensation that I'd forgotten something very, very important.

Chapter 62

Philip felt the shaking, and his first thought ran to the idea that it was pain, pain, that glorious bitch's pain from her touch. As the next slap descended he realized it was not her, but Liliana who was slapping him awake, the sting knocking his jaw asunder, the stale air of their new hideout hitting him in the face as he awoke in the darkness.

Liliana raised her hand to him again and he caught it this time, the descent halted in midair, her fingers inches away from making contact with his jaw again. "I'm awake," he said with a searing anger.

"Nightmare?" Liliana asked, staring at him from those black eyes. "Or succubus dream?"

"That latter, I'm afraid," he said, rubbing his jaw. "She has my name and she knows my power."

"How did she get them?" Liliana asked, her voice tinged with fear.

"Because you shouted it so loud it bled into the dream," Philip said, letting the sting of his cheek carry into his words. "I think it's time we sever her connection to the Metropolitan Police Department. Do you have Antonio's detonator?"

"I took his spare before we fled the warehouse," she said, producing a small black object from underneath her coat. "It's limited by range."

"Go do it," he said. "I'll watch our guests." He could taste a hint of blood in his mouth where she'd slapped him hard enough to break his lip open. He watched her walk toward the open door, the faint light of distant illumination casting her in silhouette in the doorway. "Do hurry."

Chapter 63

My head hurt, but I put it through its paces anyway, trying to review everything Philip had said.

He was a Cassandra. He could read the future. His name was Philip, no middle, no last name to work with. He had a mad-on toward Omega for personal reasons. He was irritated at the UK government for presumably also personal reasons. He hated me. He hated that I was a hero. And…

And…

Perhaps you need a repeat of the lesson in order for it to sink in.

It didn't even take my sleep-addled brain more than a few seconds to process a nasty possibility on that one. "Marjorie!" I shouted as I threw my pants on.

I heard the light click on down the hall as I opened the door to my bedroom, hobbling down the narrow, darkened hallway. I thumped against the wall and dislodged a picture, sending a glass frame shattering to the ground behind me. I heard her door open in front of me and wondered if Marjorie had meta instincts.

"What is it, dear?" She wore a bathrobe and clutched it tight in the front. Dressing gown? Whatever. "You look as though you've seen a—"

"Villain," I pre-empted her. "I think he's going after Matthew. I need to get to his apartment *now*." I put all the urgency into the last syllable.

She rushed for the stairs and I followed behind her. She was moving pretty quickly. Not as quickly as I could, but as quickly as her older joints and human reflexes could carry her. She ran for a door on the far end of the hallway and grabbed a set of keys off a ring as she threw open the door to a garage.

"Get in!" she shouted as she hit the garage door opener. It started to creak as it lifted automatically. I threw myself into the passenger seat, still buttoning my blouse, and pulled my shoes after I slammed the door so hard I shattered the window glass.

She was going before the door was all the way up, and I heard the top of the car scrape as we passed underneath it. She hit the road and the car bounced, the bottom scraping the road. We were in a little Volkswagen of some sort, and she did not spare any of the horses as she streaked down the street into the night.

Chapter 64

To her credit, she didn't ask me any of the stupid questions like, "How do you know he's in danger?" Maybe it never crossed her mind; maybe she just didn't care. Maybe she ascribed to me mythical abilities that were no more in evidence than a tail hiding in the back of my pants. (I don't have one, just FYI.)

Whatever the case, "bat out of hell" was an apt descriptor for how she drove, taking side streets and going down alleys with a precision and ability that would not have looked out of place in the footage of a NASCAR driver but looked ridiculous from an older English lady in a dressing gown.

We came out of the mouth of an alley in a drifting slide that made me worry she was going to roll the car. She hit the curb and I heard the hubcap pop off, flying into the night and caroming off a nearby tree like Captain America's shield. I saw it in slow motion and then it was gone, and we were onward, making our next turn.

"How far?" I asked. I still hadn't quite caught my breath after the dream, and part of me wondered if that was the point. Maybe Philip was idly threatening. And maybe he'd give up his life of crime if I asked politely.

Sarcasm. I haz it. All the time, not just when it's appropriate.

Marjorie came around one last bend and brought us to a screeching halt, mounting the curb and stopping in the

253

middle of a patch of lawn outside of an apartment building. I was out of the car a second after her, and she was already running toward the entry, gown flapping behind her.

"Which floor?" I asked.

"Ground," she replied, breathless. She pointed to a sliding glass door just around the side of the building. "Right there!"

I veered off course without missing a beat, taking flight and crashing through his sliding glass door like a cannonball. It hurt. A lot. But I didn't care, using Wolfe to pull my skin back together and healing the otherwise serious lacerations that resulted. I could feel the trickle of blood running down my skin in various places as I stood there, in the still living room, night air flooding in around me. The place smelled faintly—very faintly—of sweet tobacco smoke, like Webbo liked to have a cigar or a pipe every now and again.

I heard movement in a room off to my right. I flew through the open door and surged into the dark of the room. The light clicked on and there he stood, in his underwear, a flat-headed cricket bat clutched in his hands. As he registered who I was, his expression changed.

"What the hell—?" He let the bat drift downward. "Is this that same argument again?"

I stared at him in weak disbelief. And a little relief. "What?"

"About the whole gun thing?" He shook his head. "Because I would have shot you just now, if you'd have been anyone else—"

"We have to get out of here," I said, clamping a hand on his wrist.

"Why's that?" He stared at me. I was briefly distracted by his well-muscled chest. Well. Muscled.

"I think Philip is coming after you," I said, getting ahold of myself.

He glanced at the bat in his hand. "Well, I might need more than this if that's the case, so point taken, I guess—"

"We have to go," I said and pulled him forward.

He took stumbling steps as I jerked him toward me. "Hey, I do need that arm—"

"No time for this," I said, and picked him up, *An Officer and a Gentleman*-style. I wrapped my arms around his bare back and lifted him up, reversing my course and flying through the bedroom door.

"What, like this?" I felt him squeeze tighter to me, like he was afraid to be dropped. "Can I at least put some trousers on, first? This isn't quite how I imagined I'd end up naked with you—"

I passed over the threshold of the sliding glass door a second later, and saw Marjorie coming a little more slowly toward me, crossing the lawn as—

The apartment exploded behind us, and it felt like a great hand struck me in the back, swatting me out of the sky to the ground. Webster hit first and I landed on top of him, my conditioning allowing me to roll out of the impact with him still pressed against me.

The world was echoing around me, a sharp ringing in my ears. I realized I was lying on something and I pushed off quickly, landing on my back, the black night sky hanging above me like a blanket of darkness. The smell of something burning filled the air, and I saw the crackle of flames in the wreckage of the building behind me.

There was a crater in the side of the building where Webster's apartment had been, extending three floors up, like someone had taken a God-sized pickaxe and just brought it down and out, removing that section of the brick facade. I could see every floor where the concrete hung out of the gash, where bedrooms and kitchens had once stood and were now replaced by empty air and smoke.

I could see Marjorie, pulling herself up from the ground, her dressing gown hanging limp around her. She wobbled as she drew herself to her feet and staggered toward me, reminding me what—who—I'd come here to protect.

Every part of my body ached, but I pushed myself up to one elbow and looked over at Webster. There was a layer of blood running down from his scalp, and his skin had a dirty, scraped look to it. I put my hand against his cheek and felt the hints of life there, but as I shook him and shook him, he did not even once stir.

Chapter 65

I sat in Commissioner Marshwin's office, staring across the desk at her sullen façade. I knew I was in deep shit. Not just because it was the wee small hours of the morning and not just because Alistair Wexford was there looking utterly defeated, but because Ryan Halstead, U.S. Ambassador to the United Kingdom, was sitting the chair across from Mary Marshwin's desk, and he had a look on his face that told me he was the cat that had eaten the canary.

"I know silence is supposed to be golden," I said, staring at each of them in turn, "but it's more like turds spray-painted a yellowish color when this ass has that look on his face." I pointed to Halstead, who didn't look any less self-satisfied. I waited to see if Marshwin would crack first and break the silence, but she did not. "Fine, I'll just guess. The law passed Parliament."

"Got it in one," Halstead said, snapping his finger at me and then pointing it at me. What a cool guy.

"Awesome," I said, "it's always fun to watch people flail ineffectually about. When does the removal start and where are you sending them?" I caught the stricken look on Marshwin's face. "Tell me you're not setting up concentration camps."

"Incarceration, then deportation," Marshwin said. "Though we haven't found a country that will take them yet."

"So, basically incarceration for now," I said, rolling my eyes. "Camps. Why does that sound familiar? You're not going to give us a symbol to wear on a patch, are you? Like a yellow DNA helix in place of the Star of David, are you?"

Marshwin looked utterly revolted. "I am not in charge of this. I am in the charge of the Metropolitan Police Force."

"So what are you supposed to do if a metahuman crosses your path?" I prodded her.

"They're forming a unit for that," Marshwin said abruptly. "Again, not my department, not my concern. Mine ends with enforcing the laws of London and the surrounding areas. To that end—"

"You want me to leave," I said and watched her deflate as I said it.

"I want no such thing," she said. "But I am in charge of law enforcement, and as much as I don't like it, this is now the law."

"It's a good law," Halstead opined, clearly gloating. "I wish we could get one like that in the United States. Once again, Europe leads the way—"

I slapped him in the back of the head just hard enough to send his head into the desk. He hit it and bounced back, flipping over backward in his seat as his body recoiled from the force of impact. I glanced down at him and he was limp. I wouldn't have bet he was unconscious, but I would have bet he was smart enough—or at least averse to pain enough—to quit while he was only slightly behind.

"Oh, thank goodness," Wexford said, a cup of tea in his hands and a tired look on his face. "Perhaps now we can get to the crux of this without interruption."

"You know every single cop movie gets to the point of the lead detective getting thrown off the case," I said, looking from Wexford to Marshwin. Neither looked impressed with my comparison.

"We are not removing you from anything," Marshwin said primly. "And as you're hardly a lead detective, I don't see how this applies. My lead detective is suffering from a concussion in the hospital."

That was true. Webster was a little out of sorts, but I'd heard he'd regained consciousness. He was definitely out of the game for a bit, though, and I hadn't spoken to him since he'd woken up.

"It's not as though we have the power to force you in any direction," Wexford said. "Nor would I care to, in any case." He stirred his tea with that little spoon. "I prefer to retain the shape of my face as it presently is."

"It's a good look for you," I said. My comment elicited a slight smile from him in return, as he raised his teacup in salute.

"However," Marshwin said, "you do have a problem coming. The government will call for your expulsion, since you are presently the most visible metahuman in our country."

"Is there a list of other ones?" I asked.

She shook her head. "Angela Tewkesbury would be the only other one I've heard of, and you can be well assured I'm not listing her as such on my report."

I stared at her through narrowed eyes. "Worried she might get carted off and gassed?"

"Och," Marshwin said, her disgust evident. "No, I don't think she'll be treated any such way, but it doesn't mean I think any good will actually come of it, either."

"I guess you could let Antonio Ruelle be the test for you," I said. "Since it looks like he'll be staying regardless, and he's known."

"Ah, yes," Wexford said, "he will be a guest of Her Majesty for an indefinite period, and I suspect you are right. He'll be an excellent judge of what's to happen to metahumans in the United Kingdom, though from what I've heard his future won't be particularly sinister. More boring, I'm afraid, being in confinement roughly all the time."

"He could do worse," I said with a grunt.

"He could indeed, as you have pointed out," Marshwin said and glanced at the clock nervously. "I'm afraid I don't have a great deal of time left to humor you, Ms. Nealon. I can't allow you to remain in the building, not with this bloody law. As for this investigation," she looked almost contrite, "I am assigning it to another detective inspector. I think it's fairly obvious, given the direction the winds are blowing, that our conversations are at an end for now. If you plan to do something about this 'Philip,' whoever he is, make it soon."

"You've got nothing on him?" I asked. "From the description I gave you?"

"Nothing," Marshwin said and set her knuckles on her desk. "I wish you the best of luck in all your endeavors, but do your endeavoring elsewhere now, if you please." She stood straighter. "My department has enough problems without having the whole of the government land upon my head."

"I shall be glad to walk you out, Ms. Nealon," Wexford said, suddenly on his feet. He had his coat draped over his arm, and a thin smile on his face. "If you wouldn't be averse to my company."

"I could not imagine a politer way to be thrown out of a building," I said and walked through the door, which he had opened for me.

"You mustn't blame Mary for her circumstances," Wexford said, putting on his coat as we threaded our way through a quiet and near-empty bullpen, "she's caught quite in the middle of this unpleasantness. I suspect you know something of being given orders from on high that make little sense to you."

"I have a passing familiarity with it, yeah," I said, thinking of the ten billion rules and regulations I'd been forced to adapt to after my agency, which had been so easy to run back when it was only the work to worry about, got a lot more complicated after the war once we'd gone public and the oversight had gotten serious.

"This Philip has left us with a bit of a black eye," he said, letting me lead the way through the door out of the bullpen. "Extreme measures will have to be taken in order to soothe the unease among the populace. I apologize if these measures cause your life to be more difficult."

"Why? Did you vote for them?" I asked sourly.

"Indeed not," he said with a chuckle, "nor would I have were I able to." He let a little sigh. "I came back to London with the Prime Minister after a few lovely years on my country estate. I can tell you at this point, given all that is going on, I wish I had stayed away."

"Why didn't you?" I asked.

He stopped as we stood in the hall, waiting for the elevator. "I should think it would be obvious to you, of all people. How did Tennyson put it? Oh, yes: 'How dull it is to pause, to make an end, To rust unburnish'd, not to shine in use! As tho' to breathe were life!'" He straightened, standing tall. "There is more to life than merely surviving, or living for one's self, after all."

"Lot of that sentiment going around lately," I muttered as the elevator dinged. I stepped in and Wexford followed a step behind me.

"Have you ever dealt with this type of meta before?" Wexford asked, facing the front of the elevator as the doors shut. "Cassandra, I think you called him?"

"Kindasorta," I said, letting the wheels turn on their own. "I knew a girl—Adelaide—who was like me, a succubus. She'd absorbed one at one point." At the behest of Omega, no less, which was trying to stuff her full of powers.

"Do you know the limits of their powers?" Wexford asked. "How they operate?"

"Not really," I said with a shrug. "They can see the future somehow. Beyond that... I've got nothing."

"Knowledge is power, as they say." Wexford had his hands clasped in front of him, and he moved them to start buttoning his coat. I didn't see his motion, it was so smooth, but he reached in the coat and came back with a manila folder that he slipped behind him. It took me a moment to realize that he was holding it there because there was a security camera in the corner of the lift, and that section of his body was hidden from it by the way he stood. "One gets the feeling that one is always being watched in London. It doesn't exactly inspire me, but it is a different sort of knowledge, I suppose."

"Probably didn't get watched constantly on your country estate, huh?" I shuffled slightly and took the proffered folder, rolling it up and slipping it up my left sleeve while using his body as cover. I tried not to look too obvious about it, but I suspected I failed miserably.

"Good luck, Ms. Nealon," Wexford said as the door opened. A couple cops were waiting to get on the elevator, and Wexford slipped off between them. "May you find all the knowledge you are looking for." With a last smile, he disappeared down the hall before I could get out of the elevator, and by the time I managed to get out, he was gone.

Chapter 66

I got the hell out of New Scotland Yard as fast as I could, slipping down the first alley I came across. I parked my back against a wall, feeling the hard concrete against the back of my head as I leaned, and tried to ignore the smell of the dumpster nearby. It was worse than the smell of the one I'd been thrown in, somehow. I looked at it out of the corner of my eye as I slipped the folder out of my left sleeve, which was, not coincidentally, the sleeve on my coat that was intact.

A street light hung over my head, and the dark horizon was showing only the barest hints that it might eventually have a sun over it somewhere. I stood in the alley, catching my breath, and checked for nearby surveillance cameras. I saw none.

I paused for just a second, realizing I probably looked like I was homeless, given that part of my clothing was ripped, part of it was burned, and—oh, yeah, I still didn't have any money. Son of a bitch. I also had no place to stay, since there was not a chance in hell I was going to go back to Marjorie now that I'd gotten her son's apartment blown up with him nearly in it.

I stared at the manila envelope in my hands and channeled all that rage, that nearly-make-me-cry rage that I had been bottling up since I'd tried to shake Webster awake and failed, and I poured it all into thinking about Philip.

Then I opened the folder and saw his face in a photo, looking back out at me.

MINISTRY OF DEFENSE was stamped all over the damned thing. With a C instead of an S in defense. It took me about two seconds, even given how exhausted I was, to realize that this was a personnel file. Philip Delsim had worked for Britain's defense ministry until he'd been canned about five years ago for—according to this—stealing secrets and selling them to an unknown source. They had a little of the evidence, pictures of him with a lady who didn't look too unlike a British nanny.

"Son of a bitch." Her name was Eleanor Madigan, and I knew her.

I scrambled and pulled my phone out of my coat pocket, fumbling to dial a contact I'd put into the damned thing just this afternoon. When I heard someone pick up on the other end of the line, I started talking before they'd even said anything. "Karthik, I need you to plug the name Philip Delsim into the Omega database."

"All right," he said, sounding a little stilted, like he'd just woken up. "Is there some reason I'm doing this at four o'clock in the morning?"

"Yeah," I said, "because he's the son of a bitch who's about to get his ass kicked by me for all this shit he's started."

Chapter 67

"Philip Delsim?" The words echoed from the speakerphone, bouncing off the concrete walls. The room smelled stale, like air that hadn't been circulated in a very, very long time. The dank of the underground setting crept in off the walls, and it almost sounded like water was dripping faintly in the distance. This far beneath the Omega building, that would hardly be surprising.

Philip Delsim stared straight ahead as Karthik spoke. He had one of Liliana's daggers right at his throat, the blood trickling down his deep brown skin and turning the collar of the purple dress shirt he was wearing nearly black.

Philip held a single finger to his lips, now using it as an aid for contemplation as he listened to Sienna Nealon's voice on the other end of the line while she fed instructions to Karthik like he was some trained lap dog. He listened, watched Karthik, and waited. And then he prompted Karthik toward the keyboard inches away, setting him to motion typing.

"Philip Delsim," Karthik said. His voice was flat, about on point for a man who might have been woken in the small hours of the morning. Philip considered it fortunate timing, since he'd been waiting to start Liliana working on Karthik. He imagined it might have been somewhat worse had Nealon called only twenty minutes later; answering the phone while he was screaming would have been quite out of the question for this lad once he'd lost twenty or thirty percent of his skin. Karthik glanced at Philip, a silent look asking permission.

Philip nodded once, glancing over the monitor quickly. "I've got a file here," Karthik said. "Ten year veteran of the Ministry of Defense," Karthik said. "Was working as a double agent with Omega, feeding us… feeding them… secrets, other things. Details of interest."

"Is there anything there about him being a Cassandra-type?" Her voice came through tinged with excitement. She thought she was a clever girl, she really did. Her breathless thrill at putting elementary pieces together was no more impressive than a full-grown adult knowing how to add one plus one, but she was foolish enough not to be aware of this.

Once again, Karthik looked to Philip for permission, which Philip gave with a nod and an arched eyebrow. This was power.

"Yes, he's a Cassandra-type…" Karthik's voice trailed off as Philip reached out to a section of the text with a single finger, and when Karthik's eyes met his, Philip shook his head once, a simple no that was communicated perfectly. "No family."

"So he was Omega's rat inside the British government," her voice came through. "Now he's mad at both of them for some reason." The dull sheen of frustration clipped her words even with that dreadful American accent. "Any idea why?"

Philip shook his head once. "The file doesn't say," Karthik spoke in proxy for him.

"Any last known addresses?" Sienna asked, voice crackling through the phone.

Karthik waited just a second while Philip nodded and pointed straight to the only address on the page. "There is one." He gave it, slowly, repeating it back to her twice to make sure she had it. All the while, Philip listened with a sweet sense of satisfaction. Either this would end her—this bullheaded, charge-into-everything-shoulder-first bitch—or it'd put her out of the way long enough for him to do the last thing that needed to be done. He could feel the probabilities shifting, knew the trend and the direction they were heading. It might not be long now, if he was lucky. He glanced at Karthik. And if his current hostage was indeed the right one.

"Thanks, Karthik," she said, and her enthusiasm was amusing in its supreme idiocy. "I'll check it out." She hung up without a word of farewell.

"The quintessential rude American," Philip opined once he was certain that the line was dead. He took the phone out of Karthik's outstretched hand and nodded to Liliana, who tugged at his neck, pulling him out of the chair upon which he sat. "That should keep her busy for a bit." He smiled at Karthik. "And now you should be busy for a bit as well, I think."

"I have nothing against you," Karthik said, the knife against his throat. Philip stared at the welling blood, the crimson seeping into his collar. "I have done nothing to you."

"Of course not," Philip said, standing. "And if it was just you and me, there would no reason to do what I'm about to have done to you." He planted a firm hand on Karthik's shoulder. "But it's not just you and me, you see…"

He let his eyes drift over to Janus, where he sat bolted to a chair, secured with actual bolts, with chains, hand and foot bound the metal legs. "It's you, Janus, and I," Philip said. "And Janus… he just does not wish to yield." He turned to look back at Karthik. "So I suppose it's down to you to convince him to." He waved faintly at Liliana. "She'll do her best to persuade you, with blade and pain."

"But I did what you wanted," Karthik said, in faint disbelief. "I did what you wanted!" Liliana pulled him, dragged him toward the center of the room.

"Indeed you did," Philip said mildly. "But you don't actually have what I truly want." He pointed at Janus. "He does. So I suppose now we'll see if he favors you more than he values himself." Philip did not blink, the words sounding harsh even to his ears. "Because so far I've yet to break him enough to guarantee that he'll give me what I want."

Chapter 68

When I hung up with Karthik, I realized I had no frigging idea where the address he'd given me was. I had no money with which to pay for a cab, or a map, and so I did the next best thing I could.

I went into a corner store and asked.

The guy behind the counter looked at me from beneath dark eyebrows. He looked Russian maybe, or eastern European, and when he opened his mouth he confirmed it for me. I had a hell of a time understanding what he was saying, and he gestured emphatically with his hands as he spoke, telling me to go this way two streets, that way for four blocks—

The gist was that I wasn't far away.

I thanked him and headed in roughly the direction he'd faced me. I walked quickly, trying not to attract attention to myself. Not sure how well that worked, since I was missing my right sleeve all the way to the elbow. My clothes were shredded, and I had a dozen or more holes in my coat. Not the small kind, either.

I wandered for about forty-five minutes before I got frustrated. I pictured London in my head. I couldn't quite get it.

So I went down a back alley, made sure it was clear, and went supersonic as I shot into the sky.

After I did it, I realized it probably wasn't the best idea to let off a sonic boom just before I tried to get high enough into the air to see the whole city, but whatever. I'd been playing by the rules as laid out before me for two whole years. I'd dealt with a string of assholes like Ryan Halstead, U.S. Ass-ador, except they'd all had titles like "The Distinguished Gentleman from California" and "the Senior Senator from New York."

I'd eaten enough of their shit to have a bellyful.

It was all grating on my nerves now, the sum and total of it, set to a boil by sitting in that office across from Mary Marshwin, watching her get the edict dumped down on her from above. That was me, in my own seat. Not nearly as bad, but the vampires from Washington wanted to tell me what to do every day of my life, and I had to listen.

For the job.

For the last couple years, I'd been playing softball with the kids I'd been up against. I ran into a real meta once every three months, and they were almost all kids. Almost all. Kids waking up to their power and pushing the limits. Society's limits. The limits of decency, in some cases. And I was the one who was there to push back.

But without even realizing it, I'd hit limits of my own. Limits to my patience. Surprisingly, they were farther than I would have guessed them to be. I didn't even care at this point that I'd originally entered government service because I'd been blackmailed into doing it; I had a job to do, and it was an important one. I'd bought in.

When they said, "Do it this way," I'd said yes.

When they said, "Don't kill anyone," I'd said yes.

When they said, "Go here, do this, don't tell anyone, now go here—"

You get the point.

Somewhere along the way I'd become a slave to the job, to the voices up the chain who told me what to do. The person I'd been before wouldn't have eaten a spoonful of what they fed me on a daily basis, let alone the acres of it I'd ingested since the war ended.

But everybody has limits.

And now I'd reached mine.

I visualized London in my head, saw the river with the wavy line run through it like I'd seen on an internet map ages ago, and again in the tourist shop just a few minutes earlier. I pulled out my phone and looked at the cracked screen. I wondered if...

It still said "Vodafone UK" in the upper right hand corner, even this far up. Three bars.

I typed the address into the search bar of the web browser, and it took about a minute before it came back to me with a map. I clicked the directions button and it laid it out. Two point one miles away.

I let myself drift downward, easing toward the dot on the map that indicated where I was supposed to go. The map compensated, then compensated again, alternating the route as I drifted in a straight line, as the crow flies, straight toward my target.

It was time to stop letting other people put limits on me. If the UK government didn't want me around, that was fine. I'd be on my merry way.

But I'd be damned if I was going to leave town before I solved their problem for them.

Because there was a limit to how much crap I'd put up with from Philip Delsim, too, and he'd gone long, long past it even before he'd put the first guy I'd been interested in for a long while into the hospital.

Chapter 69

The screams were exquisite, the sound and volume filling the stone room, seeping into the walls. Philip wondered, not for the first time, if a telepath came into a room where something like this torture had occurred, would they be able to feel it later? Would there be residue of the emotional horrors left behind for others to witness? Could the mind detect the echoes of screams and pain?

He stood idly by while Liliana did her work on Karthik. It was definitely her usual standard of care, and Philip paid close attention for the first ten minutes or so.

Then his attention shifted to Janus at his right, as he reached out with his powers and felt the probabilities shift.

Since this endeavor had begun, he'd been reading Janus at every opportunity, watching his resolve. It was an easy thing for a Cassandra-type; you merely looked into their future. The future was a fluid thing, with multiple possibilities in many cases. As the event you were watching drew closer in the present time, the probabilities often shifted, something he could both see and feel, a sort of overlay he had never been able to explain to anyone.

Except Clarice, of course.

He had watched Janus as the old man endured torture of his own. He had watched Janus and the probabilities as he went through an endless cavalcade of former Omega operatives whom Janus had worked with, cared for. He never once made mention of what he was looking for from the old man, not even a whisper.

Because he didn't need to.

All he had to do was focus on the old man and run the scenario in his brain.

If we go to the Highshire Bank and attempt transfer of all of Omega's accounts, what will he do?

The answer had come back in pieces, fragmented, as it always did when there were so many probabilities in play. For a while, the leading contender was for Janus to inform the manager through body language or a passed message that he was a captive, and the silent alarm was pressed. No trouble for Philip, really, being able to read the cracks in the bank's defenses and escape safely, but that wasn't exactly the point, was it?

But now, in this very moment, the probabilities were shifting. They were dropping lower as Philip watched the event in question. Now he was docilely going along, doing as he was asked, making the transfer.

And Philip could not help himself from smiling as the sound of screams across the room intensified and the probabilities all hit zero.

This was it.

Janus had broken.

This was the moment he had been waiting for.

Chapter 70

I entered the building via the back alley. I did it quietly, breaking the lock and slipping in. It was an apartment building, with shoddy carpeting that looked like someone had tracked oil in on muddy shoes and just danced a conga all around the hallway. The place smelled, too, like someone had come in and peed into every electrical socket. You know, to hide it in the walls.

I wondered why you would even lock the back door to a place like this, and I snaked my way through the hallways in quasi-stealth mode. What did that look like? Basically, walking normally. Trying to hide and darting from corner to corner is a dead giveaway in an urban environment. Pretty suspicious.

So instead I roamed the hall of the building looking like a homeless person, shuffling in my torn and burned clothing. I heard movement ahead, around a corner, and I knew there was nowhere to hide so I just kept walking. Two guys in hard hats with construction vests that glowed with fluorescence passed in the hallway ahead.

I looked around, wondering if this place was slated for demolition or something. It wasn't quite to the level of a condemned building, but it wasn't too many degrees off, either.

I found a staircase and ascended, the wooden steps squeaking underfoot as I rose. I thought about flying, but if there's one thing that looks even more suspicious than a person darting about, it's a girl levitating. The way people look at you, you'd swear they'd never seen anyone defy gravity before. Which means they should probably watch more Idina Menzel musicals.

I climbed in a hurry, darting up the stairs and coming out on the second floor. This hallway was no better than the last, just a long, narrow corridor with piss-poor lighting. It still smelled, and the air barely stirred as the door closed behind me. It had an eerie feel to it, but nothing exactly screamed trap at me. It wasn't like Admiral Ackbar burst out of a nearby door to shout or anything.

Okay, maybe I was getting just a bit of a trap vibe.

It could have just been the building, though, or the upkeep of the place. It was certainly rough around the edges, which may have explained the construction guys. I didn't hear any pounding or sawing, though, which made me wonder what the hell was going on. Maybe one of the downstairs residents was carrying on a renovation.

I arrived at the door in question and stood outside it, looking at it warily. It looked a little weathered but not battered, like it had aged about as well as the rest of the building. This was it. The last known address of Philip Delsim.

And I knew as I stared at it that there was no damned way I was going in that front door.

The guy had a fricking bomb maker on his team. He had to know that the police could eventually get a lead on him and tumble to his last known address. What would be their next logical step?

Kicking in his door.

I went to the side, to the next door in hallway. I knocked politely and it opened without effort, squeaking on its hinges as it cracked a couple inches.

I wasn't a vampire, so I considered that an invitation to come inside.

I swept in and closed the door behind me, making my way through a kitchen that had been stripped of all appliances, to the wall bordering Philip's old apartment. I put my head against the wall and listened, just listened, waiting to hear anything on the other side.

Not a damned noise.

So I placed my hand on the wall and pushed. Plaster cracked under my fingers and palm, and I gently applied pressure until it shattered and my hand passed through. Once it had, I hooked my arm inside the drywall and pulled, ripping it open. I grabbed each side and made myself a little entrance, opening the wall like a surgeon until the studs were exposed and I could see Philip's wall on the other side.

Then I cracked three of the studs and removed them before smashing very delicately through Philip's wall.

I made just enough of an entrance to pass through without wasting my time, leaving a gaping hole big enough to drive a truck through. I found myself in a kitchen that didn't smell nearly as bad as the one I'd just been in. The smell of piss had faded, replaced by that scent of stale, undisturbed air that builds up in places where no human has trod for some time.

The walls were stark, with empty brown stains where things had obviously hung once upon a time. There were no curtains, and the light of the rising sun lit the whole place with an orange hue. I tried to wipe the drywall dust off my shoulders but failed. I quit bothering after a moment, resigning myself to the fact that my construction dandruff was just the icing on my homeless girl cake.

I stepped out into the main room and stopped, blinking, my jaw probably somewhere down around my knees from the sight of what was waiting.

Six big black barrels waited in the apartment's entry, all arranged around a central device that looked like a couple of foot lockers stacked one on top of the other. There were wires crossing the whole damned thing, and one leading to the doorknob that was tight with tension. Even for an amateur like me, what I was looking at was clear.

It was a bomb.

One big enough to destroy the whole damned building.

Chapter 71

"You'll need to look the part," Philip said, watching Janus as the old man buttoned his own shirt with shaking hands. "You will do exactly as I say, in the moment I say it." The old man nodded fervently, the lines of his face deeper than they had been only the day before. The shadows in the room lay long upon him, and his straw-thin grey hair hung limply over his forehead.

"How long will you be gone?" Liliana asked, her knives at rest and neatly sheathed. She did not look like she cared, but he could see the look in her eyes, the hungry one. This was what they had been waiting for, what he had promised her when he'd recruited her to his plan.

"A couple of hours," Philip answered, not bothering to look into the probabilities for himself. They always shifted on trips such as these, and he preferred to keep the focus where it needed to be. The more probabilities he examined, the more convoluted things became in his head. The farther forward one looked, the easier it was to get overwhelmed, to watch the courses branch out on an ever-widening delta—

It hurt his head to even consider it. Clarice had gone farther in that realm than he, had told him one night with shaking hands of her own that she had seen it, had seen—

Philip felt his chest grow tight and put the memory aside. He forced the smile back to his face, remembering that the triumph was not far now. All he needed to do was focus on the near term, to keep a weather eye out for the close-at-hand probabilities. That would keep him safe, that and the knowledge and preparation with which he had approached the entire matter.

"Are you ready?" he asked Janus, who stood still, shuddering, while Liliana put a tweed jacket over his shoulders with surprising delicacy. The old man gave only the smallest hint of a nod. "Good," Philip said. "Then let's begin."

Chapter 72

I'd nicked a card off Mary Marshwin's desk, to use a word out of the British parlance. It had her number on it, and as I hurried my happy ass out the gaping hole in Philip Delsim's booby-trapped flat's wall, I dialed like mad. When she answered, I didn't even let her get halfway through her greeting before I cut her off. "It's Sienna. I tracked Philip Delsim back to his last known address and there's a big-ass bomb here."

Her Scottish accent came over the phone as comically exaggerated. "Who is this?"

"Sienna Nealon," I said.

"Och, dear Lord," she said. "You found what?"

"A big damned bomb." I read off the address and could hear her scrawling on a paper, repeating everything under her breath as I spoke it. "It's huge. Wired to the front door of the flat and big enough to at least level the building, if not a whole city block."

"How did you find this place of his?" Marshwin asked. "How do you know so much about this?"

"We don't have time to discuss it," I said tightly. "A Cassandra like him can see the future, at least partially, and that means I need to figure out how to catch him. I need to come at him from the blind side."

"None of that makes any sense," she said on the other end of the line. "What the bloody hell is a Cassandra?"

"Never mind," I said. "Just deal with the bomb."

"Bastard just keeps widening his swath, doesn't he?" I wouldn't have wanted to be the one she was talking about, the curse was so deeply implied in her tone.

"He's going to be widening a damned crater if anyone goes through that front door," I said. "Have them come in through the adjoining apartment. I'll leave the door cracked." I adjusted it just so as I entered the smelly hallway, wrinkling my nose as I did so.

"Where will you be?" she asked.

"Trying to find his blind side," I said, hurrying back toward the stairwell, my footsteps echoing down the empty hall. "I wouldn't want to cause you any problems, after all."

"A giant bomb in the middle of my city," she said, "no, that's no problem at all." She hung up on me before I could properly protest that it wasn't me who built the damned thing.

Philip had covered his ass again. He just kept doing that, I reflected as I thumped down the stairs. For every action I made, he seemed to have a plan in advance. Come at him at Angus Waterman's house, he booby-traps the place and lets me blow my own leg off. Chase him after the gallery robbery, he and his Wonderfriends ambush me, toss me in a dumpster and leave me to die with a slit throat and more perforations than a serving of Swiss *queso*. I attack his headquarters, he falls back and tosses me one of his dogs without so much as a hint of remorse. Then he chucks some poor bastard off a rail platform so he can escape with his injured hostage.

I crinkled my nose at that one. He must have really wanted Janus to suffer if he was willing to drag him along like that. Clearly he didn't care all that much about human life, given how quickly he'd dispatched the poor guy in the wheelchair, but to go to the inconvenience of making his escape with Janus in tow rather than just cutting his throat to the bone and being done with it? That was a serious level of loathing.

Where did it come from?

I hit the street and emerged in the middle of a construction area as I came out the front door. A bunch of guys in hard hats were working around me, and I felt the steady, thrumming vibration of a jackhammer going off to my left. The sidewalk was completely covered with tarps and scaffolding, and in addition to the work they were doing on the ground, they were also redoing the facade of the building. At least, for now they were. Once the bomb squad got here, they'd be on a layoff.

I stood there in the middle of the sidewalk, not really caring about the hard hat regulations in Greater London, letting the vibrations seep in while I thought. I'd just nearly walked into a trap, a bomb big enough to maybe even kill me. Probably. No coming back from that. If I'd been just a hair or two more enraged and less cautious, I'd have flown in there at full speed for sure. A couple days of getting bushwhacked repeatedly had made me exercise more caution than was the norm.

Still, this whole thing, this whole trap, it had a different feel to it. And with the thrum of the jackhammer vibration, it occurred to me what it was.

I'd very nearly just been walked into it. By someone I trusted.

Like someone had turned the jackhammer loose on the back of my head to shake loose a stubbornly-wedged thought, it occurred to me why Karthik had sounded so stilted over the phone. I'd thought it had been because he had been sleeping, but he wasn't sleeping at all—

I cursed myself for an idiot. After all, where would someone who had a mad-on for Omega, who hated Omega, where would they go if they lost their own headquarters...?

I felt a surge of fury, the burning feeling of long-accumulating anger and desire for sweet, sweet revenge. I glanced around the construction site around me, and my eyes fell on a pile of rebar, stacked neatly along one of the walls in lengths almost four feet long.

I made my way over to the pile and grabbed a piece, folding it neatly until it broke in two, leaving me with one for each hand. I swung them through the air, flurrying off a quick practice round in the way I used to use my eskrima sticks. They cut through the air with purpose, crisp as if I had been practicing for the last two years instead of letting everything slide, letting my skills get slack while the world came down around me.

It was time to get back to basics.

I flew into the sky, blithely ignoring the sonic boom that cracked through the air.

Chapter 73

Philip stood with Janus at the iron gate of the Highshire Bank when opening time rolled around. They were there a few minutes early, owing to Philip's planning more than anything. Seeing the future was quite helpful when it came to predicting the best traffic route.

As the guard rolled back the gate and opened the path into the lobby, Philip stood as calm as he could manage, just behind Janus. The old man stood with his head down, and Philip kept a close watch on his immediate future. He only bothered watching the next twenty minutes or so, because that was all that concerned him. Any longer than that and he wouldn't be able to carry on a conversation or keep an eye on events around him, because of the immersive nature of the future. It was always in motion, and it was easy to walk down a street and try to take in the entire future of a person you passed.

Sometimes that was helpful, especially when it a lovely lass who might have a predisposition to immediate intimacy. Sometimes it was less helpful, such as when it showed you a vision of the horrific, soul-rending deeds that a person was off to commit. That had always bothered Clarice more than it bothered Philip, though. He'd long since learned certain actions helped abate any emotion that were dredged up by those sort of glimpses; for example, the first time he'd glimpsed the future of a pedophile on the street, he'd ambushed the man in a nearby alley and crippled him for life.

Clarice had never crossed such a line; he could read it in her future as surely as she had read what he would do in his own.

The gate clanking open cued Philip to poke Janus slightly in the shoulder, stirring the old man into motion. He walked slump-shouldered, his steps shuffling. Truly, he did look like an old man now. Philip had thought he had been worn before, but now he was a disastrous mess, a senior citizen walking with only the purpose that had been given to him by fear.

The bank was a small one, a prized front for less legitimate elements of society because of their failure to ask pertinent questions. Their reputation was well known in certain circles and probably whispered about in the realm of law enforcement. As yet, through either bribery or luck, the long arm of the law had not reached out for them at all.

After today, Philip did not care whether the law tap-danced on their bloody genitals with a pair of steel-soled shoes.

"Mr. Janus." A man in a suit stood in the middle of the bank's sumptuous lobby. For a small location, it was certainly posh: a two-story water feature fell over a stone inscription of the bank's logo, with a private banking section upstairs behind white-clouded glass. "Is there something I can help you with today?" The man was an obsequious sort of bastard, inclining his upper body forward enough to appear solicitous to the needs of his client.

Janus cleared his throat, taking his time to speak. When he did, he sounded distinctly… frail. "Indeed, Mr. Glaser. I need to make a wire transfer."

"Ah, please," the helpful Mr. Glaser said, moving his head in such a way that a thinly obvious comb-over showed itself as he moved, "right this way, up to the private bank and we can accommodate that request." He smiled and stretched an arm out to indicate an elevator in a private alcove. "Who is your associate?"

"My name is Mr. Baker," Philip lied, giving Glaser a smooth smile. "I'm helping Mr. Janus iron out his affairs."

"Are you his solicitor?" Glaser asked, not missing a beat.

"His successor," Philip said as they stepped into the elevator. "I'm taking over for Mr. Janus and helping him close out his accounts."

"Ah, I see," said Glaser as the elevator door closed, locking them tightly in the box as it started to move. "How... fortunate for you."

"Indeed," Philip said, keeping his eyes on the steel doors in front of him and his mind firmly on the immediate future of Janus. "I can feel my fortunes rising even now." The elevator thrummed as it carried them upward.

Chapter 74

I crashed through the window of the Primus's office at Omega headquarters—my old office—not bothering to do much in the way of slowing down. The window shattered inward and I tilted as I came in, shooting right through the open door into the bullpen. I was pretty sure anyone who was here would be alerted to my arrival by the explosive nature of my entrance, but I was relying on surprise rather than giving a damn about sneakiness. There was no good way to sneak into this place anyway, other than maybe gently removing the glass from one of the windows and creeping in.

And maybe I just didn't have the patience for that.

I didn't hear anything, so I shot back into the Primus's office and looked straight at the bookshelf. It was closed, the copy of *Hard Times* back in its place, so I pulled it and let the door open.

Then I drifted into the stairwell and hovered in place, looking down.

Nothing.

I could hear motion in the downstairs room, and I let myself drift slowly toward the concrete floor, threading my way through the staircase without touching anything. I made no noise, disturbing nothing but the air as I passed. I wondered if it was possible that my entry through the office window had gone unheard; this was several stories down, after all, and the bookshelf had been closed. It was possible all the distance and heavy insulation had kept them from hearing my approach, especially since now I was virtually silent.

I kept living in that hope until I reached the bottom of the stairs and peeked into the room to see Karthik chained to a chair, his eyes wide and staring straight at me in the entry.

He was missing—by a conservative estimate—about half of his skin.

I didn't rush in to go to him, because that's what unthinking fools do. While I had certainly played the part of an unthinking fool a few times in my life, in this case I was trying not to get hit by a sidewinder again.

And there were definitely a couple of them in play.

I kept my position, eyes barely peeking around the door's frame, locked on Karthik. His moved, subtly, to my right, telling me exactly where my enemy was waiting.

Thanks, Karthik.

I pulled Wolfe to the forefront of my mind, knowing that if knife-lady was in there, I'd need his assistance more than anything. I thought about bringing Eve to the party, with her nets of light, and immediately dismissed the thought.

Liliana Negrescu was going to try to kill me. She was unlimited in her viciousness, cold in her approach, and skilled by her training.

I was behind in my training, only now becoming frosty in my approach again, and my viciousness had been constrained by my government job's limitations for the last couple years.

One of those could go by the wayside immediately, and I'll leave it up to you to figure out which I threw out the window before I came roaring into that room.

I smashed through the concrete wall, leading with my shoulder. I felt it break and felt Wolfe's power stitch it back together even as I collided with something on the other side, knocking them down as I entered. I landed and staggered, the injuries from my surprise entry taking a few seconds to heal. I turned, placing myself between Liliana and Karthik.

"Whaddup, bitch?" I asked as I stood there, watching her pick herself up from beneath a pile of shattered concrete. Her dark hair had turned grey-white with the powder and dust from the busted wall, and her skin looked as white as mine had been when I'd done that damned TV interview with Gail Roth. Which I still regretted to this day.

Liliana rose, her knives still gripped tightly in her hands. She hadn't lost them in my attack, which was both surprising and annoying. I'd broken through a concrete wall and hit her; you'd think that would have been enough to dislodge them, but no.

I gripped my makeshift eskrima sticks tightly in my hands, felt the ridges of the rebar against my palms, a little sweat and a little dust forming a layer of grit between me and my weapons. I came at her hard.

My first strike hit her wrist, but it didn't break, surprisingly. It was a glancing blow that she pulled away from, letting out a little cry of pain. I expected the knife to go flying, but to her credit, she still held on. She danced back, out of my range, and I followed, pursuing doggedly as she moved toward the door.

She stumbled on the wreckage of the concrete I'd left as I entered, and I swooped in on her. My speed was superior, and I tapped her in the ribs with enough force to hear them breaking from where I stood. She tried to riposte, but the range advantage was all one side, and she grunted in pain from the movement. This time I pulled back, leaving her to favor her side as she stood, slightly hunched, protecting the ribs I'd just broken.

"You're different," she said in a cold voice, keeping her distance from me, blades extended. The fact she hadn't dropped one yet was incredibly impressive, really. Most people can't hang on to something small like a knife through searing pain like she had to be experiencing. "You're fighting differently."

"Before I was playing by rules I didn't believe in," I said, meeting her eyes with my own. Before I might have looked away, but now I was anchored on them. I didn't need to watch her body; her eyes told me everything I needed to know about her. They were the eyes of a predator.

Like mine.

"I know something of this myself," she said, still hunched to one side. She watched me, carefully, and I knew she was going to make her move a second before she did it.

But I never could have predicted the move she made.

She jumped straight up as I settled into a defensive stance. I expected her to come at me, to go left or right and blindside me, trying to catch me with speed—even though we'd established I had her overmatched in that department.

Instead she went vertical.

And clung to the ceiling.

"Son of a…" I murmured as she began to skitter across the concrete ceiling like a spider. Now it made sense why she hadn't let go of the knives. I'd seen her kind before in the form of a guy named Henderschott, a man whose skin could anchor itself to any surface. In his case, he used it to attach steel plates to his body with his power, keeping them effectively welded to his flesh as protection.

Liliana Negrescu apparently used them to keep her hands on her knives at all times and to scramble across the ceiling like an insect.

"This is why I need a gun," I muttered as she shot to my left, skittering out of my reach while I stood there, still a little stunned by the turn of events.

She bounded down to a wall and launched off at me. If she'd been smart and kept her distance, I probably couldn't have caught her. She could have gone for the door, or maybe outsmarted me long enough to at least draw me away from Karthik. Hold him hostage, prey on whatever milk of human kindness I possessed. (I know, hah, right?) Instead, she'd tried to get what she thought was a better angle of attack and thrown herself at me with wild abandon.

I whipped one of my rebar sticks around and greeted her jaw mid-flight. The breaking noise included the sound of shattering teeth, and the force of it altered her course into another wall.

She managed to catch herself before she slid down it, slapping a hand against the concrete and dragging herself up. It was a feat of strength, agility and dexterity, and she held herself upright even with a broken jaw that had been split halfway up her cheek. That'd leave a Joker scar for sure.

I started to ask her, "Why so serious?" but she started climbing the wall again. She still clutched her knives in her hands, darting over the computer servers that lined the left-hand wall. Not one to sit complacently while someone who had severely pissed me off tried to escape, I followed, ramming my eskrima stick up into her haunches and eliciting a scream. She kept moving, but it delayed her flight by a half a second as I sunk a piece of iron two inches into her buttock. She clenched the muscle and tried to tear it out of my hand.

It didn't go so well for her, and she screamed again as the metal withdrew from her flesh. She shot back up to the ceiling, but she had a distinct hobble to her movement from where I'd taken that leg out of action. I watched it sag behind her as she hung five feet above me.

"I'd be tempted to do to you what Philip does to me," I said, staring at her dark eyes from where she hung, upside down, on the ceiling, "taunt you and taunt you about how you can't win, about how I'll beat you at every turn, but we both know that'd be false bravado. You're damned good. You're clever, you're fast, and that whole Jessica Drew thing you've got going on here—mad props on hiding it for so long." I kept my eskrima up, ready for what she might try. "But I think we both know that the odds are running long against you here. You're injured, and the more this drags on, the more likely you are to bleed out, giving me the win." I looked at her over the rebar eskrima. "If you give up now, you can go to jail. I don't know how badly you want to die for Philip's scheme, but I'm hoping there's some reason left in you. If not, then I think we both know it's a battle to the death."

"It was always…" she said, rattling a little as she spoke, "… a battle to the death. That's what… life is."

"That's kind of dour, even for me," I said. "But have it your way—"

She launched at me with almost no warning. My sticks were positioned defensively, not in a great place for hard striking power. I got a little momentum out and tapped her hard enough to break a shoulder—

But not hard enough to stop her from crashing into me with all her body weight.

I felt one of her blades sink into my guts as she landed atop me. At this close a range, my eskrimas were next to useless. She didn't exactly have me pinned, but she had me down. I didn't doubt that I'd be able to overpower her, but the stab of agony in my stomach slowed my reaction.

Unfortunately, she used that time to perforate my stomach with her knife about a half a dozen more times. I heard the blade clacking against the hard concrete floor as she drove it into me over and over.

I stared, stunned, into her black eyes. I could see the weariness, the pain. I could feel the blood running out of her and onto me, mixing with the volumes of my own that were pouring out.

"Now how do you favor your odds?" she said with a strange croak.

The pain in my stomach was fierce, my innards reduced to a fine puree by her swift knife work. I wanted to say something, anything, but she'd diced the bottom of my lungs in the process.

Wolfe, I called out in my head, but he was already there.

She stared at my eyes, triumphant, and I kept them glassy and drifting, watching her while pretending I wasn't, just for a moment—

Just long enough for my abdominal muscles to grow back while she wasn't looking.

I stared into her eyes and brought mine into focus, letting the strength pull through me. I blotted out the pain, let the worry fade as the adrenaline shot through me just long enough to tense every muscle in my stomach, my back and my neck.

And I brought my head forward like a battering ram against a castle gate.

My forehead hit her nose and cheeks with force beyond the comprehension of most people. It was like a Maserati cruising two hundred miles an hour down a freeway and then channeling all its force into a two-inch square of space—the point of my forehead—and smashing into the delicate cartilage structures of her nose and beyond.

She flew, of course.

This time when she hit the wall, she didn't cling to it. Bones broke, sinews tore, flesh was rent asunder by her skeleton ripping through her body from the force.

Oh, and her head dissolved into a mist of blood and bone, but that mostly happened before she hit the wall.

When the sack of butchered meat that had been Liliana Negrescu sagged to the concrete floor, it was barely recognizable as human. It made a couple of wet sucking sounds and twitched, like a jello in a pan that someone had tapped, for about ten seconds before it went totally still.

"I like my odds just fine, thank you," I said as I felt the last threads of my wounded flesh pull back together. "You Stalinist bitch."

Chapter 75

"Where would you like the transfer to go?" Mr. Glaser asked.

The private bank smelled like luxury. Every seat was made of wood and covered with expensive leather. Glaser's desk was a mahogany of some sort, a rich, dark wood that perfectly suited his well-appointed office.

Philip sat next to Janus, the cup of tea that Glaser's secretary had brought him cooling in front of him. He reached into his jacket and pulled out a thin slip of paper. "There's a bank in Liechtenstein that I have in mind." He pointed to the numbers. "Here's the account."

Glaser gave him a look of some regret. "Is there any way we can persuade you to keep it with us?"

Philip gave him a polite smile. "I think you know as well as I do that with the nature of banking regulations in the UK, as well as the changing nature of our relationship with the British government—" at this Glaser's smile thinned; he knew at least a little about Omega's state, then, "—it's best if we make a clean break and divest our interests from the country."

"As you well know," Glaser said, "I do have to report this to the authorities. This size of transfer—"

"Of course," Philip said. "But you'll wait until after the transfer is completed, I trust?"

"You'll have until end of business today, of course," Glaser said. "If Westminster isn't paying attention, perhaps they won't notice until tomorrow, as much as they have to sift through."

"I'm sure they'll send a notice of concern to the bank in Liechtenstein," Philip said.

"Which said bank will certainly ignore," Mr. Glaser added with a smile of his own. "This should only take a few minutes to complete the transfer."

"Thank you," Philip said and picked up his cup and saucer. He gave the tea a gentle stir with the little spoon, keeping an eye on the probabilities directly in front of him. Glaser was being truthful, and the only thing in his future of interest was a cup of tea for himself in the next half hour or so. He wouldn't be talking to the authorities any sooner; naturally he had a reputation of his own to uphold. Janus still sat in utter silence, head bowed;, if he was listening to what was transpiring around him, he gave no sign of it.

Both futures were still absolutely clear, allowing Philip to settle back in his seat, take his first sip of tea, and admire the flavors as he swished them about in his mouth before swallowing.

Chapter 76

I pulled myself up a few seconds later, dragging to my feet. Most of the pain was gone, but I dug Liliana's last knife out of my belly to let the wound heal, barely noticing it as it fell to the ground with a clatter. I'd cast my rebar weapons aside.

The smell of blood was thick, and not just from what Liliana and I had left behind. There was a big damned puddle of it on the floor where I'd fallen, and I'd made a shape a little like a snow angel in it as I'd gotten up. No halo, of course.

"My God," Karthik said around the gag that was in his mouth. I'd kinda forgotten he was here during most of the fight. Facing off with a crazed spider monkey will do that for you, I suppose. "You killed her. With... with..."

"When you fight as much as I have, you make a weapon out of whatever's handy." I spat blood on the floor. "Like you've never seen me kill anyone before." I slouched over to him, breaking his handcuffs by twisting them until the metal fractured from the stress.

"I was surprised you didn't kill me yesterday," he said. "Time was, you would have struck first, smashed through my ambush and annihilated me in a matter of seconds, only checking to see who you'd killed after the fact." He rubbed his wrists while I snapped the chain around his ankles. "I was beginning to worry you'd lost your edge."

"Lucky for you I found it again," I said. I didn't help him up, because with so much of his muscle and bone exposed to the air, I was pretty sure standing would not be a good thing for him. "Where's Philip?"

"He took Janus with him," Karthik said, rubbing the spots on his wrist where the handcuffs had bitten through the flesh. Liliana had not been gentle to him in any way. "I don't know where they went, but from what I could hear over my own screaming, this was part of some plan of theirs."

That was not good. "Their plans have not typically ended in anything but pain and agony for everyone who's not them," I said, tapping my head. "I take it he was holding the proverbial knife to your throat when we talked earlier?"

"She was, yes," he said, bringing up a hand to check on his own neck with a touch. I grimaced because he found exposed veins and tissue waiting for him there. As a meta, he'd heal, but it would hurt a lot in the process. His fingers came away bloody, but only drabs of it, not torrents. Fortunately for him. "He was prompting me on what to tell you."

"He wanted me sent to his last-known address," I said, glancing over at the computer that Karthik had used the day before to access the Omega database. "There was a big-ass bomb waiting. Would have killed me, I think." I blinked and thought that over. "He doesn't care about saving me for last anymore, even though there are others in Omega he hasn't killed yet." I stopped speaking, trying to figure out why the hell that would be. "What did he leave off?"

Karthik stared at me through dull eyes that were glassy with pain that was just starting to catch up with him. "He had family in the file."

"Leverage," I said. "A weak point for him."

"No," Karthik said, shaking his head and causing a little blood to dribble down out of his neck. I grimaced in disgust. "He had a sister, but she's dead."

I stared straight at him, feeling a tingle run over my scalp. "How did she die?"

"The file didn't say exactly," Karthik said, his words slowing out of either caution or hesitation. "But it did have one thing written on it—an Omega project tag that gave a pretty good hint about her fate."

"What did it say?" I asked, waiting expectantly, like this would be the answer to the questions I'd been asking since I'd first run across Philip, pondering his mysterious motives.

"Only one word," Karthik said, staring back at me, his face going slack. "*Andromeda.*"

Chapter 77

"… and that concludes the transfer," Mr. Glaser said with as happy a look on his face as he could probably muster after watching almost half a billion pounds in deposits disappear out of the back door of his bank. "Is there anything else I can get for you, Mr. Janus?"

"Hm?" Janus looked as though he'd just been awakened. Probably had, Philip reflected; the poor sod had had a few very traumatic days, and they hadn't included much in the way of sleep.

Which was how Philip had planned it, of course.

"No, I require nothing else," Janus said in that peculiar, old-world accent of his. "Thank you, Mr. Glaser."

Nothing he said so much as hinted at a negative probability in Philip's analysis of his near future. Philip drained the last of his cup of tea—just perfect in the amount of milk and sugar—and set it back on Mr. Glaser's desk before standing and placing a hand on Janus's shoulder. The good son, giving his father an arm to stand up with. "Come on then. Let's go conclude our other business." Not even a subtle movement in the probabilities from Janus. He simply stood and shuffled out of Glaser's office, utterly resigned to his fate.

Chapter 78

"She left her phone," I said, staring at the black cell phone— mobile phone, over here—sitting on the desk next to the computer terminal. I crossed over to it and thumbed it on, and the first thing my eyes alighted on when the screen came up was a GPS tracking app.

"No way," I muttered. "No chance." No one could be this arrogant, could they?

I tapped it with a thumb and it came up with a map. I held my breath while it loaded, and it came up with a flashing indicator that said, "NO SIGNAL."

Without even a backward glance toward Karthik, I flew out the door and up the stairs into the main room, hovering in the office and waiting for the screen to change.

The "NO SIGNAL" message disappeared, and the map reloaded, with a pin showing me exactly where I was on it, squarely in the middle of the block that I knew was Omega headquarters.

And then another pin appeared, with the name "Philip," on it, and my question about who could be this arrogant was effectively answered.

A villain who not only thought he was smarter than everybody else but could see the future. Because why bother to hide what you're doing from people whose future you know?

I guess he hadn't seen this coming.

I studied the map and started to zoom in on Philip's position when the screen lit up and the ringtone sounded, warning me that a call was coming in from—yep, you guessed it—Philip.

Chapter 79

"Dispose of Mr. Karthik," Philip said as he rode the elevator down. He hadn't waited for Liliana's greeting, of course, because why would he? There were things to be done.

"I'm afraid I can't do that, Philip," came the female voice from the other end of the line.

Philip's eyes widened, and he felt his stomach drop, his fingers clenching tighter on to the phone. How had he not seen this? He felt a swell of fear, replaced by the sickening sense of something forgotten in the scramble to get to the bank—

He'd forgotten to look into Liliana's future.

This was exactly how he'd gotten caught at the Ministry. He'd gotten complacent, sloppy. He'd failed to do the basic checks, the probability watches on the people who were closest to him. Because it was always them that screwed up, always them that got rolled up first.

This was why he preferred to work alone.

"I suppose you've deprived Ms. Negrescu of her phone," Philip said, smoothly, recovering quickly. He put a smile into his reply.

"I deprived her of her damned life," came the answer, the voice hazy with static.

Philip felt his eyebrows rise as the lift doors opened. He glanced left and right and saw a staircase leading up the left side of the room, disappearing back up into the private bank.

He checked the probabilities and saw it clear to the top. The roof seemed like the direction to go, but his mind was rabbiting so quickly, trying to track the staircase, the lobby and Janus, watching the probabilities for all three, that he felt his cheeks burn. Flustered. This was how it always went in the stressful situations. Too much to manage.

"What's the matter, Philip?" her voice came again, taunting. "Surprised?"

"More than a little," he admitted, talking without being able to filter due to his distraction. "I would have expected her to at least slow you down."

"Like good cannon fodder, right?"

Philip felt a grin from the banter as he narrowed his focus to the stairs. Clear for the next minute, and that was what he needed. He tried to reach beyond but failed, needing to have eyes on it to see the future. He glimpsed back at Janus and saw the man doing nothing but slumping and falling over for the next twenty minutes, at least. He was useless. "Well, yes. What else are they good for? It's not as though I kept them around for the dinner conversation."

"That's cold."

"It's necessary," he said, letting truth spill out. "You let others get close, it gives them the ability to be a weakness for you. You should know all about that."

"So should you," she said. "What with Clarice and all."

Philip felt his blood run cold, the fury pump anger into his face. "So you found out about her."

"Yeah," her voice came back. "You did all that spying for Omega and they went and used your sister as a sacrifice while trying to beef up Andromeda. She was the Cassandra they fed to Adelaide in order to make her more powerful. That was how she saw the future. Because of Clarice—"

"Do not say her name again," Philip said, his voice dripping with a menace he did not often employ. The fact that this tart would talk about Clarice—sweet, dear Clarice, betrayed by the damned legion of Omega, by *him*—

"Or what? You'll do a tarot card reading and tell me that the King of Cups is going to whoop my ass?"

Philip forced himself to relax at the landing, looking up. The staircase curved at the corner of the square bank building, stretching up past the private bank. From there, he'd be able to get to the roof, to start crossing from building to building and go underground. His head was spinning with the emotion, the thrills. The fear. This was beyond his ability to track, and with the frustration came a certain element of heady freedom. "You'd need to be a lot closer for me to read your future, but I will say that the little I delved into when last I left you did not leave me hopeful that you were going to live to a ripe old age."

"Oh, yeah?"

"Oh, yeah," Philip said mockingly, trotting out his American accent. "Your future is blood and pain, trial and turmoil." He hadn't gone too deep, just a surface level reading of it, afraid to see it in detail. Still, he'd looked closer at her probabilities than he did with most people, and it was a frustrating muddle of a million branched possibilities. The only thing they had in common was a shocking level of violence.

"You might know my future," she replied, "but you don't have a clue about my past beyond what you've read in someone else's report. I've fought impotent weasels like you—" he felt his jaw clench at her goad, "—people who would take whole cities hostage in order to make me curl up and surrender. I've sacrificed myself before to save people. It's what I do. I have no life so other people can live a normal one—and so I can put the fist and the foot to assholes who want to shape the future in their own perverted image."

"And here I was, betting on you not having enough self left to sacrifice," Philip replied, scraping the truth out as he concentrated on the door ahead. It led to the roof, and try as he might he could not reach past the steel. Janus was little help, ready to curl into a fetal position at the sound of a loud noise. A door slammed and Janus wobbled as if he were going to collapse. Philip grabbed him by the lapel and shoved him onward on unsteady legs. "Even I can see there's little enough left of you to quibble over. You may be a hero for now, but your fall is imminent. If you somehow manage to survive that death wish you've been carrying around, then the press will eventually latch onto your past and feed on your carcass until you do the job yourself." He grinned. "You came close enough to giving them a body in that last interview, after all. It's just a matter of time."

"Too bad you're not going to be around to see it," she said, static-y again.

"Oh, don't be a fool," Philip said. "Bluster will do you little good. I think we both know that you can't find me unless you're left a trail of breadcrumbs or unless I hide somewhere in plain sight. Well, newsflash—I don't care about you now that my business is done. You were the last bit of leverage that I kept alive to break Janus with in case all else failed. All else did not fail, and now I've got what I wanted, so you'll never see me again. And of course you'll never catch me," he said with a delirious sort of triumph, "because while you're playing checkers, barely surviving your own desire to die one day at a time, I play chess. I've set everything in motion to lead to this, drawn you along with an offensive strategy that's kept you exactly where I wanted you until I needed you elsewhere, and I've been holding you up this entire time. Well, it's endgame, now, my dear, and I have no desire to play any longer. I would wish you au revoir, but I think in this case it's better if I just—" He shoved the door open with his free hand, pushing Janus out onto the rooftop, the light rain coming down around him—

And he saw the probability of a punch coming at him just in time to duck and roll, the rooftop gravel crunching under his shoulder as he dodged out of the way and came up to see Sienna Nealon standing before him, hovering a foot off the ground, her complexion flushed red with anger and her clothing shredded and hanging loose in the breeze.

"Well, damn," was all that came to Philip's mind, and consequently, his lips, as he stood there while the rain continued to fall.

Chapter 80

"What's the matter?" I asked as he stood there, staring at me with his mouth slightly open. "Magic eight ball a little cloudy? Maybe you should ask again later."

Janus was prone, lying on his belly between us. I'd never seen the old guy in quite such a state. He looked like he was unconscious, but I hadn't seen any reason for him to be. I caught a glimpse of an eye, open beneath his glasses, which were askew on his face.

I thought about waiting for Philip to monologue, but I wrote that off as stupid before the thought even bubbled up, throwing myself at him in a kick that sent him scrambling. He dodged, avoiding my attack and giving himself room to maneuver.

"You realize you're fighting a man who can see every move you're going to make before you make it?" He smiled, smoothing the lapels of his suit. I shot a fist out at him and he dodged expertly, perfectly, only inches before I was going to make contact.

"You don't even have to be that fast when you know where it's coming from, do you?" I launched into a series of attacks from memory, running off a martial arts form of pre-sequenced moves in my head. I'd done it thousands of times, simply modifying the direction of my attacks to keep constantly on him, not bothering to vary anything but the direction it was pointed in. It gave me the brain space to just let go, flowing into a sequence as natural to me as the motions required for swimming or walking.

"I don't have to be fast, no," he said with that grin, "but I am." He moved fluidly but with a little bit of a stutter as I pushed him left, then right, driving him backward. His lack of experience was clear, but so was the fact that he knew every single attack before I launched it. "Keep going until your arms wear out and the strength fades from your legs." His grin widened. "This is what they call a stalemate."

Chapter 81

She kept coming, admirably enough, not letting up even though it would have been obvious to anyone with half a brain that her attacks were doing little to nothing. He wasn't even breathing hard, evading her every move with greatest ease, his hands tucked neatly behind him just to infuriate her more. He wasn't under too many illusions; she was fast, fast enough to see any counter attacks he might launch before he could finish them. She wasn't making any bold moves, anything that would leave her exposed. He cursed his lack of practice in these arts; were he a little more experienced, it might have been possible for him to exploit her trifling weaknesses. As it was, he would simply have to wear her out.

"I think you see the limits of your incredible speed and strength now," he said, dodging again, this time to the left. "They're all very impressive, but if you can't land a hit on your target, what's the point?"

"I guess I just can't play the game like you can," she said, nearly breathless from the speed of her maneuvers. Still, she came at him, hands and fists a blur. At least she had stopped trying to kick him; those had become clumsy to look at. "I just can't give up."

"It's a matter of patience," Philip said, the answer just slipping out as he ducked a high swing. "You watch. You learn. You analyze your opponent. You see them for who they are, underneath it all. You prepare yourself for their best attacks, and when they come at you…" he sidestepped, "…you've anticipated your way out of their path. Patience. Good things come to those who wait, after all."

"You know what else comes to those who wait?" Her breaths were coming fast. She was tiring herself out, the fool. He wondered if she would realize it before it happened, if she'd even slow down. He was watching seconds into her future, could see every move in definites, not probabilities. She was attacking with a surety that left no doubt. Her course was certain, and though he didn't care to admit it, it was taking all he had to avoid her furious assault. "Death. Excuse me if I don't wait patiently for it."

Her blue eyes were tinged with green, and the anger had them ice cold. She grunted with every exertion, and he had to concede she was pretty enough, her pale cheeks flaring red from her efforts—or possibly her emotions. Frustration was evident in the twist of her lips.

He started to reply as he made his last dodge, and his foot slipped, just slightly. He caught himself and looked back, the edge of the rooftop waiting for him. The next building over was a solid jump away, but he couldn't make it without a moment to prepare—

He narrowly dodged the next attack, only centimeters between him and her hammerblow. He escaped by instinct alone, and the follow-on attack he avoided by only a little more. This time he felt the edge before he slipped, and knew that his left foot was on the very corner of the building. A glance back left him with no doubt—

It was a four-story plunge to the street below, and he was completely out of room to maneuver.

Nowhere left to run.

Chapter 82

"Chess, not checkers," I said to Philip, his face stricken with horror at the realization that he was trapped. All his fancy dodges and maneuvers had required space to execute, room to work.

And he was fresh out.

"Checkmate, asshole," I said.

"Wait," he said, holding up his hands in front of him. "I have—"

I kicked his ass off the edge of the building so hard I was able to watch his mouth open in terror as he flew out into the middle of the street—

And got hit by a red double-decker bus going about thirty. A taste of London.

He bounced, coming to rest behind a Volkswagen down the road.

I just stared down at the middle of the street, where he'd left a pretty decent puddle of blood at the site of the impact. "I guess your Spider-sense failed to tingle on that one."

Chapter 83

Philip felt the broken bones, every last one of them. There were too many to count, too many to feel, but he had so little time. He crawled along on his good arm, on his good leg, using the cars behind him for cover. He'd stayed conscious for the bus, fortunately, seeing it just soon enough to best plan his trajectory. He couldn't read his own future, not exactly, but he could read the future of the bus and could see that if he turned his body just so that he'd be able to survive by taking the hit and landing under cover.

And he had survived. It was what he was, a survivor. He scrambled, crawling as fast as he could, toward the narrow mouth of an alley. He had to move, had to rely on that bitch's arrogance. No one could have survived the bus, after all.

No one but a man who could see the course of the future. In the kingdom of the blind, the one-eyed man was as near to a god as could be imagined, because he could see.

And he *could* see.

The alley ahead was clear, and he was only a few feet away. He reached into his breast pocket with bloody fingers and withdrew the slip of paper with the bank account number for Liechtenstein. He had to hurry. Had to flee. She couldn't catch him once he was underground, and he could disappear to—

He felt strong hands seize him by the neck and turn him around. There was a face—her face—slightly rounded, the pale cheeks still red with outrage. "You're not Sherlocking your way out of this one," she said. "You think I've never dealt with a villain before?" He felt a twist, heard a crack, and suddenly he could not feel his lower body, nor anything else.

He saw the paper slip out of his fingers before he fell to the ground. He tried to breathe, but couldn't. He tried to speak, to warn her. He'd seen her future in the moment she grabbed hold of him, had seen it all like a flood of emotion, all the probabilities feeding down to one moment in her future the way water tends toward a low point. He tried to tell her—not out of any virtue, but out of pure shock for what it entailed—try to verbalize the words, say that it was coming, the Awakening—

But it died on his lips as the paralysis of his broken neck set in. And as she stood, satisfied, looking into his eyes, the world faded to black and Philip Delsim's future—all of the numerous, wondrous probabilities of it—faded with it.

Chapter 84

I'd returned to Mary Marshwin's office voluntarily, not wanting to leave her in the lurch with a few bodies and a mess on her hands. I did it after returning Janus to Karthik. Janus had said only a perfunctory "Thank you" to me after I'd helped him up. I don't think he really knew who I was.

"Well, you've made a right mess of things, haven't you?" Marshwin said after Wexford had walked in. "Left us with a body on a street, no less—"

"A tragic suicide, if you were of a mind to explain it," I said. I had carefully descended in a nearby alley before I'd killed Philip, so it wasn't like anyone had seen me flying to or from the area.

Marshwin's arms were folded, and her face was unmistakably grave. "I suppose you think we can just clean it up that way?"

"You can clean it up however you want," I said, folding my own arms. "It's your country and your mess. I was just suggesting that if you wanted to do it with a nice, neat little bow—"

"'A nice, neat little bow'?" Marshwin asked, working her jaw open and closed after she finished speaking. She rummaged on her desk and brought out a newspaper, throwing it down in front of me. "Do you really think that's possible now?"

There was a picture of me flying into the sky on the front page. "An American Metahuman in London," was the headline. Kinda cliché, I thought. They had a blurry inset of a close-up of my face; it did look like me, enough that I wouldn't have been able to lie and say it wasn't.

"You asked for help from American authorities and it was granted," I said with a shrug, "since you have no metahuman policing apparatus of your own—yet."

Marshwin looked apoplectic, but her voice came out low. "Stop… offering me suggestions… on public relations. Being as you are hardly an expert on knowing your own bloody limits when it comes to giving an interview to the press."

Man, that Gail Roth thing was going to haunt me forever.

"I think Ms. Nealon is offering very reasonable suggestions," Minister Wexford said with a faint smile, "and I for one feel very relieved to know that a serial killer has been 'taken out of play,' I think is how you Yanks put it."

"It's a black eye for the department," Marshwin said.

"It's a minor public relations gaffe," Wexford said soothingly. "With public sentiments against metas running a bit… high, the merest mention that Ms. Nealon, acting in concert with New Scotland Yard, dealt with the threat at hand should play well enough to give us the breathing room to work with this." He straightened his lapels. "Mr. Delsim's suicide upon the realization that he could not flee from the long reach of the Metropolitan Police force is a very acceptable outcome, I should think. I doubt after the incident at the gallery that you'll find many in the press who'll mourn his loss, and those who do will all be on the fringe, of course."

Marshwin looked like she was about to vomit. "Acceptable enough, I suppose. But the matter of Delsim's efforts at the bank is an open sore. He managed to move quite a sum of money outside our reach. Seizing five hundred million pounds of illegal assets would have been quite a balm."

"What can you do in these instances?" Wexford asked, giving me a sympathetic smile. "Make your inquiries in Liechtenstein, of course, but I think we all know how that will turn out."

"How will it turn out?" I asked. I didn't really know anything about Liechtenstein, having only seen it on the map.

"They're what Switzerland was to banking a few years ago," Wexford said, "a black hole for most of the rest of the world. Money goes in, and if it comes out again, it's virtually untraceable."

"So it was all about the money all along," I said, shaking my head. "Philip's revenge was just a cover for his robbery of Omega's assets."

"It sounds as though he was at least a little angry with them," Wexford said. "And he certainly did you a little bit of damage in the process, didn't he?"

"He was keeping me around as the last person to torture in front of Janus if all else failed," I said. "Probably knew containing me would be a nightmare, so he just kept one step ahead. Arrogant bastard, but then again, if I could see the future of everyone around me, I might be a little cocky myself." I pulled my shredded coat tight, huddling in Marshwin's frigid office.

"Well, he's good and sorted now, as you say," Marshwin said, sitting back down in her chair. "Now we're just left with the matter of you."

I sighed. "I know when I'm not wanted. I'll head home." I stood, reaching into my pocket for my phone. When I pulled on it, it came out in three pieces. "Sonofa... I guess they'll know I'm coming when they see me."

"I'll walk you out, Ms. Nealon," Wexford said, already heading toward the door, his silver hair as perfectly in place as ever. The man was simply unruffled by anything, apparently. "Good day, Ms. Marshwin."

"What the hell is good about it, exactly?" she grumped as he closed the door behind her.

"Thanks for your help," I murmured to Wexford as he walked me through the bullpen, a hand resting lightly on my shoulder.

"Officially, I have no idea what you're talking about, of course." He said this low, under his breath, letting it dissolve in the natural chatter of the room. "Unofficially, of course, the PM is quite pleased about the outcome. Keeping Mr. Delsim in prison would be a headache of no small proportions."

"Glad she sees it my way," I said, still hugging my coat tight around me.

"I suspect if you were to meet her, you'd find you both have a great deal in common," Wexford said as he tapped the button to summon the elevator.

I blinked, putting a couple things together. "You called Philip a Cassandra-type before I'd told you what he was."

Wexford made a harrumphing noise. "You assume that the file I gave you was the only one we had on him."

It was a lie, and it was obvious to me. When I looked him in the eye, I knew he knew it as well. "You lived in the country and just came back to London a year ago?"

He knew I knew, and in spite of being caught, his eye twinkled. "When the PM formed her government, yes. She... left for the duration as well, you see. A little time in the country."

"Holy shit, you're metas," I said, scarcely believing it. "You bailed out of London to avoid the extinction."

He steered me into the elevator and pressed the door close button once, with confidence. "Ms. Nealon... I can tell by looking into your mind that delicate matters of this sort are something we can trust you to keep... discreet." I just watched him. "Especially given that there is a great deal of work to do in changing attitudes in this country." He straightened and tapped me once, gently, tugging on the torn lapel of my coat. "Besides, I think you have a few things of your own you'd prefer to keep under wraps?"

I swallowed hard and tugged my coat closed even tighter around me. Indeed I did. I didn't even need to say it, because I knew he was reading my thoughts.

"Perhaps you should visit Detective Inspector Webster before you leave," Wexford said, giving me a patient smile. "I'm sure he would rather enjoy making certain that any unfinished business between the two of you was settled before you left." The elevator dinged and opened, and once more Wexford slipped out before I could pull myself together and follow him. He paused just before rounding the corner, turned back to me and said, "Aim low." Then once again he disappeared down a hall, leaving me more than a little mystified at what he'd meant by that.

Ambassador Ryan Halstead's face popped around the corner, and he slid into the elevator and pushed the button for the fourth floor. It took him a second to look back and see me, standing there in my shredded clothes, and his distaste was evident a second before the loathing, and the anger followed a second behind that. "You," he said. "You are in so much shit, you have no idea. Washington is so friggin' pissed at you, you'll be lucky if you can get a recommendation to find a job as a dog-catcher after this crap, you—"

I slapped him on the chest and felt something stiff beneath his suit. Kevlar, I realized after a second. He was wearing a bulletproof vest. "Aim low," I muttered, realizing what Wexford meant, and I raised my knee to land in Halstead's crotch.

The man dropped; I'd been about as gentle as I could be while slamming my knee into his balls. I suspected he wouldn't appreciate it, but dammit, he should have. I could just as easily have hit him so hard he'd have had to squeeze his throat to jerk off.

I left him in a pile on the elevator floor and stepped out, listening to him whine quietly as the doors closed behind me.

Chapter 85

I knocked on the door of the Webster house a little tentatively. I didn't know how I'd be received, but I needed to do this before I left, that much I knew.

The birds were chirping, the garden was looking surprisingly fresh—maybe not so surprisingly given how much rain they'd had since I'd gotten here. The sky was blue and the sun was shining down. A better April day I could not have asked for.

I just hoped it wasn't all clouds and thunderstorms waiting behind the door.

Marjorie clicked the lock and opened the door, staring out at me with as good a poker face as any I'd seen. I stared back at her and felt myself withdraw a little, hesitant, ready to run. I'd been in a knife fight to the death earlier today, but now I was ready to run at the sight of a motherly English woman.

"Sienna, dear," she said, relief flooding across her face, "oh, I've been so worried! And you haven't answered your mobile! I've called and left messages!"

I thought back to the shattered pieces of my phone that I'd given up and tossed into a garbage can outside New Scotland Yard. "Yeah... I kinda need a new one."

"Come in, come in!" She stepped back from the door to allow me to pass. I slipped off my shoes, gaping holes all over them, and let my bare feet fall on the hardwood.

"Matthew just got out of the hospital this very morning, I know he'll be happy to see you."

"Where is he?" I asked.

"In the shower, dear," she said. "But come along, you must be hungry! Come on, to the kitchen." She disappeared through the sitting room in a flash, and I knew she wouldn't be dissuaded. Besides, I was hungry.

She laid out a spread of cold meats and cheeses, and I attacked it like someone who hadn't eaten since... well, yesterday. I counted myself lucky that Webster himself wasn't around to witness it and tried to keep my ears open over the sound of my own chewing in order to keep from having him surprise me. I had my pride, after all.

"I can't thank you enough, dear," Marjorie said after a few minutes of idle chitchat. It probably surprised the hell out of me, because I stopped eating altogether. I looked at her in curiosity, completely unsure of what she could be grateful to me for. I'd only landed her son in the hospital and caused his apartment to be bombed. I waited, almost expecting her to take a right turn into condemnation. "I always worry about him, you know," she went on, "but having you watching out for him... you know that madman would have killed all of them if you hadn't been there to stop the flames?"

"Oh." I'd definitely forgotten about that. I tried to find a way to say it without sounding stupid, but came out with, "Well, I don't know if that makes up for getting his apartment bombed..."

"His flat?" she scoffed. "That dreadful place? They probably would have done it anyway, since he was on the investigation. You saved his life."

"Maybe," I said, almost shrugging it off. "Doesn't feel that way to me, though."

She didn't take her eyes off me. "That's just guilt talking. I watched that interview with that awful Roth woman, the one you did a few months after things changed?"

I thought I tasted something sour in my mouth. "You and the rest of the world."

"She was a perfect representation of the worst of people," Marjorie said. "The absolute dregs of our nature. She turned everything around on you, and I'm glad you didn't just sit there and take it. They live to see heroes fall, you know. It's what makes them money—the tabloids and the telly, those vultures."

I pursed my lower lip. "I don't know how much of a hero I am, Marjorie."

"Nonsense, dear," she said, and reached out to pat my arm. "Can I get you some tea and biscuits?"

"Hello, there." Matthew Webster's voice chimed in, and I realized he'd slipped into the kitchen without me noticing.

"Uh... hey," I said, before I could come up with something cooler.

"I've just realized," Marjorie said, rummaging through the cupboards without looking back at us, "I'm all out of biscuits." She shut the cabinet door and I saw her disappear toward the side of the house. "I'm off to the supermarket. Do either of you need anything?" She didn't wait more than a second for our answer before I heard the door close, and I met Webster's eyes as he smirked while we listened to the garage door go up.

"I got the guy," I said, maybe with a little pride in a job well done.

"I heard about that," Webster said. His arms were folded in front of him, and the way he was leaning against the door frame I noticed that he was wearing a pretty tight t-shirt. "Well done, carrying on in my absence, breaking the case. I'm a little confused, though—was he a terrorist with schemes of revenge?"

"A robber using revenge as his cover," I said as he crossed over to me. "Very Hans Gruber. It was pretty clever on his part, but he got overconfident toward the end. It was his downfall."

"Overconfidence can lead to that, I've heard." He leaned against the back of the chair next to me. "And, uh... not to wade into those waters, but... it would appear I missed our date for yesterday."

I stared into his eyes. "I think... we could probably reschedule. You know, since you had a concussion and all that."

"Oh, well, the doctor has cleared me for duty," he said, knocking a hand against the side of his head and grimacing. "Though I imagine it would have been a slightly different story if someone hadn't carried me out of my flat before it exploded."

"Any restrictions?" I asked, looking at the way he leaned. It was... kind of a suggestion all of its own.

"I am fit for anything," Webster said, assuring me. "Though I'll admit, I'm a bit curious about this whole... touching without touching thing you mentioned."

"Ah," I said. "Well..." I turned my head to indicate the direction his mother had gone. "How far away is the supermarket?"

"Oh, she's gone for the afternoon," he said, waving a hand behind him. "She's got a reserve of biscuits to cover the end of the world. She left for our privacy."

I felt a newfound respect for Marjorie blossoming in me, but it was somewhat quickly replaced by something else, a desire to fulfill a promise I'd made—quite eagerly. "Well, then, Detective Inspector," I said, "in addition to the normal materials, I have to ask you... do you have any latex gloves?" I pulled out my most mischievous smile.

It turned out he did have some, by strange coincidence. We kept busy with each other until well after nightfall, and I fell asleep with him next to me, fully re-dressed. For safety's sake, you know.

Chapter 86

Karthik listened to Janus shudder well into the night. He didn't speak, just shook, making almost no noise. An occasional quiet groan escaped his lips, echoing in the dark. The smell of blood was still heavy in the air, neither of them in a fit state to clean. Karthik could taste it on his tongue, dripping down his throat. He lacked the will to fight his injuries and do anything about it. He could only watch, feeling his strength fade, until finally he passed out somewhere in the night himself.

He was awakened by Janus shaking him, the old man's breath heavy with blood. Or was it his own body, still healing, that gave off that smell? Either way, Janus was shaking him awake, murmuring quietly.

"What?" Karthik found himself asking. The gentle jarring was only enough to disquiet him, not enough to distress him. "You're safe now, Janus." He had a feeling this nightmare would recur. He'd seen the look in Janus's eyes when Sienna had brought him back, knew a haunting lay within. But now they were different. Wild.

"Did you tell her?" Janus asked, barely speaking audibly.

"You mean the woman with the knives?" Karthik asked, still feeling the pain of his wounds and the bleary edge of the sleep he'd happily embraced.

"No," Janus said, shaking his head. "No, not her. She's dead, what do I care if she knew? No… I'm talking about Sienna. Did you tell Sienna?"

Karthik listened carefully, processing the older man's words until the light came on for him. "No, no, I did not tell her. Not a word."

Janus's posture sagged, and the fire that burned in his wide eyes died down. He relaxed, sliding back to the concrete floor and huddling there, arms around his knees like a child. "That's… that's good. She can't know. Not about this." Karthik watched him stare off into the distance, at the red splotch on the concrete wall where the woman with the knives had died, and listened as Janus continued to mutter to himself, that breath of lucidity gone as quickly as it had come.

Chapter 87

I left early the next morning. I thought about checking on Janus before I left, but I'd burned more time in England than I had available, so there wasn't time to say goodbye. Besides, I wasn't a psychologist, and whatever damage he had experienced wasn't something I could easily fix. When I'd parted ways with Karthik before I'd returned to New Scotland Yard to make my report, I'd told him I'd check in on them via phone when I got home. I already knew that I'd offer to bring Janus to the Agency for care, and if Karthik wanted to take the offer, I'd be fine with it.

It was the least I could do for Janus after all we'd been through.

I'd parted ways with Webster on good terms. The best, really, since we'd had a repeat the morning before I'd left. He was a quick learner, and he dealt with the constraints against direct skin-to-skin contact like a champ, figuring out exactly what to do to maximize the experience for both of us. If the United Kingdom hadn't just happily kicked out my entire species, I might have already been planning my next trip back.

If I could find the time in my schedule, I might have to come back regardless.

I headed southeast out of London, flying until I saw the channel, and crossed before the sun was fully up. I kept low, not chancing setting off radar for most of Europe. I had one last nagging thing that needed to be dealt with, and I meant to do it before I blew back across the pond.

I took my time, stayed subsonic, and dipped down to look at road signs when necessary. Air navigation without signs or GPS isn't exactly the easiest thing in the world to manage. I crossed the border into Switzerland sometime around mid-morning, and by the time I'd found my destination, it was getting close to noon.

I made my landing in an alley just down the street from a lovely old building in Vaduz, Liechtenstein. I checked the blood-stained scrap of paper that I'd kept in my coat's inner pocket, just to be certain I had the right place. Once I was sure, I walked in through the lobby of one of the nicest banks I'd ever seen.

It was pretty impressive, I must say. It wasn't full opulence on display or anything, but they had nice paintings on the walls, the furniture in the lobby was top notch, and the man waiting to greet guests at the door wore a polite smile even for me, and I suspected it wasn't because of how nicely I was dressed, with my coat still riddled with holes and all.

"Madam Nealon, if I am not mistaken," he said with a thick German accent.

"You know me," I said, nodding as I took in my surroundings.

"I do indeed," he said, with a subtle nod of the head. "And I know you are with American law enforcement. I welcome you to Liechtenstein, and hope you will have a wonderful stay with us. My name is Nils." His smile now looked forced. "What can I do for you?"

I held up the blood-stained scrap of paper that had his bank's name on it with an account number. "I don't know if you heard, Mr. Nils, but I had a little trouble in London yesterday with the owner of this account."

His face did not waver, though his smile slightly dimmed. "I'm afraid I cannot discuss matters regarding any of our customers with American law enforcement officers, not even to confirm or deny. We prize confidentiality about all else."

I stared into his smoky eyes. "How do you verify the identity of your account holders?"

That got him to raise an eyebrow. "As I said, we prize confidentiality." He fidgeted slightly. "However, speaking in a general sense, many of our account holders are anonymous, interacting with us via the internet, making transfers as necessary. It has been a boon, I think you would call it." His smile grew flat. "This has left us in the unique position of not always knowing our clients' identities."

"Who owns this account?" I asked again, pointing at the account number.

His lips wavered, just the slightest bit. "I am afraid I cannot cooperate with you. It is nothing personal, but we do not discuss our clientele with outside parties, especially law enforcement officers for foreign countries, and our laws do not compel us to—"

"You know who I am," I said, dull intonation ringing out. "You know what I can do, yes?" I leaned closer, and he did not flinch away, though I saw he had to try mightily not to. "What I could do to you?"

He held himself straighter than I would have thought he would have. I could see guards easing out of the wings, and he looked with me, shaking his head to warn them off. "*Ja, Fraulein.* I know who you are. I know what you could—and would—do to me were you to turn loose your wrath. But I cannot give you what you want."

I stared him down, looking for a hint of weakness. There was none, not a bit, not even beneath the plain, vanilla fear that covered him from head to toe.

"Fair enough," I said and relaxed, easing back from him a little. I saw his posture change, the fear dissolving just slightly. "I need to talk to you in private."

He grew stiff again. "I am sorry, Ms. Nealon, but I cannot give you the information you ask for. To compromise our clients by cooperating with foreign law enforcement is anathema to—"

"I'm not here to talk to you as a law enforcement officer, Mr. Nils," I said, shaking my head. I felt a tingle of nerves as I drew slow breath.

"Oh?" His eyebrow raised again, curiosity plain as he prepared to reach for the bait I dangled in front of him. "Then what are you here to talk about?"

I reached into my coat again and pulled out the second part of the blood-stained paper I'd taken off Philip Delsim's corpse. The one that contained his password to access his account. "Retirement planning," I said, staring at the banker. "I've got a future to consider."

Chapter 88

I left Liechtenstein hours later, the sun already down and with a few dollars and euros in my pocket after I'd made a quick stop and gotten some clothes. Nils had done me a favor in this; we'd had a discussion that went very late, and he'd had the owner of a local boutique open her doors just for me. I'd gone simple this time—black pants, a dark tank top, and a watch I'd picked up on my way out. Figured it'd help to gauge my flying time if I strayed off course over the North Atlantic.

I went supersonic over the Alps and went "feet wet" over the Atlantic a little while later. I could only tell after I'd caught the moonlight reflecting on the surface of the ocean below. I was hauling ass, going about as fast as I wanted to be traveling. The air was cold, but I didn't care. I kept Aleksandr Gavrikov close to the surface of my mind and let my skin heat up to near-flaming whenever the chill got to be too much.

I made landfall somewhere over Virginia late. I was racing sunset, trying to see if I could catch the glowing edge of the horizon before I made it to Minneapolis.

Looking at my watch, I figured I'd missed it by a half hour or so when I landed outside of town. I stopped somewhere in Dinkytown, pausing for a breath on top of one of the big residential buildings on the east bank of the

Mississippi as I stared into the downtown skyline, lit up for the night.

My town. My city.

I'd failed to place the proper limits on myself and I'd ended up dragging my ass all over hell and gone for some really stupid reasons, exhausting myself and completely burning down to nothing.

But here... this was where I was supposed to be. Minneapolis was the city I owed my debt to. Not like I wanted to see anyone else in the world get hurt, but I needed to start doing a better job of focusing on what mattered. I needed to stop seeing how much of myself I could roast off before there was nothing left.

My city.

My life.

It was time to recognize my limits.

With a last look, I vaulted back into the sky and flew over downtown on my way home.

Chapter 89

I landed on the roof of the dorm because I didn't want to break my own sliding glass door to get into my apartment. Stupid, I know, locking it when I knew I was going to be out, but I was obsessive compulsive that way. It's not like it would even prevent a halfway dedicated meta from gaining access to my quarters, but I still locked my doors anyway. Call me crazy.

I descended the interior staircase and exited on the top floor. I was halfway down the hall when the door next to mine opened and a tall man with long, dark hair and an olive complexion stepped out to greet me with a grin.

"I was getting worried," Reed said, catching me in a hug I didn't even know I'd offered him. "You don't call, you don't write, you catch a serial killer halfway around the world and end up taking another day plus more to come home." He pulled back and looked at me. "You all right?"

"I'm fine," I said, only meeting his eyes a little bit. "Just... had some business to attend to before I came back."

"With that cute detective guy?" He bumped his shoulder softly into mine. "Amirite?"

"When you're right, you're right," I said, pasting a smile on my face. "So... what's the word for tonight?"

"The word is silence," Reed said. "I've still got everything shunted so the shit rolls downhill and away from us for at least another day. It's actually been kind of nice not having you here; I get to tell more people, 'No, no and hell no,' without feeling guilty about it."

"Let's do that more often," I said with a solemn nod.

"Seriously?" He perked up. "You mean that? Because whenever I've suggested it before, you're always all serious, with the, 'We have a job to do...'" he lowered his voice in what I presumed was an imitation of me being serious.

"Yeah," I said. "To hell with it. Let's be human for a while. Priorities only. Let the rest of the government sort their way through the thousand bullshit sightings a year that we've been chasing down. We need to save ourselves for the real enemies, because they're still out there." I thought of Philip. "Not as many of them as there used to be, maybe, but they're still out there, and they're not going to politely wait for us to be ready to face them."

"I hear that," he said, nodding like I'd thrown down some sage wisdom. "So... want to get a drink?"

"I think I'm just going to go to bed," I said, giving him my fake smile.

He got it and stepped out of my way. "If you change your mind..."

"I'll let you know," I said and reached for my door handle, turning it and disappearing into my quarters.

I closed the door and waited until I'd heard Reed's footsteps recede down the hall, until I'd heard his door shut behind him.

Then I crept my way to the bedroom.

I stood there and stared at the empty bed for a minute, remembering the last time it hadn't been empty. That was a long time ago. The night of the interview with Gail Roth, in fact.

I could hear the raised voices in my head if I listened.

I didn't want to listen. Not tonight.

Not any night.

I made my way to the windows and shut the shades, closing the moonlight outside and leaving only a faint glow in the bedroom.

That was plenty enough for me to see by.

I made my way over to the closet and listened, just listened, to see if I could hear anyone else in the building. I couldn't.

I slid my closet door open and stepped inside. It was a small closet, really, a couple feet deep and maybe four feet wide. A shelf at the level of my head forced me to duck as I entered.

The new construction smell still lingered, more obvious to me now that I'd returned after a long absence than it would have been otherwise. I kept the clothes in the left side of the closet, because... well, hell, I didn't have that many.

The right side... that was for something else entirely.

I put my back against the wall and eased to the ground, feeling my spine against the smooth drywall as I sat, pulling my knees to my chest as I slid the closet door shut.

When I was a child, my mother had punished me by locking me in a metal box not much bigger than the space I currently inhabited.

I listened to the slow drag of my breaths coming in and going out, and I felt the sense of malaise I'd been carrying with me since Liechtenstein gradually disappear. I stared straight ahead into the darkness, listened to the slow rhythm of my heart drumming in my ears, and rested my head against the wall.

Sleep would come soon. It always did when I was in here like this. In the dark.

I drifted off to the slow sound of my own breathing, and the memory of a time long gone.

In the Wind

Out of the Box
Book Two

Coming Late 2014/Early 2015!

Note From the Author

First off, if you want to know when future books become available, take sixty seconds and sign up for my NEW RELEASE EMAIL ALERTS on my website at www.robertjcrane.com. Don't let the caps lock scare you; I don't sell your information and I only send out emails when I have a new book out. The reason you should sign up for this is because I don't like to set release dates (it's this whole thing, you can find an answer on my website in the FAQ section), and even if you're following me on Facebook (robertJcrane (Author)) or Twitter (@robertJcrane), it's easy to miss my book announcements because...well, because social media is an imprecise thing.

Come join the Girl in the Box discussion on my website: http://www.robertjcrane.com !

Cheers,
Robert J. Crane

Acknowledgments

My thanks to all these people.

Jo Evans – Co-conspirator, namer of Webbo and Marjorie, the British anchor that kept the English parts from drifting into the realm of American rubbish.

Nicolette Solomita – Vindicator of my crazy literary decisions, enabler when it comes to some of my language choices, and chronicler of some of the crazy, hilarious shit I say in passing. "Wikipedia: Foundation of All Truth and Light!"

Karri Klawiter – Creator of beautiful covers or possibly the imagineer of the crazy amusement park in my mind. Whichever of those sounds least insane, it should be her job title.

Sarah Barbour – Error-catcher, prose-smoother – she's like my literary janitor, honestly. In the best possible way.

Jeff Bryan – Final reader extraordinaire.

My kids – Because sleeping too much is not good for you.

My parents – For encouraging.

My wife – For believing.

About the Author

Robert J. Crane is kind of an a-hole. Still, if you want to contact him:

Website: http://www.robertjcrane.com
Facebook Page: robertJcrane (Author)
Twitter: @robertJcrane
Email: cyrusdavidon@gmail.com

Other Works by Robert J. Crane

The Sanctuary Series
Epic Fantasy

Defender: The Sanctuary Series, Volume One
Avenger: The Sanctuary Series, Volume Two
Champion: The Sanctuary Series, Volume Three
Crusader: The Sanctuary Series, Volume Four
Sanctuary Tales, Volume One - A Short Story Collection
Thy Father's Shadow: The Sanctuary Series, Volume 4.5
Master: The Sanctuary Series, Volume Five* (Coming Late
    2014!)

The Girl in the Box
and
Out of the Box
Contemporary Urban Fantasy

Alone: The Girl in the Box, Book 1
Untouched: The Girl in the Box, Book 2
Soulless: The Girl in the Box, Book 3
Family: The Girl in the Box, Book 4
Omega: The Girl in the Box, Book 5
Broken: The Girl in the Box, Book 6
Enemies: The Girl in the Box, Book 7
Legacy: The Girl in the Box, Book 8
Destiny: The Girl in the Box, Book 9
Power: The Girl in the Box, Book 10

Limitless: Out of the Box, Book 1
In the Wind: Out of the Box, Book 2* (Coming Late
    2014/Early 2015!)
Ruthless: Out of the Box, Book 3* (Coming Early 2015!)

Southern Watch
Contemporary Urban Fantasy

Called: Southern Watch, Book 1
Depths: Southern Watch, Book 2
Corrupted: Southern Watch, Book 3
Unearthed: Southern Watch, Book 4* (Coming Late
    2014/Early 2015!)

*Forthcoming

11692209R00193

Printed in Great Britain
by Amazon.co.uk, Ltd.,
Marston Gate.